"A LADY DOESN'T RESPOND TO A KISS WANTONLY, I CAN ASSURE YOU!"

Angered beyond endurance, Vanora plastered the flower against Holton's lips. But upon seeing his jaw jut again as he spit away bits of leaf, she suddenly knew she stood in greater danger than she had in her bed chamber.

"Do you truly believe that, you little innocent? Do you doubt that you can perform the same sweet dance as your sisters of the stage, indeed? Perhaps Sir Charles wasn't the man to teach you the steps!"

Holton got both arms about Vanora and put his lips firmly to hers. Vanora gripped his shoulders to steady herself, then found herself slipping both arms about him. Feeling her treacherous lips succumb to his insistence, Vanora knew this was a battle she couldn't win by fighting Holton. She pressed herself bravely against his chest, took his head between her hands, and gave her entire being into surrender.

A DANGEROUS DANDY

PAT CODY

HarperPaperbacks
A Division of HarperCollinsPublishers

This is a work of fiction. The characters, incidents, and dialogues are products of the author's imagination and are not to be construed as real. Any resemblance to actual events or persons, living or dead, is entirely coincidental.

HarperPaperbacks   *A Division of* HarperCollins*Publishers*
10 East 53rd Street, New York, N.Y. 10022

Cover illustration by Rick Johnson

First printing: December 1994

Printed in the United States of America

HarperPaperbacks, HarperMonogram, and colophon are trademarks of HarperCollins*Publishers*

❖ 10 9 8 7 6 5 4 3 2 1

For
James Donald Cody
whose sixty years of elected public service
set a Tennessee state record
and
Martha Eva Templin Cody
who taught in Cocke County
for forty-three years.

The agent's son married
the squire's daughter
to live the best romance.

1

Holton's mood *was* more funereal than festive as the coach bearing him and his mama toward a house party swayed along the oak-lined avenue. From ennui, Holton tapped booted toes alternately with an ebony cane, earning attention at last from Lady Fenmore's elbow.

"I'm sensible you dislike riding staidly inside," she coaxed, "but must you vent your fidgets in that way?"

"The prospect of Christmas at Keathley Manor is enough to daunt a bishop," Holton grumbled, speaking only half in jest. "You're in my debt for this duty!" The best thing about arrival would be straightening his legs, after folding up like a pocket handkerchief in this curst carriage all day. Riding in an icy mist was very nearly preferable to the confinement of being driven, even in this well-sprung coach.

"Don't play the bear with me," said Lady Fenmore, "for you never put yourself on too high a form to enter into any entertainment offered. I don't regard that glum face, for meeting people is meat and drink to your tastes for remarking the absurdities of your fellow creatures!"

Clasping her yellow-gloved fingers, Holton replied, "And you know where I learned the habit, Mama, for you find little more diverting than the doings of acquaintance." He eased cramped shoulders against the squabs, wishing knotted muscles might be pressed out along with his coat.

"I can't regard this occasion as holding out the highest promise of entertainment," Holton continued. "Family parties bring together people who know each other far too well to trot out their best behavior, and people fascinate most when they endeavor to show you just what they wish you to see."

"The company's family, but not altogether familiar," his mama objected, pushing aside the glass curtain as though seeking a glimpse of the manor through mid-afternoon's half-light. "Your father promised to join us by Christmas Eve. You've known my cousin Mary since you both wore petticoats, and Squire Plewes, since they married. You don't regard meeting Alicen and Chalmers together with any discomfort?" asked Lady Fenmore, referring to their hosts' daughter and her husband of less than a year.

Holton waved the notion aside with the negligence it deserved, setting a glossy Hessian on the opposite seat. "They're welcome to the wedded state. You know that I was relieved my little cousin had the good sense to turn down my impetuous proposal, for I should make a shocking husband!"

Lady Fenmore sighed. "You'll make the sort of husband you set yourself to be, if you ever come to do the thing at all. Don't pretend you've forgotten that Chalmers's family is to be represented among us. You never miss an occasion to best the other bucks by meeting young ladies before anyone else in the *ton* makes their acquaintance!"

Holton leaned a shoulder against his mother's in a

surge of affection tinged with annoyance. "I know what you're about; no need to wrap it up in clean linen. You're match-making again, and it won't fadge! Though to your credit, you're less obvious about it than Pater."

Holton grimaced. "If a little gem twinkles at me in a taking way this season, it won't be one of Chalmers's sisters, I dare swear! Both are bound to be as broad as he, even if they don't wear his craggy features. My tastes are far too nice to appreciate less than the daintiest of morsels."

"I protest; Chalmers is perfectly agreeable," said Lady Fenmore, tucking her hands under the fur lap rug once more. "Why assume the worst of his features for his sisters? I can allow them to be blue-eyed, with fair, curling hair, from what I recollect of his person."

"Chalmers's eyes are a chilling blue; his corkscrew hair, plain sand in color; and his fairness allows of spots. You fail to whet my appetite for this encounter." Holton cast a teasing look his mama's way, leaning with the coach's lurch.

"Your appetites have proved too voracious for me to be certain what tidbit is likely to appeal at this late date," Lady Fenmore replied. "Having watched you flirt your way through countless seasons, I've despaired of your setting up a nursery while I'm this side of the grave!"

Lady Fenmore's fond smile assured Holton that she bantered in their usual manner. He felt a grain of guilt, for his mama touched lightly on the topic his father dug at like a badger. The succession was assured through two younger brothers, but Lord Fenmore wouldn't desist until his firstborn had done his duty, Holton thought grimly.

Holton jabbed the seat opposite with his stick, feeling more strongly pressured toward marriage by Mama's gentle prodding than by Pater's heavy-handed shoves. The baron insisted that his son meet an obligation; the baroness longed to dandle her favorite son's child on her knee. *Love is ever a greater spur than duty,* Holton mused.

"Are you set on lending consequence to the Chalmers chits' come-out?" he asked to distract his mama's attention.

"I'm not committed to doing so thus far," Lady Fenmore said, staying his stick once more. "Time enough to decide if I'll take a couple of Scotch sisters under my wing when I've seen how they conduct themselves through a quiet holiday."

"Shall I save you consideration of so tiresome a task and tell you now that the rustics won't be worth the candle?"

"But you often assure me that any lady sparkles in the light of proper male attention!" Lady Fenmore teased.

"Improper attentions spark far more dazzling displays from the fairer sex," Holton drawled. "But my interest in these particular ladies fizzles. One expects no brilliance from females of little background and less family beauty."

"Granted, they come from a cadet branch of a Scottish-titled family," Lady Fenmore conceded. "But the girls are well-enough connected, for their mama was an earl's daughter, and adequate dowries allow for unexceptionable matches, Mary writes. I'm far more concerned to learn if they're well conducted, coming from Scottish society."

Holton countered, "Beauty, Mama, beauty is the sole bolt required to rivet chits suitably! A pleasing face and form will take any Miss farther than perfect conduct. Only old tabbies are best pleased by pleasing manners."

Lady Fenmore replied with mock plaintiveness, "How can I credit that argument, when diamonds of the first water have failed to fix your interest for well above a dozen seasons?"

Vanora entered her younger sister's chamber after the most perfunctory of knocks. "Eva, I must impress upon you— Whatever is the matter, my dear?" Vanora hurried to seat herself on the bed, where Eva lay in a flurry of white flounces and a flood of tears. Laying a consoling arm about the trembling shoulders, Vanora begged, "Won't you say what's amiss? Are you unwell?"

Eva lifted a tragic face from her book, long lashes laid against damp cheeks like dewy fronds. "I'm not ill; it's lovely to cry! She adores him, you see, and now he's gone into battle. They may never meet again, and then she must harbor an unrequited love for the rest of her days!"

Vanora recoiled from the words. "Most affecting, I daresay! I thought you had the toothache at the very least!"

"A heartache is far more painful, you must allow!"

Vanora sprang off the bed and strode to the window. "I'm aware that heartache is painful at first hand, though why you shed tears over fictional ones is beyond me. Attend to reality instead of romance, for the lady whose good offices can assure you a successful season arrives today."

Eva scrambled off the bed, sending the dampened book flying. "I don't mean to tease you," Eva said. "I ken you avoid reminders of your own come-out, and I apprehend that you've overcome an aversion to Society to present me."

"You know I'll do the necessary to see you settled in life, and my own mishappens determines me to set you properly on course," said Vanora. "Not that you rightly say I shall present you, for even my twenty-six years don't make it proper for a spinster to act that role. We must win the support of our connections by marriage for that courtesy."

Vanora seated herself upon the couch and beckoned Eva. "Come sit by me and attend, Eveleit. It's imperative that you act with the utmost propriety to gain this sponsor."

Eva alit on the edge of the chintz-covered couch like a butterfly already lifting wings to the next breeze. "You admit at last that you aren't a proper chaperone! Now will you attire yourself attractively as you did in your own come-out? Off with these old-crone caps!" Eva snatched at the offending headgear and twitched Vanora's drab sleeve. "Away with these dun-colored gowns! You must wear silks and muslins as pretty as mine, so the Scotch Chalmers sisters may take the *ton* by storm as did the Irish Gunnings!"

Leaning away, Vanora resettled the plain mobcap that hid hair and face. "Mind that only I am Miss Chalmers, and you as the younger are Miss Eva Chalmers, in proper address!"

"Chance would be a fine thing! You never let me forget propriety for an instant," said Eva. "Nor shall I allow you to forget what's due Miss Chalmers as we enter Society."

"Let's make an end to a tired argument, for even dressed fashionably, my hair lacks your curls," Vanora said with finality. "Without doubt, you and Mama exemplify the family beauty, for our brothers and I resemble Papa far too nearly."

She could have named other differences from her pretty sister, Vanora thought. Eva wore perfect features within an oval shape, while her own ordinary face stretched squarely, except for a pointed chin. Eva was petite rather than overly tall, full of fun rather than sober, hopeful rather than resigned. Comparing herself to Eva was like laying a dull charcoal drawing next to a delicate watercolor.

Eva threw both arms about Vanora, unsettling the maligned cap once more. "I shan't listen to a word against you, even from yourself, for you could look charmingly again if you chose. Recall that you allowed me to hand pins while our maid dressed your hair becomingly before you came out. You wore colors other than sparrow-brown and dove-grey then, for a bright bird flew off in the right plumage to draw London gentlemen's eyes!"

Vanora returned the embrace to hide her expression

as she put away memories of the hopeful girl she, too, had been at eighteen. "You must think of me now as a rain-goose, which mates for life," she said, "for nearly achieving that end makes another pairing unthinkable to a person of sensibility. Our entire attention must focus on presenting you to good effect; I've no mind to further efforts myself."

"If I'm to bait suitors, I'll share them with you," Eva insisted. "Those below thirty shall be mine, and I'll turn those above in your direction!"

"Don't speak pertly about serious matters," chided Vanora. "You must control these coming ways if you're to impress Lady Fenmore as suitable to present to her friends. You tend to flirtation, you can't deny, and I won't have you lay yourself open to approach by the wrong sort of man."

Eva flitted from the couch to waltz about the room, arms lifted to an invisible partner. "But the wrong sort of man is invariably the most attractive, you will allow. May I not enjoy the company of unsuitable men whilst I encourage the advances of those plodders you approve?"

Vanora swallowed dread like a peach pit in her throat. Had she erred, to believe she could guide Eva through the pitfalls of a season, when she had muddled her own come-out?

Dismissing doubt, Vanora held out a hand to the sprite who wafted by to silent strains. "Please, Eveleit; this is your best chance to marry well. Before the day is past, we'll meet connections who may introduce you to friends' notice, if you don't behave like a hoyden before them."

"I shan't regard a quizzing, for my come-out was your notion, not mine! Besides, a son accompanies the lady, who will likely remark that I move like thistledown," Eva lilted from her circuits round the furniture.

"Men don't marry romps they disport themselves with," Vanora warned, suppressing thoughts of long-past flirtation. "We must be particularly on guard, for gossip calls Lady Fenmore's eldest son a very devil with ladies."

Eva stopped in mid-sway, running to lay a flushed cheek against Vanora's cool one. "Only a *gruntie* would tease you, when getting on terms with such a person must cost you pain! I've observed that you avoid flirts above all things." ·

Vanora turned from Eva's pitying expression, determined to sound unaffected as old memories clawed for attention. "It's all of eight years since I was a foolish girl. I'm prepared to confront a dozen triflers on your behalf, if needful. And from all reports, we'll be presented to a man who's both dandy and rake before dinner this night!"

"What a time has passed since we tilted a glass in company! Come into the library and let's mark your arrival," Chalmers invited, crunching Holton's frozen fingers.

Giving in gracefully to the inevitable tête-à-tête, Holton wished Chalmers' sisters at the devil rather than at Keathley Manor, where he must meet them.

"You enjoy this Burgundy, as I recall," said Chalmers, pouring from a decanter on a leather-topped table centering the long library. "The level's low, but we can drain a glass or two before resorting to the cellar, I apprehend."

Moments later, the men faced the library fire from leather-wing chairs, companionable glasses in hand.

"I'm glad of the chance to bend your ear before you meet my sisters," said Chalmers, "for I'm beholden to your family for giving thought to greasing their paths in town."

Waving aside gratitude, Holton said, "That's entirely up to Mama. I'll do no more than stand up with them now and again, whether or not she feels up to sponsoring them. You may be assured that I'll keep them in my eye whatever Mama deems possible." *If I know where they are, I'll know where not to be,* he thought cynically.

Chalmers nodded. "But your standing with hostesses guarantees invitations where you express interest. A few minutes' conversation now and again could tip the scales for a pair of girls from above the border."

"You exaggerate my consequence," Holton said dismissively, extending his legs toward the fire. "How unfortunate that neither your wife nor mother-in-law is up to the full rigors of the season this year."

"Can't credit it myself yet, that I'm to be a papa." Chalmers beamed quiet satisfaction. "As you say, it's untimely that Lady Mary finds herself in the same delicate condition as her daughter. Alicen prefers to remain here at Keathley for lying in, but Lady Mary chooses to be close to her accoucheur in London. She'll attend such events as she's up to, of course, but Lady Mary can hardly promise to stay the course for a come-out."

"Just so. Have your sisters been much in Society?"

"Vanora came out with our cousin a few years back, though she don't talk about it," Chalmers said. "I was amazed when she proposed herself to accompany Eva this year; but Eva is a lamb needing a shepherd, for she's too trusting by half. Eva's only attended local assemblies and balls, which you'll consider small beer."

"Any social experience helps young ladies feel less gauche in company," said Holton, thinking both sisters like to be graceless indeed. The elder must have blotted her copybook in some way, and the *ton*'s old cats had nine memories. The younger rustic was of no possible interest to one of his sophisticated tastes. Holton knew his credit good enough to carry off bucolic connections, but the season threatened tedium with the Scotch sisters underfoot.

"Mayhap I should warn you against Vanora's managing ways," said Chalmers. "She likes to get the bit between—"

A presence had made itself felt in a good servant's way. Holton turned with Chalmers to find the butler at hand.

"Beg pardon, sir," said the man to Chalmers. "You're needed urgently in the stables. The new hunter took exception to stalling, and the squire hasn't rode in as yet."

"I'll come straight away," Chalmers replied. Rising, he addressed Holton. "Sorry to rush off in midstream, old man. Warm your feet and your innards with the fire and wine, and I'll rejoin you in two shakes to present you to my sisters."

"Don't hurry yourself on my account," said Holton, meaning every word. He poured another glass as Chalmers departed. *Best fortify the spirit against the ordeal ahead.*

The Scotch sisters stepped off the last tread of the staircase into the vacant entrance hall. In its imposing hush, the whisper of skirts and slippers against the veined marble tiles was magnified.

Vanora observed, "How like Chalmers to send for us urgently to meet guests when no one's about." She twitched her brown merino skirts straight as though girding for battle.

Eva stepped to a pier glass on the long wall of the entrance hall. "Shall we await him in the drawing room?" she asked, arms raised to tuck up a curl so that her full bosom swelled into prominence against a short bodice.

Across the way, Holton emerged from the library, an empty decanter in hand. Hearing voices from the entrance hall, he had expected to find servants to replenish the wine. Instead, he beheld an intoxicating vision.

A golden sylph of a girl stood reflected in the glass, arms upraised in graceful pose. Holton saw nothing more than the enchanting reflection, isolated in glowing perfection like a painting on his consciousness. His attention fixed about it like a living frame.

Holton crossed the hall on an indrawn breath. "My life has been as empty as this decanter until this moment, and seeing you, I finally know why!" he drawled languidly, handing the wine vessel to the brown shadow near the vision without a glance away from the glass.

"See to filling that," Holton ordered the shadow without removing his mesmerized gaze from the goddess in the glass, "while I drink in the wondrous charms of a female Narcissus before a glass instead of a pool. Yet there must be a pool, for I find that I'm drowning! And I must be Narcissus, for it's I who worships the reflection!"

The sylph turned with a ripple of laughter that swamped his senses. Holton took her hand in his, long fingers flicking between glove and sleeve to expose her wrist. He pressed his lips to her pulse as though slaking a thirst.

Holton's hand was snatched away abruptly, the palm slapped with the cold cut glass of the decanter he had just disposed. A pair of freezing, pale blue eyes shattered his contemplation of the goddess of the glass.

The brown shadow spoke, every syllable a splinter of well-bred ice. "You may give your own orders for wine, sir, unless you wish me to direct your affairs for a particular reason. And I should order you to drink less, so you may conduct yourself in a more seemly fashion!"

"I beg your pardon!" said Holton in embarrassment, looking directly at the female in brown for the first time. "I mistook you for a servant. No one said that a governess accompanied the sisters!"

2

Following tea with the entire company, Holton hurried out of the drawing room in an exit wholly unlike his usual languid movements. "One moment, Miss Chalmers, if you please!" he called after the stiff, somber figure crossing the entrance hall toward the stairs.

Vanora stopped but didn't turn. "I'm retiring to my room for solitude, if you please, sir." Her voice placed a greater distance between them than the vast hall allowed.

"But you must permit me to apologize," Holton said with assurance, stepping squarely between her and the staircase to shed his most taking smile upon her. "I don't know when I've regretted a misapprehension so thoroughly. I beg you'll be gracious enough to overlook a frightful mistake and allow me opportunity to recover myself in your opinion."

Her tone was as colorless as the face half hidden under the mobcap. "An honest mistake requires no explanation or apology. Without proper introduction, you couldn't know my sister or myself. You might refrain from addressing ladies before you're presented to them in future, however!"

Holton endured a dispassionate stare from eyes the cold grey-blue of a winter sky. As bare branches bordered such skies, a darker hue rimmed the lady's pale eyes. The effect could have been fascinating, found in warmer scenery.

"While I enter into the sentiments that prompt your stricture, I assure you that I meant no disrespect," he said, offering his most chaperone-charming smile. "Coming upon Miss Eva Chalmers in a most affecting attitude drove all rational thought from my mind, and I must plead the enchantment of the circumstances in mitigation of my thoughtless words to you."

Instead of soothing the dragon, Holton's apology appeared to inflame her. She had sat like a stone throughout tea without once looking in his direction or speaking to him in more than single-word replies. Now his words ignited a blaze in her eyes. For an instant he glimpsed a passionate nature that burned away the formal facade of the last hour, revealing a creature of such heated intensity that he felt scorched. He stepped back without knowing why.

Yet, when Miss Chalmers spoke, her tone was as flat as previously. "Sentiments, sir, are best kept leashed. Don't pretend that you will ever enter into mine. You owe me no apology. The manner in which you looked upon and now speak of my sister is far more insulting to her than your heedless words to me. I forgive both as readily as I overlook the barking of a dog in the midst of family prayers; it's no more than the nature of the beast. Excuse me, if you please; I must attend to matters in my room." Sidestepping him neatly, Miss Chalmers swept up her skirts and rushed up the stairs.

Holton looked after her in angry confusion. *Devil take the woman!* He had offered his best manner and apology.

What more did she want? While it was understandable that she wouldn't care for being taken for a maid-servant, or even for a governess, what did a female of her years expect when she went about dressed like a dowdy-goody? And what was that tirade about his manner with the sister? She could hardly have acted more incensed if he'd had his way with the chit!

Typical old maid, he told himself as the stiff-backed figure rounded the turn at the landing. *Plain as a milk pudding, with that pasty face and scraped-back hair hidden under an untrimmed cap. Probably never had a man look at her twice and resents the attentions her lovely sister invites. Obviously wouldn't know a sentiment from a snake, if her empty face and voice are any indication, and natural male reactions are just about as welcome as the reptile.*

Yet, just for a moment, when anger had melted her stiff-necked demeanor, she had appeared almost magnificent. *Must have been a trick of the imagination,* Holton concluded, *some momentary reminder of the beautiful Miss Eva.*

Vanora had never felt so relieved as to reach the safety of her room, following a tea that had threatened to choke her. The urge to choke had been twofold, for she had also longed to get her fingers round the elaborately cravated throat of the dandy laying siege to Eva.

Mortified by Holton's perception of her as a servant or governess, Vanora's fury at the dandy exceeded the offense. Unwilling to search for the leak in her mind allowing a deluge of anger to gush through, Vanora blamed Holton entirely for her agitation.

"Vanora, may I come in?" Eva asked from her doorway.

"The question seems redundant, as you've entered as

you ask it," said Vanora waspishly, wishing Eva home in Scotland. She sat up on the window seat where she had flung herself.

"Are you displeased with me? Your tone of voice is the same you used to the delightful Mr. Holton," Eva observed.

"I'm hardly delighted that you made yourself conspicuous by playing up to the odious man throughout tea," snapped Vanora, feeling somehow betrayed by her sister.

"But you were conspicuous by abrupt replies to his unexceptionable efforts at conversation," said Eva. "I can't conceive what Lady Fenmore thought of you! I scarce know what to think myself, considering that you cautioned me to behave with the utmost propriety not an hour before!"

"After the man's horrid rudeness to us both, I doubt he wonders at my attitude, at any rate," said Vanora grimly.

"Did you find him rude?" Eva hugged herself. "I thought him by far the most handsome creature I've ever set eyes on. He puts me in mind of a cat, a lean, glossy one that looks to be lazy as a summer's afternoon, yet springs to the fray in a blink when the occasion warrants."

"Take care that he doesn't toy with you in a cat-and-mouse game! Without fail, handsome men bear the most watching." Vanora reflected that Eva's admiration gave her every reason to watch Holton with great vigilance herself.

"Certainly it's more entertaining to observe handsome men," Eva said. "Such elegance in dress and person! I held my breath when Mr. Holton seated himself, in case his seams couldn't withstand the strain. I never saw pantaloons fit to the form like a rain shower had slicked them to the skin!"

"If you're so enamored of clothing, you might just as well set your cap for his tailor and valet," said Vanora, wishing Eva had not brought Holton's form so vividly to mind. "The dandy goes hand in glove with fine dressing; this one's nothing out of the ordinary."

"Do you pretend not to notice such elegance of motion?" Eva's sigh was too lusty for a lady. "Few men will undertake to pass a plate or cup, for to do so with any appearance of grace is beyond them. Yet Mr. Holton performs such services without the least loss of a most masculine air."

"The drawing-room dandy makes a study of appearing to perfection," warned Vanora. "Trust my greater experience! When you reach London, you'll learn that Holton is hardly unique. He's little above average in height, for instance." Vanora thought how nearly her inches matched his and caught herself stooping. She straightened her spine at once.

"He's quite tall enough to make me feel my daintiest," said Eva, giving Vanora an urge to shake her. "Perhaps it's the way he holds himself, so erect, yet at ease, that makes him appear taller than he is."

Vanora made a sound of impatience. "If you're ready to swoon at a glimpse of a dandy, you'll faint every moment in Society. A dandy is all show and no substance; he's full of easy promise without being dependable in its fulfillment; he inspires heart stirrings without giving heart's ease."

"No doubt you know far more about dandies than I," Eva said, "but if Mr. Holton represents the type, I quite look forward to meeting more of them!"

"I don't know how you find him at all remarkable," Vanora said shortly, recalling every detail of the man's face and form with perfect clarity. The lean elegance of narrow hips and shapely calves was topped by shoulders wide enough to block a green girl's view of more worthy men.

"But his fair hair falls in perfect golden curves, as though spun from sunlight, Vanora. His eyes touch upon one like the caress of the finest-silk Norwich shawl," Eva enthused. "Have you remarked how blue-grey eyes appear to change with the hue worn? A celestial shade would turn Mr. Holton's eyes blue as summer skies, I don't doubt."

"'Changeable' perfectly describes the dandy! You may depend upon his eyes altering in more than hue, if you encourage an association with a man who makes an easy show of emotion. A person of discrimination doesn't flaunt feelings like so much flapping laundry on the line!" Vanora's lips compressed as she recalled how Holton's eyes had caressed Eva but slid from herself as though she didn't exist.

Eva sighed and clasped a cushion from the window seat to her high waistline as she danced it round the room. "Surely you heard the musical tone to his voice, the way it lowered when he addressed me, in a manner to make me feel that he spoke for my ears alone. Though his speech was perfectly correct, his voice enclosed us in a space that left no doubt the rest of the world was excluded!"

"Take care that you listen to the true purpose behind this expressiveness, for the dandy drowns gullible young ladies like lemmings in their own tears," said Vanora sharply, with a promise to herself to hear every enticement the rake offered her inexperienced sister.

Vanora warned, "Holton is precisely the sort of man I'm here to protect you against."

"Yes, I was afraid that was the case," said Eva with a saucy smile.

After his valet had readied him for the night, Holton took to the black passage in a puddle of flickering light, shielding his bed candle from sudden drafts.

Holton needed one of the dissections of the day's events that he and Lady Fenmore often shared at house parties.

She was too observant to have overlooked the sisters' divergent reactions to him, which probably prompted her invitation for a coze in her room at the evening's end. Besides, she might be expected to understand confounded females.

The evening's efforts to include Miss Chalmers in conversation while entertaining Miss Eva Chalmers had met with the cold civility of a grand duchess. Holton was baffled that the affability for which he was noted among ladies of all ages and stations in London served him so poorly with Chalmers' spinster sister.

Holton kicked at the hem of a new quilted silk dressing gown in celestial blue. He stopped for a moment in the flickering circle of candlelight to consider the gown's length. The blasted thing required shortening.

A door opened immediately opposite Holton, causing his candle's flame a nervous shudder. Against a slit of faint light, a white-wrapped figure appeared dimly, a plait as thick as his wrist loose over the emerging feminine back.

Holton's breath caught as he anticipated an intimate glimpse of Eva, out to visit her sister. The shadowed figure turned from closing the door, and a muffled squeak showed that his presence had startled the lady.

Holton shifted his candle to cast faint yellow light on the curving form, thinking how deliciously it swelled even a simple wrapper. He raised the candle higher, expecting to reveal a lovely, laughing face. Instead, outraged eyes flashed from him to the door beside him, marked by the least line of light, bringing it to his notice for the first time.

Miss Chalmers' accusatory stare impaled him where he stood. Why did this cursed woman spike him with guilt each time they met? "I'm merely on my way to my mother's room," he said, the words sounding false even to his own ears.

"Indeed," said Miss Chalmers with no sign of belief. She crossed the passage like a vengeful specter to stand guard at the door he assumed to be Miss Eva Chalmers'.

"You may proceed to your sisterly good nights; that was never my destination," he said, nettled to be assumed capable of the kind of nighttime visits he had enjoyed on numerous occasions at house parties.

"I shall instruct Eva to turn the key on this door as I leave," said Miss Chalmers in a prim voice that Holton thought accorded poorly with their attire.

"Shall you lock yours as well?" Holton was stung enough to retort in an insinuating tone. He had the satisfaction of seeing the pale square of her face in confusion before Miss Chalmers whipped into her sister's room.

Feeling unaccountably better, Holton paced further along the passage to his mama's door. Opening it at her invitation, he swung inside in a swirl of silk.

Lady Fenmore offered a scented cheek for his salute, indicating an upholstered chair near the hearth from the couch where she reclined. "Are you cold?" she asked. "Bring a quilt from my bed for your lap if you like. Fires never warm rooms adequately in December."

"I'll fetch it if I grow chilly," said Holton, knowing that she wouldn't insist, or bustle after it herself, as did some women. Mama had the rare talent of showing that she cared without fussing one.

She smiled quietly, brows faintly raised, asking nothing beyond his company. Perhaps this was why he found it easy to confide in her, to talk as readily, and nearly as openly, as he did with friends of his own sex and age.

"What do you think of the Scotch sisters now?" he asked with a mocking smile.

"What do they think of *you?*" she returned.

Holton laughed at the repartee. "You probably can answer that question as well as I, Mama."

"I would venture only to say that their reactions seem markedly at odds." Lady Fenmore sounded idly interested.

"Which may relate directly to differing actions with them," Holton admitted ruefully.

"I never thought to see a female actually appear to take you in aversion," said Lady Fenmore. "What did you do, to earn such antipathy from Miss Chalmers?"

"How like you to assume that Miss Chalmers's attitude toward me is wholly deserved, rather than deciding like the usual fond mama that the lady harbors unreasoned prejudice."

"I may be prejudiced on your behalf, but that doesn't close my eyes to your shortcomings." Lady Fenmore settled under her quilt as though for a bedtime story. "Tell me when you first encountered the sisters and how you managed to give Miss Chalmers a disgust of you."

Holton stretched his length in the chair, hooking a footstool into place with one toe, and, in succinct words, made Lady Fenmore acquainted with the afternoon's scene in the entrance hall. He decided not to mention the brief encounter in the passage, preferring to hold it back for some reason he hadn't examined as yet. "And that's how I discovered my goddess of the glass, Mama, and stirred the wrath of the brown dragon who guards her."

Lady Fenmore had uttered only one sound during the story, a choked counterpoint to his calling Miss Chalmers a governess. When he was silent, she said, "I've never known you to be maladroit, Holton."

"Certainly not with ladies! It quite destroys my good opinion of my skill with the fair sex," Holton drawled.

"I'm delighted to hear you say so," said Lady Fenmore.

Holton straightened in his chair, hardly expecting such unfeeling sentiments from this parent. He crossed his legs at the ankle and disposed the silken folds of the dressing gown more precisely before he replied. "You seem pleased to find me discomfited in my latest attachment."

"Love and comfort are rarely close acquaintances, at least until love is an old friend," she said. "Lasting love must come as a new experience, Holton, for if you've felt much the same emotion before, what you feel isn't love."

Lady Fenmore observed her son closely for signs that he recognized the similarities between this headlong tumble into adoration to previous ones. She remembered his sudden infatuation, less than a year ago, with his pretty, petite cousin Alicen. Eva and Alicen were even much of an age.

Lady Fenmore found Holton's gaze fastened on the flames as if they suggested graceful feminine movements. She tried once more. "Loving is as individual an experience as the person who inspires it. You can't give any two people the same regard, for true sentiment grows from appreciation for what each person is. When you find yourself swept up in sudden, familiar passions, it generally indicates that you're taken with an ideal, not a person at all."

"Then you, too, believe that I've finally found true love in a reflection in a glass?" asked Holton.

"Allow time to tell you that." Lady Fenmore sighed. "It isn't what I believe, but what you know, without requiring my opinion, that tells the tale." Observing Holton's rapt expression, Lady Fenmore suspected that he had heard only what he wished to hear.

"She's the loveliest little creature who ever looked into a glass," mused Holton aloud. "She embodies every requirement of form and innocence I seek in a wife."

"You've listed points for a wife like a horse, without finding one lady to match them during all these years?" Lady Fenmore's tone could be heard as teasing or incredulous.

Holton joined his hands behind his head and stared toward the ceiling, shrouded in deep shadow. "You know I've ever been attracted by Pocket Venuses, Mama. Perhaps petite ladies bring out a protective urge in me, but I've never cared for Long Megs. I knew I would recognize her instantly, when I met the girl I could love."

"You believe a young girl will suit you best, even as you enter your own thirty-fifth year?" asked Lady Fenmore.

"Without doubt," Holton said languidly. "I want to be the one love of my lady's life; I want her to feel the first stirrings of the heart at my side. I want to lead her into the fullest experience of loving, and I want her to make every step of that delicious journey under my guidance. Even in her second season, a young lady has become a bit tired, like a muslin that's been worn too long. No, I never doubted that the love of my life would come to me fresh as dew."

Lady Fenmore cast her own eyes to the ceiling, recalling barques of frailty who hadn't been too tired to attract Holton's attentions. "You might well consider that *love* has no *I* in it! However, my part in the Scotch sisters' foray into Society is decided," she said. "I couldn't refuse to sponsor your latest romantic ideal through this season."

"Miss Chalmers will enchant the *ton* as she charms me," said Holton. "Your task will be no more difficult than securing the first invitations."

"Miss Chalmers?" queried Lady Fenmore with a taunting lift of tone and brow.

Holton waved aside his tongue's slip. "Miss Eva Chalmers, I should say, Mama. Don't tease me. The brown dragon has long since been at her last prayers."

"How do you plan to get round the dragon to claim the younger lady? I comprehend that Miss Chalmers accompanies Miss Eva *in loco parentis,* with the responsibility of recommending a suitor to her father. Do you allow that you've won Miss Chalmers's approbation to the point that she will urge your suit for Miss Eva upon him?"

"You know that I haven't." Holton's tone set the query aside. "But every female can be charmed; I simply haven't discovered the line to take with this one as yet. Even a crotchety spinster has her vulnerable point. I shall study Miss Chalmers until I discover what will win her approval of me as brother-in-law." He leaned toward his mama. "You've such a way with people; pass time with Miss Chalmers to learn what may further my cause with Miss Eva!"

Lady Fenmore's half smile in lurching firelight appeared faintly malicious for an instant. "Be assured that I shall encourage this matter to its best conclusion," she said.

Holton took his leave well satisfied.

Vanora's door was unlocked, as she had no intention of dignifying the dandy's words by precautions. Yet she lay awake still when Holton left his mama's room. The whisper of a silk dressing gown passing by her door started an undefined frisson through body and spirits.

A hot brick at one's feet made cold company in the black hours of the night.

3

Approaching the breakfast parlor next morning over the thick runner laid down the passage, Holton heard polite but contentious tones from within. He recognized the feminine voices escaping the partially opened door as those of Chalmers's wife, Alicen, and elder sister Vanora.

"You must allow us to honor you as a guest," came Alicen's soft but decided speech. "Please don't fret yourself with household responsibilities on this visit."

"Please permit me to explain what took place," said Miss Chalmers, in typical commanding tones, Holton judged.

"No explanation is required, indeed, but I deemed it best to delay any further discussion until we could be more private," said Alicen stiffly.

Holton hadn't spent years gathering the tidbits of talk that engrossed the *ton* without taking advantage of chance-heard conversations. He stepped to the hinged side of the cracked door and leaned his shoulders against the wall to eavesdrop in greater comfort.

"I merely formed an intention to prepare a special dish and took myself below stairs, not realizing it would raise such a *fashery*," Vanora protested. "I didn't think to seek your permission, before you might have left your bed."

Holton's lips lifted in amusement as he thought of his mama's superior French cook. Guizot would likely chase this interfering harpy from his precincts with a carving knife, should she dare intrude upon his domain.

"I was very nearly dressed when Cook sent word that my presence was urgently required in the kitchens," replied Alicen, sounding defensive to Holton's ears.

"Truly, you mistake my implication, as you misinterpret my intention," Vanora interrupted. "I wished to save you bother, not to set your kitchen at sixes and sevens!"

"I regret you were balked in your good intentions; for when Cook requires my presence before I breakfast, I assume our staff is disturbed," answered Alicen. "You must consider yourself on holiday here."

"I thought to have my dish dressed before you were down, for I never expected your cook to take offense at a request for simple ingredients. Nothing was out of the way in my manner to him," Vanora said, sounding genuinely puzzled, to Holton's ears, that she had been denied.

"I hope that you will feel comfortable enough to give your orders to the servants for any dish you fancy," said Alicen with a hint of exasperation in her voice. "It's hardly necessary for you to invade our kitchens, give your orders for foodstuff, and set about cooking for yourself."

"Not for myself; I went to the kitchens with the intention of making a Black Bun for Chalmers, thinking to help holiday preparations along by making the Scottish New Year's cake he favors," explained the forceful Miss

Chalmers, endeavoring to sound apologetic, to the eaves-dropper's mind.

Holton chose to believe that Vanora had attempted to seize the household reins from the manor ladies.

Alicen's voice climbed higher in tone but not volume. "Please don't provoke yourself with fears that your brother's comfort isn't of first consequence in this house."

"Forgive my unfortunate way of expressing myself," said Vanora, quite humbly for her. "I don't mean to imply that you fail Chalmers in any way. But a Black Bun must be prepared two weeks before it's served, and one couldn't expect a Southron household to know the recipe or tradition of serving it at midnight to welcome the new year. Chalmers relishes my Black Bun particularly, and I couldn't let the season pass without preparing it for him as I always have done."

"Papa's mama was as Scots as yours, Vanora; our household is fully sensible of Scots traditions." Alicen's tone was amused. "Cook prepared a Black Bun yesterday; no wonder he was insulted when you insisted on making your own!"

Holton smothered a laugh as silence stretched on the other side of the door.

"Indeed!" said Vanora, sounding mortified. "I must beg your pardon for my unwarranted interference. Please endeavor to forgive me, if you can!"

Scurrying steps from within caught Holton unprepared. Before he could do more than stand erect, the door slapped back, slamming his shoulder against the wall painfully.

Miss Chalmers shot out of the room like a fox with a pack on its tail.

"Damnation!" Holton swore, clutching his shoulder.

"You!" Vanora cried, flushing as she saw him. "You're well served, sir, for lurking about listening to private conversations!" She was off with a snap of brown skirts.

Easing his hand inside his coat to nurse offended flesh, Holton watched Miss Chalmers run away from him down the passage. He wasn't too bruised to notice that, in spite of her drab attire, Miss Chalmers sported a trim ankle.

Holton entered the bright breakfast room to find his diminutive cousin by a window, hands clutching her arms below the puffs of the tops of her long sleeves. "Hot at hand, isn't she?" he asked Alicen cheerfully.

"Holton! Were you actually listening in the passage, or did you approach at an unfortunate time?" asked Alicen with a disapproving shake of her dark head.

"You know I listen where I shouldn't," Holton said, "so be a good girl and tell me what ails that female. Is she at odds with the world, or do you and I occupy positions of special distinction with her?"

"Don't ask what can't be answered, Holton. You know I mustn't gossip about my sister," said Alicen.

"Sister-in-law, my dear. And I'm a cousin, so it's hardly gossip, just family chitchat," Holton cajoled. "Chalmers mentioned that his eldest sister tends to ride roughshod, so you hardly speak out of turn."

"You make Vanora sound horrid, which is far from the case," scolded Alicen. "If you wish to understand Miss Chalmers's motivations, you must apply to her."

"That's a difficult proposition, when she hardly speaks to me," Holton replied, trying a pitiful tone.

Alicen laughed. "Eva told me about the contretemps when you met yesterday afternoon. I couldn't credit your saying the wrong thing to a female!"

"Obviously, I made a mull of it with that one," Holton admitted, escorting Alicen to the sideboard, where various dishes waited under covers. "You see that I require assistance in learning how to get on her good side. Since you claim there is one, the least you could do is point the way. Help me to placate the lady!"

"You don't require assistance with ladies, Holton; you need handicapping where females are concerned. I shall only say that you must try to make allowances. Vanora's sensibilities appear easily overset by your kind of male," said Alicen, taking up a plate, "and your introduction couldn't have been calculated to make a worse impression."

Holton clattered down the ham's cover to face Alicen squarely. "Don't stop with so little when you've said so much. I wasn't aware that my sex came in varieties, like turnips! What kind of male am I, pray tell?"

Alicen contemplated a dish of kidneys doubtfully. "I should never have said so much, but I quite like Vanora in spite of managing ways. You might even improve each other by acquaintance, if you can get past your dread of direction! Just overlook her prickly side and show your kind nature, rather than the ladies'-man you enjoy to enact."

"I protest that my appreciation for ladies is no act; it's one of my greatest kindnesses!" Holton insisted, offering Alicen a roll. "Won't you tell me more about the dragon with hedgehog tendencies?"

Alicen accepted the roll and considered buttered eggs. "Must you banter on every subject? As for your great reputation with females, no gentleman who loves ladies as you profess to do would remain unwed in his thirty-fifth year!"

"You could, and you would, be helpful toward that end," Holton wheedled. "Point the way to appeasing Miss Chalmers, so I may pursue acquaintance with the lovely Miss Eva."

"I've given you the best advice of a true friend," said Alicen, turning to the table. "More than that I can't say."

"Very well," Holton said, following. "You leave me no option. I must apply all my considerable resources to learning what in the dragon's dark past makes the lady so skittish that men need take care in approaching her!"

Vanora had taken refuge to nurse her embarrassment after pulling caps with her sister-in-law. Knowing Eva didn't hesitate to enter her chamber, Vanora sought sanctuary in the library. The room was little occupied of a morning, she had observed, so she could count on solitude to compose herself.

How presumptuous to assume that Alicen needed my help in holiday preparations without asking, Vanora thought. *Mama warned me about this tendency to snatch reins and drive to my own destination, so it isn't as though I didn't know better. Why is it that knowing one's faults takes one such a short distance toward mending them?*

Vanora paced the long room, entering an alcove lined by bookcases at the far end. Of all the ill luck, she fretted for that toplofty tulip to lurk outside the door and witness her embarrassment! Shame shuddered through Vanora like a chill. Showing Alicen her besetting sin was bad enough, but displaying her worst fault before Holton was beyond agony.

The only reason she desired the man's good opinion was that his mama's assistance was essential to Eva's season. What could he report of her conduct to his mama now? Vanora flung herself into an upholstered barrel chair in the alcove, buried a flaming face in her hands, and groaned.

Half an hour later, Vanora still sat in the alcove, punishing herself by reading diligently from an excessively dry volume of Sherlock's *Sermons*. She heard the door into the library open. Thinking a servant entered to tend the fire, Vanora remained quiet. She couldn't face even a servant as yet.

"Speak as you find her," came her brother Chalmers's voice clearly from the main body of the room. "Vanora speaks her mind plainly enough, so there's no need to hide your teeth on that topic with me."

Vanora sat bolt upright. She didn't expect Chalmers to speak of her in that tone, even to Alicen. And she could hardly credit that Alicen had tattled to him about the morning's misunderstanding.

The drawl that answered Chalmers was plainly masculine, appallingly familiar. "How can I disparage a lady I know so little as yet? I merely hope to learn how I might approach her in a way to inspire civil relations. Distressing her on our first meeting weighs heavily, and I wish to atone."

Vanora felt as though her stays were too tightly laced.

"Nora's nose gets out of joint on occasion," said Chalmers. "But she generally works out ill humors in her own time. Mama and Papa may have overindulged her along that line, which accounts for the odd kick in her gallop."

Vanora gripped the book of sermons so firmly that she marked the pages. How dare Chalmers discuss her with no more discretion than if she were a family pet, or as if she were subject to taking a pet without provocation!

"You call Miss Chalmers 'Nora,'" Holton observed. "Have I also heard her designated 'Vanora'?"

"Indeed," Chalmers answered. "Mama gave her the Scot form of the name 'Guinevere.' I consider myself fortunate not to be lumbered with 'Lancelot!'"

Holton laughed. "Names might be more appropriately assigned after one's character forms. Miss Chalmers's given name could be said to fit Miss Eva Chalmers more nearly."

Vanora's lips clamped tighter than the mantrap in which she wished Holton caught.

"Nora's normally a better sport than you've seen," Chalmers defended. "Too bad you got off at the wrong gait with her. A fellow couldn't ask for a more staunch friend, even if she gnaws on one as a mark of regard."

"Naturally, I don't ask that you speak out of turn," said Holton, "but I should appreciate being set on the right road to dealing more pleasantly with Miss Chalmers."

The sounds of bodies settling into leather chairs came clearly to Vanora's burning ears as her mind supplied a picture of Holton's sinuous grace in performance of the action. How sincerely the ferret spoke!

Chalmers's voice dropped to a confiding tone. "Nora's never seemed herself after her season eight years since. Nobody tells me aught, as Nora's my senior, and female to boot. But I formed the distinct impression after her come-out that events hadn't come out right, somehow."

Vanora fell back in her chair, the book of sermons over her heated face.

"Indeed!" said Holton. "And you received no impression of what, precisely, might have gone wrong?"

"Not exactly," said Chalmers, adding, confidentially, "but I expect it was something to do with a man."

Vanora slid down in her chair onto her spine.

"It so often is," came Holton's hateful drawl.

"This is purely conjecture, you understand," said Chalmers. "I was at school during the actual events. But before Vanora went to town, she encouraged quite as much male attention as Eva does now. She came back from London acting as though eligible men had ceased to exist."

Vanora slid out of the chair quietly, turning her face into its cushioned seat.

"You mean she invited the attentions of young men

before she came south for a season, but those attentions were no longer welcome on her return home?" asked Holton in a voice full of false concern to Vanora's outraged ears.

"Not just young men, single men! She's perfectly cordial to long-married males and the parson," Chalmers answered. "Like Eva, Vanora took the eye at one time. She never sat out a dance in her life, until she came back from London. Then she put on caps and dull colors, not to mention die-away airs, till one wouldn't know her for the same girl!"

"Quite remarkable," observed Holton. "And you don't know any more to the story than that?"

"Not a jot. Mama told me to leave Vanora to come about in her own time, when I asked what had changed our Nora so. You see why I say that the parents should have pushed her to behave normally again, rather than indulge her in whatever freakish fancy she brought home from that season."

"I appreciate your concern," Holton said. "Certainly she can support your parents' latter years, but eventually you'll have the responsibility for her keeping. I doubt she would marry now, not at her age."

Vanora's head shot up from the chair seat and she half-turned where she knelt.

"I should be glad for her to come to us, if need be, though she might prefer living with my elder brother or Eva, come the day. I'm right fond of the old girl," said her blasted brother. "Not that she's really so old as she makes herself out to appear. What age do you think Nora to be?"

Vanora put her handkerchief to her lips and leaned forward. She listened so intently that she felt blind, as though all senses were concentrated toward hearing the reply.

"That's hardly a fair question. A gentleman never notices a lady's age and certainly never comments on it if he does so." Holton dared to laugh at so serious a subject.

"Give it a guess; I promise never to divulge what you say," Chalmers urged. "Allow me to prove a point about what she's done to herself from some silly notion."

Vanora held her breath so as not to miss a syllable.

"I surmise the lady's reached the far side of thirty, though I won't remark how far," said Holton.

Vanora stuffed her handkerchief into her mouth to quiet the screams she needed to indulge.

"That's just the way a female looks when she don't present herself well," said Chalmers with odious satisfaction. "Nora's barely twenty-six."

"Fancy that!" Holton said in equally odious wonderment.

Vanora crawled quietly behind the chair, vowing to hide there until dinner, if necessary, rather than show herself before these detestable men.

4

Vanora picked up her skirts and took to her heels. Through the shrubbery, round the kitchen garden wall, out to the orchard she fled from the twin torments of anger and pain.

Fruit trees stood in ladylike ranks, barren in the face of winter's cold disdain. Empty aisles stretched between rows of short stock, where carpets of dead thatch caught at Vanora's slippers. Vanora bolted like a mad rabbit, down one long corridor and up the next, running headlong until a stitch in her side slowed her at last to a staggering walk.

Falling against the stocky trunk of a cherry tree, she flung back her head to gulp breaths. Chill air, or colder memory, seared her throat. Blinking rapidly at grey, serrated clouds, Vanora fancied that bare branches crazed the sky like lines netted across old china.

A glacial gust whipped the woolen cloak against Vanora's exposed ankles and flung her cap's ribbons into

her gasping mouth. She spit them out, wishing she could
as easily be rid of the bitterness caused by the overheard
exchanges.

She had set out to drive anguish into the ground with
pounding steps, once out of sight of Keathley Manor.
Like her heart belabored her ribs, fury beat at her mind.
Only as the tumultuous gallop in her chest followed the
pace of painful breaths to a semblance of normalcy did
coherent thoughts form once more.

At first, black incantations roiled within. As Vanora's
breathing slowed, logic intruded, until reason wrestled
with rage for ascendency over her thoughts.

*How could a brother betray one's most grievous
secrets,* rage asked. *He knew only guesses to reveal,* reason pointed out in Chalmers's defense.

Charles! thought Vanora and flinched from the
specter of that long-ago season as from a threat.

Vanora stumbled away from the cherry tree on ruined
slippers. She had snatched a cloak without taking the
time to change into sturdy boots. Frozen turf stabbed the
soles of thin kid slippers like memories jabbed her mind.

The far side of thirty! rage recalled. *You chose to clothe
yourself in the trappings of a woman who has put away
youth,* reason reminded her.

Vanora tugged at her cap's ribbons, finally freeing it
with cold, stiffened fingers. She snatched the despised
object off her head and threw it to the ground like a mor-
tal foe. For several minutes, she expelled pent-up vexation
by grinding the fine fabric into the dry turf as thoroughly
as thin slippers could manage it.

Charles! Vanora's heart cried. *How could you claim my
youth and abandon me to age without you?*

Feeling the wind's rasping breath on naked ears,
Vanora pulled the cloak's hood over her bared head. For-
lorn, she walked on.

Frigid air, flung though a break in the line of trees, doused Vanora. Shaking with cold, or nerves, she spotted a short stump where a damson must have sickened and died. Her parents couldn't live forever, and her home would die with them. Vanora couldn't bear life on the estate once they were gone, with a sister-in-law as mistress. Holton had pointed out that a brother or sister must be prepared to take her in, for she was unlikely to marry now.

How dare he say so? cried rage. *It's no more than you planned for yourself,* chided reason.

Following that insupportable season, Vanora had returned home to stay. She had planned to be a prop to her parents in their last years, and afterward, to act aunt to her siblings' children. Vanora hadn't pictured time beyond that. Must she live sterile years on the fringes of family groups, where she was cheerfully tolerated, benignly neglected, as were so many old-maid aunts of her own acquaintance?

This plan for her life had seemed comfortable, even safe, until now. Holton had spoken of Chalmers having the responsibility for her keeping. Could she avoid usurping Alicen's place for a lifetime when she couldn't control her interference for one visit? Directing a household came naturally; having no right to give orders did not.

Spinsters were a subject for jests, as though lacking feelings to hurt, Vanora realized. An unmarried woman had no life of her own; she lived at the beck and call of relations. Vanora's independent nature cringed at the very thought.

Even if her dowry stretched to a cottage in which to live out her days, she couldn't properly live alone. She could think of no one to bide with her. Eva would wed, for Eva was too warm and loving not to marry.

Charles! Vanora thought, remembering a time when she had loved. *No gift enriches the giver like loving.* She pushed impoverishing torment away.

In its place rose an image of the elegant Holton. Vanora pictured him leaning toward Chalmers as the private places of her heart were stripped bare by his casual inquiry. Mocking eyes must have shone with amusement at the thought that the spinster had been young enough once to dance. Her anger rose from some lair in the past, like a snarling dog.

Rage advised, *Flout Holton as his heedless rooting about in other's lives deserves!* But reason reminded, *Eva needs his mama's support through the season.*

Vanora kicked at the stump, recalling her thin slippers too late. *Do frozen toes shatter at a blow like a heart?* As she hopped about to relieve the offended foot, Vanora pledged herself to forethought before kicking out at the self-centered dandy who roused her ire.

Showing Holton the anger he released would hurt her far more than him, Vanora thought, limping between trees. How freely he expressed his instant passion for Eva, how solicitously he quizzed Chalmers about Vanora's private affairs. An effortless display of sensibility showed how little his heart was engaged in easy expressions of emotion.

Clasping an apricot's branch with both hands, like a claymore's hilt, Vanora vowed to show her superior strength over Holton by concealing the loathing she felt for him. *A strong will controls sentiment,* Vanora chivvied herself.

Masking emotion was difficult at first, in those early days after losing Charles. Avid eyes had watched her like furtive thieves for the show she would make of her feelings. But Vanora had shown nothing. Grief was a private place.

Holton had demonstrated the shallow nature of his emotions by enacting any sentiment that might gain the desired end. Showing the dandy how she detested him would afford her the greatest satisfaction for the moment, but Eva would suffer for it a lifetime.

Eva must have her season. Eva must know happiness denied Vanora. Eva needed Lady Fenmore's backing, and she would have it, Vanora averred.

Vanora loved Eva far more than she despised the dandy, so her emotions toward Holton must be set aside. Not by a lifted brow would she betray her disdain for the dandy. She would act amiable beyond belief. She would smile, make civil conversation, flatter the rake in his great opinion of himself. Lady Fenmore would believe her a well-conducted female, no matter what the cost in self-control.

But, just for the present, rage must be served. Vanora beat upon an apple tree trunk until her fists were sore, pretending that the insufferable creature's broad chest took the drubbing.

Eva's dextrous fingers bound holly with long strands of ivy into a growing sphere. She had unlooped the buttons to long sleeves, folding them back to free ungloved hands for the task of twining greenery.

Holton licked at Eva's wrists with his eyes like a greedy boy scraping a bowl clean of icing, Vanora thought, feeling overly warm. She hadn't fully apprehended the dangers of the male gaze. No wonder ladies were taught to cover their hands with gloves in company!

Eva must be reminded to don her short primrose gloves immediately after this work was done, Vanora thought, quelling a desire to throw her serviceable woolen Paisley shawl over Holton's caressing eyes.

The three were down for Christmas Eve festivities before the rest of the company, Eva eager to join Holton in fashioning a kissing ball. Determined that the two shouldn't sit down to it alone, Vanora sat gooseberry on a nearby sofa.

Holton's long fingers fed ivy vines to Eva's efforts,

and Vanora watched him brush Eva's fingers with his own far more frequently than the task made necessary. If only Vanora had a baton, she could correct Holton in the same way a music teacher had ordered her hands at the pianoforte.

"Do you know the symbolism of the greenery you use?" Holton asked Eva. He spoke quietly, no doubt hoping only Eva could hear, thought Vanora, leaning closer.

"You'll tell me, I fancy," said Eva. "Surely one selects greenery for its color at Christmas time."

"Never make a choice based solely on what's available," Holton bantered, with a quick glance toward Vanora. "Let your heart tell you its desires in all things." As Eva tinkled a delighted laugh, he continued. "This ivy represents the female, perhaps because it clings for support as it grows. Holly's strong, sharp leaf offers protection when planted in hedges, representing the male."

Vanora couldn't resist intruding her view. "And mistletoe's pearl-drop fruit is poisonous! So the symbolism of the kissing ball is that when male and female come together, the results threaten to be disastrous!"

"Not at all," said Holton, directing a glance of appreciative amusement her way. "One might as justly observe that the female, or ivy, forces restraints upon the male, or holly, in this coming together!"

Returning his attention to Eva, Holton said quietly, "Tradition has it that when an unmarried lady is taken by surprise with a kiss under the mistletoe, she's assured of marrying within the year. A gentleman's daring assumes the risk of losing a bachelor's comfortable life to a lady and must not be undertaken lightly!"

"I expect you've made the whole notion up out of whole cloth," Vanora said loudly, feeling the outsider sitting apart on her sofa. "How unflattering, to make marriage sound like an attainment for a lady, but a loss to a gentleman!"

Bowing to Vanora before turning his attention to Eva again, Holton murmured still lower, "When I claim a berry from the kissing ball after capturing you there, I'll tuck it into my card case rather than discard it."

Vanora caught every word, her senses especially acute in the dandy's company. She determined to stay close to Eva's side so that she could draw Eva away should Holton attempt to maneuver the moment he anticipated.

Vanora watched Holton place branches of greyed mistletoe against the ball of deeper green while Eva secured them with ivy strands. Holton reached for silver ribbon, weaving a length among the greenery with the languid sensuality he would use to wind it among a lady's tresses, Vanora thought. Long, pale fingers shouldn't speak to one of latent strength. The mesmerizing effect of graceful male hands ended abruptly as Holton picked up shears to snip the ribbon.

The symbolism of allowing oneself even a moment's fancy over a dandy is clear enough, Vanora reminded herself. *Snip! and you're cut off, alone.*

Watching Holton flirt with Eva, Vanora wondered at odd emotions that niggled like gnats. She had chaperoned her sister since Eva had put up her hair and let down her skirts at fifteen, but Eva's admirers had stirred no sentiments beyond boredom. This hollow hunger couldn't be jealousy, Vanora reasoned, for that sentiment required wanting, and desires on her own behalf were long dead.

She wasn't attracted by Holton in the least, Vanora assured herself, though her vow to civility had proved easy enough to keep, more so with each day that passed. Doubtless this was because a dandy by definition was pleasant company, apart from the falseness of flirtatious ways, at least.

As he tied a knot in the ribbon to form a hanging loop, Holton teased Eva about tying another sort of knot by the end of the season. Vanora knew an urge to yank Eva off the delicate caned chair and march her upstairs. Disappointment must come, should Eva count on more than dalliance from this dandy. Concern for Eva must account for her uneasy state of mind, Vanora mused.

If the smallest twinge of jealousy existed, no doubt she regretted the dull grey silk of her gown, made from ells bought for Mama. But a gown like Eva's, white patent net over silk, was far too young for a spinster. Vanora smoothed the lace lappets to her best cap over her shoulders, her one concession to dressing for the holidays.

Holton held the kissing ball aloft as he stood. "One naturally approaches the fire on entering a room, so our creation might hang in its vicinity," he said.

"Heat could dry the mistletoe too quickly, and the berries drop of their own accord," protested Eva, tucking holly more securely under an ivy strand as she stood by him.

"Such precious fruit mustn't be wasted," Holton agreed with a speaking look to Eva. "The usual placement is a doorway, so perhaps we should honor that tradition."

"You honoring tradition?" challenged a voice from the entrance to the room. "Surely such effort is beyond you."

Vanora looked to the newcomer with interest. She had been dressing in her room when sounds of arrival suggested that Lord Fenmore had joined the house party for Christmas Eve as anticipated. She was curious to know what sort of man fathered a dandy with rakish leanings.

The elegant gentleman crossing the threshold gave Vanora an odd sense of seeing Holton as he might appear in another thirty years. Lord Fenmore held himself in the same assured posture that added to Holton's stature, and regal features provided the mold for Holton's classical face. Where Holton's hair fell in golden curves, his father's waved in purest silver strands, brushed back from his brow. Holton should wear well, in appearance, at least.

Like his son, Lord Fenmore dressed for evening in the Spartan black and white adopted often these days by men of taste. Expression stamped the two as dissimilar in more than age. While Holton's features arranged themselves in languid amusement on most occasions, Lord Fenmore looked every inch the serious politician. Vanora could believe Lady Fenmore's concern that her husband might not free himself of parliamentarian duty to join the family house party.

"You come in good time, Pater," greeted Holton coolly. "Allow me to present you to Chalmers's sisters."

Vanora stood to be made acquainted with Lord Fenmore, feeling that one should remain at attention when receiving his steely regard. By the time Lord Fenmore had instructed the ladies to be seated again, Squire Plewes and Lady Mary appeared, and Lady Fenmore entered shortly after. Chalmers arrived in time to help Holton secure the kissing ball to the door's frame with drawing pins, and Alicen, entering last, paid the first forfeits under its boughs to both men.

The squire was handing round wine when a bustle of stifled voices and shuffling footsteps followed a cold draft from the entrance hall. From the doorway, the butler announced: "The Yule log is here, sir, if you're ready to receive it."

Vanora remained in the background, watching the ceremony as cotters, headed by the estate carpenter, paraded the greenery-decked log round the entrance hall on stout shoulders. Surely the thing represented the whole of an oak tree's trunk, she thought. No trouble keeping a log this size burning for the twelve hours that would bring good fortune to the household. Vanora wished the good luck on visitors as well as residents as she stepped closer to Eva.

"Mind the furniture," trilled Lady Mary as the huge

log was carried in state to a resting place prepared for it in the hall's great fireplace. To complaints and laughter, the log was fitted into the prepared grate, filling the cavity.

"Where's the splinter?" demanded Squire Plewes, referring to the piece saved from the previous year's Yule log to light this one. The butler produced it, bearing the blackened wood in on a tray. The squire made a hearty speech about servants and masters coming through another year in company, made fond reference to his wife and daughter, and welcomed the guests and newcomers to the family, Chalmers and his sisters.

Vanora tasted homesickness as this Southron squire called her father sharply to mind. She watched the splinter being tucked into the kindling and held her breath as Squire Plewes applied a spill. If the kindling caught quickly, Eva would take well in the upcoming season, she mused superstitiously.

The fire blazed with a popping and color to the flames that suggested the kindling had received encouragement to do its job. Vanora promised herself that Eva should have whatever was required to shine brightly upon the *ton*. Feeling a hand slip into hers, she turned to find Eva glowing already, with Holton, predictably, at her elbow.

"Isn't it lovely, Vanora? Aren't you excessively pleased that we're here?" asked Eva, watching the service of Lamb's Wool to the Yule log's escorts.

"I'm well content if you're happy," said Vanora, vexed that Holton hung at Eva's side like a reticule. Noticing that the hand Eva had given her was bare, Vanora said sharply, "Fetch your gloves at once, Eva!"

Lord Fenmore crossed the drawing room to join the ladies after dinner, followed by the rest of the gentlemen. Settling near Vanora on a sofa, he leaned over to pat his wife's hand where she sat on an elbow chair to one side.

Holton drawled as he followed, "I should have expected you to beat us all out by taking the only remaining seat amongst the ladies, Pater."

"You should, indeed," replied Lord Fenmore. "If you followed my lead into politics as readily as you do upon that head, I should make no complaint of you."

Holton shot an arrogant look at his father without answering the jibe. He took a chair behind Eva so that he sat sideways to her, where he could easily lean across to speak quietly into her ear, Vanora noted with irritation.

Conscious that Lord Fenmore snipped at his son for a second time, Vanora also knew a twinge of sympathy for Holton. No greater mortification than being faulted in front of others existed, she thought. She wondered if Lord Fenmore made a habit of addressing set-downs to Holton in public.

So recently arrived from town, Lord Fenmore drew interest as he had at table. He patiently answered questions about various acquaintances in London, reporting town thin of company as the *ton* took to estates to celebrate Christmas.

"What word is there from Vienna, beyond what we may read in the papers?" Vanora asked civilly.

Looking gratified to be questioned on a topic of interest to him, Lord Fenmore said, "One begins to wonder if the allies will wage war among themselves before they reach a territorial compromise. At the moment, Poland and Saxony are the bones of contention. Watch the papers for mention of Talleyrand's doings, Miss Chalmers, if you affect interest in political maneuvering. We must congratulate ourselves that this Frenchman had no bent for manipulating armies!"

Looking significantly between Vanora and Holton, Lord Fenmore said, "I allow myself agreeably surprised to find that Scotch youth take an interest in what's toward in the world. My heir only knows of the Congress in Vienna because of the superior social life developing round it."

Vanora's hands tensed together with embarrassment on Holton's behalf. How humiliating to be made an object of public scrutiny. She spoke to distract Lord Fenmore's attention. "Perhaps you assumed that, the Scottish vote being in the government's pocket, so to speak, Scots have no need to concern themselves overmuch with world affairs."

Lord Fenmore turned his whole body to observe her, as though a statue in a niche along a wall had given tongue. "You're obviously aware that the ministry can count on the support of nearly all the Scottish vote. Are you informed as well on the advantage of that arrangement to your people?"

"As in favors between two farmers, one pays back what one owes, if you refer to the military and civil service posts put at Scotland's disposal in exchange for support," said Vanora. She noticed that Holton had left off flirting with Eva to attend her speech with his father.

Lord Fenmore raised an eyebrow, laughing in the languid way Holton did on occasion. "A lady who practices plain speaking! Two farmers, indeed! Well spoken, though our good Farmer George is past such concerns, more's the pity. You hold views on price supports for corn, I don't doubt."

Vanora kept Lord Fenmore in conversation for several minutes, until she saw his glance move away and stay. She followed the direction of his eyes to find Holton assisting Eva from her chair. Vanora thought of the kissing ball. "What a good idea, to stroll about the room," she said, rising. "I'm ready for exercise myself."

The look Holton turned on her was warm but amused. Bowing exquisitely, he murmured, "How delightful!

One can never enjoy the company of too many ladies."

As Vanora moved to join the couple, she heard Lord Fenmore remark to his wife, "Miss Chalmers and Talleyrand have much in common as machinators, I perceive!"

Lady Fenmore had just dismissed her dresser when Lord Fenmore knocked for admittance to her chamber later that night. The woman curtsied him in as she departed.

Lord Fenmore pecked his wife on the forehead before taking the chair their son occupied during late-night chats. "Holton's after the pretty little minx, is he not?" he asked crossly by way of preamble.

Lady Fenmore smiled. "I daresay he entertains himself with the company at hand in his usual fashion."

Her husband snorted. "Ridiculous! A man of his age to be chasing the nursery set! The chit could be his own child!"

Lady Fenmore leaned over the chair's back to lay arms round her husband. "Not quite that, perhaps, for I'm persuaded you never meant him to set up his nursery before his twentieth year!"

"No, indeed; but I never intended him to reach midlife without an heir, either. The boy's gone out of his way to confound me at every turn! He's never shown the least interest in what counts for something in life. Holton makes a career out of doing the pretty! It's as though he's set himself to be at cross-purposes with everything I stand for. Has he no regard for my judgment?" Lord Fenmore fumed.

Lady Fenmore kissed her husband's silver hair before crossing to settle herself on the couch. "Holton loves you, my dear; never doubt it."

Lord Fenmore snorted again. "Don't be absurd; I

require only the occasional mark of respect. But as long as he holds out against any show of common sense or purpose in his life, how can I credit that he respects the important business of government, which is my life? Can you conceive of him speaking in the House of Lords? He will require so long to dress for the occasion that he'll miss the session entirely!"

"Best not vex yourself over matters beyond control," said Lady Fenmore. "Indications this past year suggest that Holton's closer to choosing a wife than you believe. He would have married Alicen, had she accepted him."

"I've seen no evidence whatsoever," grumbled Lord Fenmore. "Alicen was just another of the games he plays to amuse himself. Chasing pretty little widgeons with more hair than wit won't get him a wife of the least help to him when there's a vote to be influenced."

Lord Fenmore sat up in his chair as though struck by inspiration. "Miss Chalmers is a lady with an understanding adequate to grasp situations of a political nature, whatever she may lack in appearance! Not that countenance counts for much in a contract of marriage. Her breeding's above reproach and could even give us an edge to sway another Scots vote or two!"

Nodding decisively, he continued, "Miss Chalmers demonstrates a strong sense of management, with that flighty sister to keep in hand. No reason she couldn't handle Holton just as well, if she put her mind to it. I believe the girl might do very well for Holton!"

"Don't so much as hint to Holton that you favor Miss Chalmers in that regard!" begged Lady Fenmore. "Any push in one direction so often sends him bolting in another!"

5

With *nine members of* their party to transport to Christmas Day services, the men had elected to ride. Grooms had taken charge of the mounts before the parish church.

A gentleman handed down each of the married ladies, and as Vanora leaned into the carriage's doorway, Holton offered assistance and his heart-breaker smile. Vanora had believed her extremities frozen past sensation, but as Holton grasped her gloved hand, an unholy tempo pulsed through her fingers. She didn't dare look into his teasing eyes.

Safely on the ground, Vanora glanced up briefly to thank Holton, to find him already turning away. He handed Eva out tenderly, and Eva displayed no inclination to keep her gaze decorously down. Vanora's lips quivered with a repressed scold on the oft-repeated subject of excessive flirtation.

Squire Plewes and Lady Mary led their guests across the churchyard studded with grave markers and into the stone structure. Lord and Lady Fenmore followed close behind.

Chalmers fussed over Alicen as though no female had ever carried a child, Vanora noted enviously. She hurried to keep pace with Holton as he handed Eva across the ground as though snares threatened her every step.

Holton and Eva would attend to each other instead of the Christmas service, Vanora fumed, watching them flirt on the very doorstep to the church. She must make an opportunity to separate the two, if Eva were to worship God instead of man.

Following the others up a central aisle, Vanora stumbled over uneven stone flags. She was aware that heads turned to assess their arrival, just as they would in the kirk at home.

Little else in her surroundings reminded Vanora of a Scotch kirk. Instead of stiff rows of upright seats, boxed pews of unmatched sizes and heights jammed the nave higgledy-piggledy. Hatchments dotted the walls.

The squire held open a door to a pew more than half-way along the uneven aisle marked with a brass plaque. Paying for a private enclosure was a sad waste of the ready, to Vanora's mind. Lady Mary showed Lord and Lady Fenmore to the far end of the pew. Chalmers handed Alicen inside tenderly, settling her solicitously before sitting beside her. Squire Plewes waved the sisters and Holton ahead of himself into the box.

Vanora stepped nimbly ahead of Holton, giving Eva a shove in front of herself before she left the aisle. A quickly-smothered titter nearby caused Vanora to compress her lips. It hardly mattered what observers thought, or Holton himself, for that matter. Eva might even benefit from this service, separated from her flirt so she could hear it.

Vanora seated herself beside Eva, ignoring her reproachful look as well as an amused one from Holton. He took the seat beside Vanora with lithe grace and no show of dissatisfaction in his placement. The squire distributed prayer books from the stack by the pew's door. Vanora found herself sharing one with Holton and took satisfaction that she had prevented Eva from flirting rather than reading the lesson.

Eva leant sideways to murmur, "Such luxury is beyond anything great; cushions upon the seats! Fireplaces would be more to the point, though, I vow!"

Vanora frowned repressively. "Hush! One doesn't attend kirk to be comfortable." Cold flagstones breathed a chilling message already, even through half boots. Vanora doubted she could move her toes by the end of services, despite the luxury of a paneled pew to exclude drafts.

Settling, Vanora eased her lined cloak from under her to allow arm movement. Her elbow brushed Holton's, and he turned to smile impersonally upon her. Vanora forgot to breathe. His smile was like a shaft of sunlight through the square-paned window, warming impartially where it chanced to fall. The man's most meaningless smiles spelled danger!

Vanora clamped the traitorous elbow to her waist, vowing not to move again. Even through her heavy cloak, she had experienced a sensation like touching her forehead by accident with curling tongs. A good thing Eva wasn't the sister subjected to such oversetting proximity, Vanora assured herself, feeling justified in altering the seating.

Eva whispered as a band filed in among villagers who seated themselves in an enclosure near the three pulpits. "Do the English hold a musicale in place of a church service? Look! There's a violin, a bass viol, a bassoon—but whatever is that strangely winding horn? And why do those people sit with the musicians?"

"Shush!" warned Vanora quietly. "Southrons employ musical instruments as part of the service. The people with the musicians are no doubt a choir, and the instrument is the serpent. Be still!" She noted that Holton leaned forward to smile upon Eva, brushing Vanora's arm as he did so. Vanora started, then froze, a difficult feat while waves of molten warmth coursed up one limb.

Holton must have noticed her involuntary movement, for he leaned to whisper, "I didn't intend to discomfit you!"

Outraged, Vanora said stiffly, "You don't! You startled me. I expected you to be attending the prayerbook!"

An hour later, Vanora's right arm, next to Holton, was still locked to her waist, alive to every brush of Holton's sleeve as he changed position. Whether he deliberately allowed his elbow to stray was conjecture, for when she turned to glare, his profile was cherubic in its innocence.

The rest of her body was numb with cold. The walker would be out of a job, if he relied on keeping her awake for his pay. Yet Vanora heard nothing of the long litany, once Holton's fingers joined hers on the *Book of Common Prayer*.

Much later still, Vanora listened in disbelief as the sermon's Latin phrases concluded in a call to pray. The vicar had turned the hourglass only once, and that a scant half hour since, yet he was folding up his papers already. Perhaps the short sermon honored the holiday, allowing more of the day for family celebrations. The English considered themselves pious, no doubt, but it was clear they spent little enough time in church, Vanora reckoned.

Rising with the rest of the party, Vanora followed Holton from the pew. He wrapped his caped great coat close, outlining slender hips. Vanora's gaze traced the lean lines tapering below broad shoulders. Catching herself in such impious observation was no doubt the reason she couldn't meet Holton's eyes when he pointedly offered an arm to her as well as to Eva in escort from the church.

*   *   *

Vanora's face felt as though it would crack like a dropped plate if she held her social smile another instant. The first duty of a guest, to appear amiable every moment, became onerous as Christmas Day crawled toward evening.

Luncheon had been more of a nuncheon for those who wanted it, with the kitchens in a swarm to produce an early dinner to mark the day properly. Discussion of seasonal celebrations had occupied much of the short afternoon, with the Chalmers siblings describing Scottish traditions, which made more of New Year's.

Lady Fenmore described the Duchess of York's holiday fair, with tables of gifts for houseguests and a decorated indoor evergreen tree in the German way.

"The *ton* rushes to ape the duchess's extravagance rather than her generosity," grumbled Lord Fenmore. "Christmas will hardly be worth keeping, if this foreign notion to make a display of gifts takes hold generally."

By four o'clock, an early dinner had been announced, a feast that had dulled Vanora's spirits as she thought of home. Only her determination that Eva should have the season she deserved draped a civil expression over Vanora's features, like a holland cover over furniture in a closed room.

Holton had made Eva the object of mild flirtation after their return from church services, which Vanora didn't doubt had delighted her sister. Vanora saw Lord Fenmore frown now and again as he regarded his son's dalliance, and the sight failed to raise Vanora's low spirits. Perhaps Lord Fenmore considered the Scottish sisters beneath his son's touch.

The servants had gathered in the great entrance hall after dinner to drink the traditional toasts to the season with the family, the squire speaking from the stairs. At last the servants began returning below to enjoy their own festivities. Family and guests turned toward the drawing room, with a longer evening ahead to fill than was usual.

A searching look about the near-empty hall indicated that Holton must have slipped Eva out in the melee of servants taking leave, and Vanora knew sharp dread. She had shadowed Eva all day to keep her out of the doorway where the kissing ball hung, only to have her creep away in the crowd like a housemaid with an unauthorized follower.

Vanora couldn't push rudely past her elders, who clumped at the drawing room's entrance exchanging pleasantries and kisses under the mistletoe. She all but danced with impatience to cross the threshold. Finally reaching the door, Vanora looked toward the sofas near the fireplace.

She failed to find Eva and Holton there. Just as Vanora turned to look toward the other half of the long room, Holton leaned to salute her cheek, for she stood directly under the kissing ball avoided so assiduously on Eva's behalf.

By turning at the last moment, Vanora received Holton's ready lips full upon her own.

The brief touch startled both; Holton and Vanora leaped apart as though stabbed with pins at the same moment. In the instant encompassed by the meeting of their lips, Vanora felt the firm warmth of Holton's mouth, smelled the sharp citric scent of his skin, heard her own heart thuds instead of the company's voices, and saw nothing but the nearness of Holton's teasing eyes.

Immediately afterward, Holton regarded her wildly, as if expecting her to strike out in retaliation, she thought. Then he pulled down the points of his white waistcoat as though getting a grip on himself.

Vanora choked back nervous laughter, wondering if this womanizer had ever kissed an old maid on the lips. Clearly, the experience hadn't been an ordinary one for him, either.

The urge to laugh receded, as she began to compare Charles's kisses with this chaste mishap and found a precious memory erased. She must be too overset by the foolish, meaningless custom to bring even a tremble of Charles's touch to mind. Holton's kiss meant nothing, for his intentions fixed on Eva, and she had no interest in her sister's beaux.

Holton stepped toward her again, and Vanora stumbled back. A smile crinkled the corners of his eyes and lifted the ends of shapely lips. One elegant white hand reached to claim a berry from the mistletoe on the kissing ball. "I believe I shall treasure this berry with the other memorable one I've collected this Christmas Day," he drawled, with a most correct bow and a complacent expression.

Vanora snapped, "With such a collection as you must have gathered over the years, what can one or two more signify?" She castigated herself because the rake had snatched his kiss from Eva, after all her vigilance to subvert it. Obviously, he had intended to kiss only Vanora's cheek, and discomposing her gave him cheeky self-satisfaction, no doubt.

Vanora turned from the encounter, affirming to herself that the kiss was only the house-party pleasantry Holton meant it to be, hoping no one had observed the seasonal silliness. Lady Fenmore stood across the room, staring with a thoughtful expression. Vanora felt herself flush as she fled to the seat farthest from telltale candles.

Watching Holton walk about the room with Eva, laughing and making easy conversation, Vanora knew envy. Both Holton and Eva found pleasure in any company or pastime. They appeared at perfect ease, carefree.

Eva found a sprig of holly overlooked in clearing up the makings for the kissing ball. Flirting her lashes outrageously, she tucked it into a buttonhole on Holton's pristine waistcoat. Vanora's lips and hands tightened. Eva comported herself in an overfamiliar way with Holton, and must be warned to more maidenly behavior.

Even as she composed a scold in her mind, Vanora wished for a measure of Eva's ease in company. How free one must feel, to cast off the fetters of convention and simply act as the moment's impulse dictated.

Holton and Eva shared a capacity for enjoying the moment. They were well matched. Yet the thought of a match between the two, eligible as the connection must be thought for Eva, left Vanora uneasy.

Vanora's longing to be left in peace for a space, to quiet a cacophony of reactions to events and her thoughts, was not granted. Eva bubbled with notions for the evening's entertainment, having heard from Holton of Christmas games his family traditionally enjoyed. Eva had secured the necessary complements to the activities, and she was not to be denied.

"Bring this card table forward into the room so we may all stand about it for Bullet Pudding," Eva directed Holton.

"At your service, now and forever," he drawled, shifting the table to her satisfaction. In the meantime, Eva urged the squire and Lady Mary, Alicen and Chalmers, Lord and Lady Fenmore to gather about for the game. When Vanora hung back, Eva took her hand to pull her into the circle.

"Now the tray with the flour!" cried Eva, and Holton brought the flat pewter dish with its white mound in the center. "Holton tells me the flour must be scraped into a peak," said Eva, picking up the heavy silver dinner knife on the side of the tray to improve the snowy mountain's slope. "Now for the bullet! Did you bring it, Holton?"

Smiling at Eva's exuberance, which Vanora found too coltish for any girl past ten years of age, Holton accepted a pistol ball from the squire. He placed it on Eva's palm, folding her fingers round it so that Vanora ached to snatch his hands off her sister, as on the day they met.

"Everyone must hold their breaths while I position the ball on top of the peak," instructed Eva. "This is a most delicate process, and the steadiest of hands is required." Eva laid the shot in place, assuming a graceful attitude that held Holton's full attention as she leaned over the table. Turning to Holton, Eva insisted, "You instructed me on how the game is played, so you must go first to demonstrate."

Holton bowed, accepting the knife she extended to him. "The game is quite simple," said Holton. "For the edification of our Scotch players, the aim is to slice the pudding without disturbing the bullet." He turned to the pile of flour and inserted the point of the knife near the peak, slicing away from it to the edge of the plate.

Holton turned from his surgery. "Who will be next?" he asked, offering the knife, handle first.

"I shall indulge you," said Lady Fenmore, "for early players fare best at the game." Her slice at the pudding was as deft as her son's, and the bullet held firm on its peak.

"You go next, Vanora!" Eva urged.

"I prefer to watch," Vanora protested.

"Don't think it an advantage to observe the science employed by the rest before taking a turn," Holton warned.

Vanora mistrusted the mischievous look on Holton's face, reminded of her brothers when they indulged in foolery. She moved to the rear of the group as first Alicen, then Eva and Lady Mary, made cuts in the flour pudding.

On the last slice, the bullet changed position slightly, sending a sifting of flour down the mound, but it remained aloft while Lady Mary endured the teasing of the onlookers.

"We've a lady who hasn't taken a turn as yet," Holton reminded the group, and Chalmers pulled Vanora from the safety she had sought behind shoulders, urging her to have a whack at the pudding.

Feeling a sense of dread, Vanora took the silver knife and stood considering the flour mound with its five narrow channels down one side. Impatient voices prodded her.

Just as Vanora sank the knife into the flour near the ball, Holton leaned forward beside her to point at the pile as if to suggest a safe entry. Finding him so close beside her, Vanora jerked the knife instead of making a smooth cut, and the bullet leaped from its pinnacle to disappear from view into the white mound.

Laughter erupted around her as Vanora stepped away from Holton's distracting presence. He apologized, but Vanora seethed at losing a game she hadn't cared to play.

"Now you must fish out the bullet with your lips!" crowed Eva. "You aren't allowed to use your hands, though you may apply nose or chin!"

Vanora cringed at the thought of the appearance one must present after rooting in the flour like a pig after truffles. The dandy's games weren't amusing. "Surely nothing so ridiculous is required as a penalty!"

Lady Fenmore spoke in a placating voice. "I protest; 'tis vastly unfair to make a player who doesn't know the penance carry it through!"

"Not in the least," said Vanora, unwilling to have anyone make excuses for her. "I insist on abiding by the rules of the game and ask no exception on the basis of ignorance—or interference from another player!"

She cast a dark look at Holton before taking a deep breath and bending over the flour mound. Finding the hole where the bullet disappeared, Vanora gamely dove in, vainly searching for the metal pellet. Her lungs burned for air. Voices urged her on from a great distance. Vanora was forced to come up for breath without the bullet.

Blinking flour from her lashes, Vanora was aware that most eyes were on her whitened face as the group joshed her to another effort. One pair of eyes searched the tray, and Vanora saw with disbelief that Holton reached a furtive finger into the mound to rake the shot into view. She looked a question at him, but Holton parodied innocence. Quickly she bent to the pewter platter, seized the ball in her lips and dropped it into her hand.

Holton stepped forward immediately to take the bullet, handing it to Eva. Drawing a snowy linen square from a pocket in his waistcoat, he turned to Vanora. "Allow me to remove traces of the penalty I visited upon you," he said, "for had I not offered advice at the wrong moment, you would never have dislodged the shot."

As he spoke, Holton wiped dustings of flour gently from Vanora's face. His compelling fingers on her chin, holding her like a child in need of scrubbing, made it impossible to move, much as Vanora desired to escape his ministrations. She could think only of the pressure of his lips under the kissing ball, for they stood in much the same positions now.

Most likely Holton's tormenting eyes haunted her because, being so much of a height, it wasn't necessary to look up to him. Vexed nearly to tears, Vanora refused to meet his gaze and allow him to see her confusion.

Holton's touch was warmth, comfort, consideration. It was exquisitely disturbing. He was far more threatening in kindness than in any practiced flirtation. Vanora yearned to lean into the hand securing her chin and nuz-

zle the strong fingers stroking her face through the fine
linen.

*Holton is a dandy and a rake, knowing just how to
foster any response he desires in females!* she reminded
herself sternly.

Vanora willed herself to take the handkerchief from
Holton to complete repairs herself and to thank him civilly
for his assistance. She hardly heard Eva's suggestion that
they play another game. Vanora felt totally played out.

Stepping to a mirror near a wall sconce, Vanora finished
wiping pale powder from her face, leaving little difference
to her color. Smoothing the handkerchief that carried the
faint citric scent of its owner, Vanora saw the drawn white-
work that embellished it. She rallied herself to disgust. How
like a dandy to carry a prettier handkerchief than she!

"Come, Vanora, we're ready for a different game!"

Vanora became aware that Eva called to her from the
card table. She straightened the lace lappets lying against
grey silk, tucking the handkerchief into her reticule absently
before turning to engage in further social nonsense.

Lady Fenmore made way for Vanora to join the circle
beside her, holding out a hand to guide Vanora into place.

Vanora avoided Lady Fenmore's eyes, as she did
Holton's. Eva beamed from beside the table, curls and
eyes dancing with the fun of simple entertainments. Vanora
conceded that a bit of flour on one's face was little enough
to pay for Eva's pleasure. The game hadn't ended so ill.

"Now we shall play at Snapdragon," said Eva, indicating the tray covered with a layer of raisins. "First I must
pour on brandy." Her actions followed the words. "Then,
once the fruit is flamed, we snatch it out and eat it warm!
Holton says raisins never tasted so deliciously, so I don't
doubt it's worth the risk of burnt fingers. If you filch them
quickly, starting round the edges, Holton says you won't
feel the flames. Isn't it excessively exciting?"

Vanora felt no desire to indulge in Snapdragon, feeling she had already experienced far more excitement this evening than was agreeable. Or perhaps she meant seemly.

Squire Plewes lit a spill from a candle nearby, teasing Eva that the snapdragon wouldn't burn nearly so brightly as her eyes. Flame applied to the brandy-soaked raisins spread a sheet of thin blue fire with a sound that sounded like a heated sigh to Vanora. Eva squealed and drew back.

Holton stepped to Eva's side, bending to urge her to snatch at a raisin and pointing out likely ones. When Eva removed her gloves, Holton took them from her and kissed them, and Vanora saw flames that weren't on the tray.

Incensed, she advanced on the table, forcing her way between Eva and Holton. "I shall get you a raisin, Eva," Vanora said, tearing off her own gloves. She bent near the tray, gauging the flames' height, until she spotted an area where the flames had already burned the brandy away.

Vanora's lace lappets swung on either side of her face, blocking her view of Holton and Eva. She quickly snatched a raisin and turned her head to see what the pair was about. Vanora straighted to put the hot, wrinkled fruit in Eva's hand, to find Eva staring in horror.

"Good Ged!" said Holton, seizing a vase of cut flowers from a side table. He flung its contents at Vanora's head.

Vanora stood in shock. She felt a cold trickle between her breasts, soaking under her light stays. Looking down, she saw that water plastered her best grey silk gown to her chest, a rose blooming crazily off her shoulder.

Holton stared, vase still in hand. His expression mixed concern with a warmer emotion, and his eyes certainly weren't on her face.

"How dare you, sir!" Vanora exclaimed from a state between tears and outrage, scrubbing at her wet bodice with her gloves.

Holton seemed to have trouble forming words. "Fire!

I assure you— I never intended your discomposure!"

Vanora looked down at her soaked gown, realizing that silk left little to the imagination in this state. Before she could loose the invective struggling for expression, Lady Fenmore was beside her.

"Merciful heavens, my dear! Your lappet must have dangled in the flames as you bent above the Snapdragon; it was smoldering as you straightened from the tray. Holton, what quick thinking, to seize upon the flowers. Eva, your sister is in shock; assist Vanora to her room at once."

Near tears, Eva wailed as she came forward, "You might have been injured! I told you to put off those old-lady caps; you see what comes of insisting on wearing them!"

Vanora allowed herself to be turned about, feeling much abused by the joys of the season. Perhaps it was due to their slow progress, perhaps because of her sharp ears for Holton's every word, but as she walked away, Vanora heard Holton speak in stifled tones to Lady Fenmore.

"I shall ever recall Miss Chalmers as the Snapdragon! With smoke rising from that lappet, the dragon seemed to breathe fire, for a certainty!"

Vanora felt a *cauld grue,* but not from her wetting. How dare the *scovie* heap insult on injury! She would singe the fop's fine feathers, if she could just figure how to do it without prejudicing Eva's come-out.

6

Vanora opened her eyes reluctantly. Thin light slunk furtively into the room as Mysie, the maid she shared with Eva, pulled back the drapes.

Vanora's first thought as the icy air of the chamber slid over her warm cheeks was of fire. The maid stooping at the grate wasn't the focus of Vanora's mental picture. Instead, she relived in an instant the smoldering lappet and Holton's splash from a vase the evening before.

Schooling her features to an expression that wouldn't alarm Mysie, Vanora piled pillows against the headboard in anticipation of the morning tray. Chocolate helped one wake pleasantly, while the room lost its worst chill before dressing. Eva would be in directly to drink a cup.

When a tall, rose-painted chocolate set was placed before her on a footed bed tray, Vanora was surprised into an exclamation. One white chrysanthemum lay across the tray's top, a sheet of pressed paper folded round the stem.

Vanora couldn't unfold the heavy sheet fast enough.

Tickling her chin with the double-white flower's petals, she read and reread the bold black spikes of ink.

May I hope that the purity of this blossom convinces you of the purity of my motive in the last flowers delivered to you unceremoniously? My desire for your good opinion is equalled only by my hope that the morning finds you fully recovered from the various indignities of last evening.

The scrawl under these lines carried but one recognizable letter, an elongated *H* as elegant as the man it identified. Vanora traced the initial with one finger as though copying it onto her consciousness.

The chamber door swung open, and Eva flew across the floor to bounce onto the bed. Vanora snatched up the tray at first sight of her sister, accustomed to the leap that landed Eva beside her. The tradition had commenced when Eva was a toddler, and each morning the sisters shared sips and chats that set them both up for the day.

Burrowing bare feet under the covers to nestle them against Vanora, Eva smiled, blinking sleepy eyes. Vanora returned her greeting, fondly noting Eva's tousled warmth, like a puppy's after a nap.

"Pretty!" said Eva, reaching for the flower like a baby attracted by a bauble. "We don't normally find flowers on our tray; is this a Southron tradition for Boxing Day?"

Vanora knew reluctance to see the leafed stem in Eva's hand. She wasn't called upon to relinquish it, for Eva was distracted from the chrysanthemum by the note Vanora had dropped in order to balance the tray against Eva's arrival.

As Eva unfolded the creamy sheet, Vanora resisted an impulse to snatch back the note. The communication was hardly private, but it was rude to read correspondence without permission. That was what vexed her, Vanora decided.

Eva lapped up the message with thirsty eyes. She beamed on Vanora. "You see what a graceful apology Holton makes you, and he expresses his concern for your well-being to a nicety. You must admit to what a pretty-behaved gentleman he is, with such evidence of concern before you!"

"It signifies only the pretty ways of a practiced dandy," said Vanora, "and I shan't refine on it beyond that. Mere civility requires that he inquire how one goes on who only avoided being roasted alive by enduring a flood at his hands! Holton's breeding would require a similar expression of concern toward any maiden lady who chaperoned you."

Vanora laid the flower negligently on the tray, carefully placing it beyond Eva's reach on the far side, as she poured chocolate for the two of them.

"I should say instead that Holton put himself out to secure a blossom from the glasshouse and arrange for it and a note to be delivered on our tray," Eva objected.

"A few words and fewer coins fixed the matter in a trice," said Vanora, unwilling to allow any significance to the gesture. She fingered the flower's stem as she sipped.

Eva breathed steamy fragrance before drinking, as though warming her nose. "You may cavil all you like; I find Holton quite the most admirable gentleman of my acquaintance!"

"And your acquaintance among London gentlemen is so wide," Vanora teased, savoring the sinful satin of creamy milk and chocolate slipping past her tongue.

"Such acquaintance will soon increase," Eva said complacently, licking a milky upper lip. "Lady Fenmore will speak to you about my come-out later today."

Vanora set her cup down, not trusting her hand to

control it in her eagerness. "Will she, indeed? How do you know this?"

Eva smiled smugly, downing her chocolate and holding out the cup to tease Vanora by prolonging the interesting revelation. "May I have more *jokalet?*"

"Not before you tell all you know," Vanora bargained.

"There's little enough to tell," said Eva. "Holton said after dinner last evening that he has begged his mama to see us launched, and she agreed to present us."

Vanora's relief that Eva would have her season felt like setting down a heavy load. But if Holton desired his mama's protection for Eva so keenly that he had begged it, Vanora found his interest in Eva disturbing. She vowed vigilance to keep Eva safe from disillusionment by this dandy.

As Vanora picked up her chrysanthemum, she reminded herself to be glad that she need not beg Lady Fenmore's support for the months ahead. The least she could do was overlook a splash from a vase, so Eva could make a splash in town. This lovely blossom had absolutely nothing to do with her change of heart.

Boxing Day occupied the manor family with distributing coins to servants and tenants. Lady Fenmore suggested to Vanora that the two of them stroll the picture gallery while they discussed the season ahead.

Vanora felt like a housemaid interviewing for her first place when the ladies entered the long space, more a passage than a separate room. Green-and-white-striped wallpaper above white-painted wainscotting formed a pleasant background for paintings in gilded frames, hung in balanced patterns from a picture rail. Formal chairs and benches stood against the walls and between windows on the north wall, and wide oak boards glowed with years of waxing under their slippers.

Chatting about the pictures hanging round them, Lady Fenmore put Vanora at ease within minutes. "Will Lord and Lady Lauder be in town this spring?" Lady Fenmore asked, referring to Vanora's uncle and his wife. "I know them in a social sort of way, as well as their offspring. Didn't you come out with one of the daughters just a few years back?"

"More than a few!" Vanora said evasively. "My uncle said they were so relieved to have no child to foist onto Society at present that they will bide at home this year. He very kindly franked Eva's season, however, saying it was the least he could do if someone else undertook to introduce her, saving Aunt Lauder the exertion."

"Little exertion will be required, with one so lovely as your sister," Lady Fenmore protested, noting that Vanora had side-stepped the hint for information about her own come-out. She wished, not for the first time, that she could recall this particular girl among the coveys presented each season.

"Mary plans that you will reside in the Plewes's town-house with her," Lady Fenmore continued, "and I shall have the pleasure of Eva's presentation for the most part, as Mary's attendance on the season must be uncertain in her condition. Mary and Plewes are situated across Cavendish Square from us, so communicating plans will be no hardship. We can easily take you up on our way to engagements."

"You speak of yourself and Lord Fenmore?" asked Vanora, not wishing to allude directly to Holton.

"My husband looks in on what functions he may," Lady Fenmore explained. "As late as Parliament and its committees sit, he doesn't appear socially as often as one might wish. Holton is good about squiring me to such events as require escort, and I don't doubt that we can press him into service on your sister's behalf."

Vanora frowned. Accepting the good offices of this lady who became a connection by their brother's marriage was one thing; finding oneself beholden to Holton was insupportable.

Lady Fenmore took in Vanora's scowl with interest. "You may rely on Holton to forward your sister's interests with hostesses and young men as well. He's made himself something of an arbiter of the flock presented to the *ton* each spring, and gentlemen follow his lead in attentions to young ladies." Lady Fenmore laughed. "Winning Holton's approval is nearly as much of a point to mamas with daughters to launch as securing cards to Almack's!"

"He already appears well disposed toward Eva!" Vanora exclaimed stiffly, irritated that Holton had apparent reason to be set up in his own opinion.

"You mustn't refine overmuch on Holton's tendency to flirtation," Lady Fenmore said reassuringly. "He enjoys the perfection of a natural beauty like your sister in much the same way he's a connoisseur of first-rate paintings."

"But a painting lacks the response to admiration that allows a young lady to be led into grave disappointment," Vanora answered quickly.

"Certainly I applaud your care for your sister," said Lady Fenmore. "But you aren't at your last prayers by any means, my dear. You should look to your own heart as well."

Unable to bear the least hint that she harbored any interest in Holton on her own behalf, as she perceived Lady Fenmore's words, Vanora interrupted. "You much mistake the matter, for I've no interest whatsoever in your son except in regard to Eva!"

"Of course you have not," answered Lady Fenmore soothingly. Lady Fenmore wouldn't have dared suggest to Vanora that she might be attracted to Holton on her own behalf; but Vanora's assumption said much about the direction of her mind. "Still, that doesn't preclude the possibility that you may attach other gentlemen of worth during the season before us."

Vanora nearly groaned aloud, now aware that Lady Fenmore hadn't referred to Holton in connection with herself, but to the season in general. Her mistaking the matter could create a false view on Lady Fenmore's part. "You must believe that I have no ambitions on my own behalf. I've quite put away all consideration of forming a connection. Such a thing is impossible, for I cannot care for any man or for the married state," Vanora insisted in mortification.

"Indeed I hope you may be persuaded otherwise," Lady Fenmore replied easily. "However, if you open yourself to finding pleasure in the season and making agreeable acquaintances, you serve yourself and your sister best."

"This is Eva's season; mine is far behind me," said Vanora, with finality in her tone.

"One should never close doors, let alone lock them, where happiness is concerned," said Lady Fenmore, ready to make use of a second mention of Vanora's come-out. "Setting aside efforts to attract attentions to yourself, it's only prudent to present yourself attractively as background to Eva. Did your own season produce no association of promise?"

"My come-out convinced me that I should be most happy serving the interests of my parents and siblings," Vanora said decisively. "Please believe that I'm not on the catch."

Lady Fenmore noted that Vanora twisted a handkerchief as they walked in a way that suggested agitation. Unwilling to leave the opportunity alone, she said, "I must admit that I don't recall much about your season, my dear, though I recall meeting you and your cousin and thinking how charming your accents were. Didn't your cousin marry that same year?"

"Yes; she's Lady George Hartlebury now. She lives in Yorkshire with her husband's family, and they have four children thus far." Vanora recognized her envy.

Hearing wistfulness, Lady Fenmore said, "How lovely for her. Do you not wish for children yourself?"

"I find great satisfaction in my role as aunt," Vanora insisted, in an effort to convince Lady Fenmore. "My eldest brother has three little ones, and now Alicen will present me with another niece or nephew. All I lack at present is seeing Eva settled in life."

Forming her own conclusions, Lady Fenmore predicted, "That modest ambition will be satisfied before summer. Knowing Lord Lauder, you were provided funds to outfit yourself as well as your sister. Dressed fashionably, you would doubtless draw notice on your own behalf."

Receiving no response, Lady Fenmore continued persuasively, "Holding your own child is an experience beyond compare to holding the dearest child of another, you know. I shouldn't like to see you exclude marriage from your dreams, whatever disappointments you may have suffered as a girl."

Vanora looked toward the paintings they passed, seeing only a future as bleak as the past. "I'm perfectly sensible of the favor you do us in presenting Eva to your friends this season. I couldn't think of imposing on your good nature with any claim beyond that," she said stubbornly.

Lady Fenmore recognized that she had pushed Vanora past what civility allowed, so she introduced discussion of the Queen's drawing room, confirming that Vanora had been presented during her come-out. Before Eva attended important social functions, she must make a bow to royalty.

Plumes and presentation dresses were under discussion

when Holton appeared far down the gallery. Lady Fenmore heard the quick intake of breath beside her and knew Vanora, too, had seen him. A glance confirmed rising color.

Vanora dropped her gaze after meeting Holton's searching look as he advanced down the long gallery. Unfortunately, this view was no more comfortable, for she was all too aware of the action of lean thigh muscles under soft buckskins nearly as revealing as silk knit pantaloons.

She pulled mind and eyes up sharply. No doubt his gaze sought to determine whether his note and flower had softened her attitude toward him this morning. She would fix her eyes on his perfectly cleft chin and give nothing away.

"Have Boxing Day gifts been distributed?" asked Lady Fenmore as Holton came up to them.

"To the last one," he replied. "And Alicen informs me that Miss Eva Chalmers means to choose a gift for herself. The head groom compared the blue of her eyes to one of a recent litter of kittens in the stables, and she's there with the squire to select one for herself now."

"We cannot travel to London with a cat in a basket!" wailed Vanora. "Will you excuse me, Lady Fenmore? I'd best get to the stables to squelch this love affair!"

"Consider it good practice for town," Lady Fenmore said to Vanora with a smile.

"Just so!" said Holton, giving Vanora a wicked grin. "No doubt any number of prowling Toms must expect set-downs from the redoubtable Miss Chalmers!"

"Mayhap I'll scorch them instead," said Vanora with a melting glance, as she turned away in a swirl of skirt meant to display a glimpse of ankle. She would show the dandy that the dragon had snap, indeed! He left for town tomorrow; no harm could come from a hint of flirtation, just enough to prove she was no old biddy.

Holton stood watching brown skirts sway out of sight,

appreciating grace of movement as well as a flash of slim ankles. He wondered at himself for looking twice at a lady with no regard for her appearance, when he was noted for his own. "What do you suppose she meant?" he murmured absently.

Lady Fenmore took Holton's arm to stroll further. "I apprehend that she overheard your unfortunate remark last evening, as she left the drawing room with her sister."

"I don't refer to that!" Holton said impatiently. "You know I meant not the least harm by the term 'snapdragon.' But what the deuce did the lady mean by the look she just gave me? Did you not see? Were I puffed up in my own consequence, I'd call it flirtatious."

Lady Fenmore looked at her son with satisfaction. Perhaps a tiny nudge toward a dowdy miss wouldn't come amiss. "What one intends and what's perceived may be quite different. You must have a care with the sisters, Holton. As they will be introduced under my auspices, I'm in a sense responsible for their welfare."

Holton laughed. "That sounds like a warning against pursuit of either sister, worthy of the Snapdragon herself."

"I'm glad I communicated so clearly," said Lady Fenmore severely, well pleased with her effort. "It was a warning. I'll not see either of those sisters pained by your pleasures, my dear."

One brow rose as Holton looked down a classical nose at his mama. "Do you accuse me of trifling with that pretty child? I thought I'd convinced you that I'm committed to charming the elder sister in order to court the younger."

"I often wonder if you know yourself what your games signify, Holton. Very likely you'll charm them both." Lady Fenmore chose her words carefully. "Make certain neither sister has reason to complain of your wiles, for I suspect that Miss Chalmers has suffered enough from charming men."

Holton stopped to take his mama's hands. "You've learned something already! I knew you had the touch for such a delicate piece of work. Tell me instantly!"

Drawing her hands away, Lady Fenmore walked on. "You're entirely in the wrong of it. Miss Chalmers can hardly be brought to speak two words about her season, and what I surmise is based more on her reactions than confidences."

Holton clasped his hands behind his back, swelling the fashionable deep-chested cut to his coat. "After my best inquiries, I know no more than the year she came out, though I don't scruple to speculate. Chalmers said the event was nearly eight years ago."

"No wonder you don't recall her; you were traveling with Mildmay to Tilsit during that season," recalled Lady Fenmore.

"Pater meant for Sir Robert Wilson to give me a taste for politics," Holton recalled grimly. "Instead, the Queen of Prussia perfected my steps in the waltz!"

"Indeed, you made a point of writing nothing home but court news!" Lady Fenmore chided. "A shame you were away that particular season, for you're far more likely to know the whole of each new crop of girls than am I," Lady Fenmore continued. "Unless a child belongs to a particular friend, I don't pay much mind. Still, I can't believe Vanora's secret such a dark one, as strict as she is with Miss Eva."

Reflecting on her brother's hint that Vanora's distaste for men manifested itself after her London season, Holton fixed his intention to learn what lay behind it. He knew how to quiz acquaintance adroitly, and few people needed much urging to talk about others' affairs. His natural interest in people, combined with Vanora's resistance to his efforts to charm her, made inquiry irresistible.

Holton answered Lady Fenmore in his bantering way.

"Perhaps she acts on the principle that turns rakes into watchful husbands and fathers: One who knows his own capabilities knows what to guard against in others!"

"You could be in the right of it," Lady Fenmore mused.

"Mama!" Holton laughed uncomfortably. "Surely you don't believe the plain lady who just left us capable of a grand passion! Who would indulge her, even if she were so inclined, which I take leave to doubt!"

"Don't be objectionable, Holton. Because you look for no more than china-doll faces, don't assume other men incapable of appreciating the finer qualities of the lady."

"I wish you will discover just one man who will!" said Holton with a defensive shrug. "Find a kind widower to keep Miss Chalmers's attention occupied during the coming season, and I shall be most humbly grateful."

Holton stopped to stare up at a painted rural scene, as though seeking a home for Miss Chalmers. "I spoke in jest, but that notion may serve. You might very well pawn the lady off onto someone who needs a second wife to take over his household. Encourage her to do something with her appearance before coming to London, for she must offer some attraction if she's to be busy about her own interests."

"Miss Chalmers resisted even the hint of making a better appearance, not twenty minutes since," said Lady Fenmore.

"Then do more than hint, Mama. Every lady has some feature to raise her above the ordinary," said Holton.

"And what is Miss Chalmers's extraordinary feature?" asked Lady Fenmore with a searching look.

"How should I know?" asked Holton, a note of irritation to his tone. "I've hardly had a glimpse of her, with a cap covering all but her disapproving nose and primmed mouth, and her high-necked drab gowns masking the rest. But certainly there's no need to hide her ankles, or the charms revealed by fashionable necklines. Whatever else you may accomplish, get her lovely hair from under her accursed caps!"

"Tell me about her hair," said Lady Fenmore innocently. "For all I know of the matter, she may have none!"

Silence swelled between mother and son. Holton looked at her defiantly. "I came upon Miss Chalmers in the passage one night on my way to you. Her glorious hair hung in a thick plait; it's very like the color of Miss Eva's."

Lady Fenmore observed, "And you didn't see fit to remark upon this meeting to me earlier."

Expressionless, Holton replied, "Slipped my mind, no doubt. The thing of it is, she's an intelligent woman, Mama, in spite of her lack of style. Leaving her on the shelf is a total waste of a lady who could do some man a world of good. Curled and dressed, she has a chance of finding a decent husband for herself. Leave her as she is, and who will look past her drab exterior to learn her finer qualities?"

"Who, indeed?" agreed Lady Fenmore. "You know I can't promise, for she's as stubbornly set on her own course as you on yours. But we shall see what may be contrived."

Holton kissed his mama's hand. "If anyone can transplant a snapdragon from the wilds to a cultivated garden, you will accomplish it. I scarce can wait to renew acquaintance with the sisters in town. Perhaps there I won't trip over my feet at each encounter with a mere spinster!"

7

Later on Boxing Day, Lady Fenmore sought her hostess. As Lord and Lady Fenmore and Holton planned to depart the following morning, she determined to set wheels turning that would bring Vanora to London in her best looks.

Running Lady Mary to earth in the stillroom, located on the lowest level of the manor house, Lady Fenmore accepted a pot of lotion from her cousin.

"Wear this balm inside cosmetic gloves of a night, and you'll find discolorations of the hands disappear in next to no time," Lady Mary assured her.

"I don't doubt its efficacy," said Lady Fenmore, setting the stoppered pot carefully on the deal table centering the small room. "Your way with enhancements for the appearance is well known, and you serve as surety for your concoctions by your own appearance, Mary."

Lady Fenmore gestured at jars, baskets, and pots crowding shelves on two walls as a medley of scents teased her nose. "Half the *ton* would give their best jewel just for copies of the receipts from this stillroom."

"One applies science to appearance as to less important matters," Lady Mary answered complacently, rehanging a sheaf of dried lavender.

"If only science could change Vanora's appearance before she appears in London," Lady Fenmore said. "I vow, she can hardly do you credit in her present dowdy state."

Lady Mary appeared to consider. "It's true that it will be generally known the Scotch sisters stay with me, though you introduce them round most social events."

Lady Fenmore sighed. "Putting Eva forward among our acquaintance will be an easy matter, for she's as pretty as she can stare. What a pity that Vanora is past improvement!"

"I daresay she could take the eye, if she put herself into capable hands," said Lady Mary at once.

"Do you think so indeed?" asked Lady Fenmore, making a display of surprise. "I doubt anyone could make a silk purse of this sow's ear."

"Perhaps every eye can't discern potential, but I assure you that I could make her appear out of the common way, were I to set myself to do so," Lady Mary said with assurance.

Lady Fenmore allowed a note of incredulity to enter her voice. "Could you, indeed? I wish it might be so. Holton believes it would be a kindness to introduce Vanora to the notice of a few widowers of our acquaintance in town. But he expressed concern that the effort would be wasted, were she to appear in her present retiring guise."

Lady Mary gave her cousin a knowing look. "No man's interest in a lady's appearance is totally disinterested! Which sister does Holton set up as his flirt this season?"

"Which indeed?" said Lady Fenmore with a twinkle. "I'm not certain he knows himself at this point."

"By all means, let's make his choice more difficult," Lady Mary said, taking a pot off a shelf.

After the other guests departed the following day, the Scotch sisters presented themselves at Lady Mary's rooms as requested. Before Vanora could knock for admittance, Eva dropped her reticule.

Stooping, Vanora caught up the netted bag just as Eva bent to seize its strings with a little cry. Vanora felt a stiff sheet within the netting, folded like a letter. No missive had waited by Eva's place at breakfast, and the late post was hours away. Taking in Eva's expression of lively dread, Vanora began a question, broken off by the opening of the door before them.

Lady Mary stood in the doorway, and the fact that she was increasing hardly showed in an excessively high-waisted morning gown made up from Anglo-merino in pomona green. Looking little older than her daughter Alicen, Lady Mary invited the sisters into her sitting room.

Vanora put aside her question about Eva's letter, suspecting the answer was best pursued in private.

No doubt Lady Mary was best placed to guide them in matters of fashion, Vanora thought, considering the deceptively simple cut of her gown. She noted Lady Mary's assessing looks at herself and felt like a looming stone watchtower beside the diminutive lady.

"We must prepare for the season ahead," said Lady Mary, urging them to chintz-covered seats in a gold-and-green sitting room. "No matter of appearance ever warrants neglect, and we must commence immediately, if you're to show your faces at their best in two month's time."

"Surely Eva requires little improvement," Vanora

objected. "We beg your guidance in the matter of ordering her gowns, but that must wait upon arrival in London."

"Attire!" said Lady Mary, waving the consideration aside. "That's the least telling part of a lady's appearance! *Amour propre,* how you feel about yourself before the gown goes on, determines the impression one makes far more significantly! Besides, I'm not concerned with Miss Eva's pretty face, but with the potential your own offers."

"That's hardly to the point," Vanora said, feeling defensive and wistful all at once. "This is Eva's season, and I remain entirely in the background to her."

"Do you not value proper background?" Lady Mary asked in the tone of one who brooks no argument. "Eva won't be seen in isolation, but in context with her sponsors. I flatter myself that my company will do her credit, even in my state!"

"You and Lady Fenmore must supply the credit required," Vanora said stiffly, "for I'm not on the catch and have no desire to appear mutton dressed as lamb in any case."

"A lady is never too young or old to strive for the best presentation possible," Lady Mary stated, looking horrified. "Making the most of one's appearance has less to do with matrimonial intentions than with proper respect for oneself. When you fail to show consideration for your own person, you invite others to take you entirely at your own valuation!"

"But I'm quite on the shelf," said Vanora, feeling an unaccustomed pang at the admission. "I have no wish to appear what I'm not. If I wear colors and uncovered hair, people will assume I draw attention to myself as an eligible *parti,* which I'm not by any stretch of the imagination."

"Public opinion deems a female incapable of the romantic passion at twenty-seven; you have a year before you can truly be said at your last prayers!" Lady Mary said, then looked thoughtful. "Though gossip indicates a vast display of some sort of passion in females beyond that age, one can't deny."

Romance is a long-buried memory, Vanora thought, pulling a handkerchief from her sleeve as though in tribute to long-ago tears. *If only it were possible to love romantically again,* she thought with regret, *but a pure love allows of no second attachments.* The character Marianne had said as much in the popular novel *Sense and Sensibility.*

"My ambitions are only for Eva," Vanora insisted.

"I have no desire that you appear the watchful nanny, ready to depress gentlemen's pretensions," said Eva. "If you won't make yourself pretty again on your own behalf, do so on mine! Lady Mary, do I understand you to say that Vanora's style will be taken into account in any consideration of me?"

"Quite," Lady Mary agreed at once. "I should hardly know where to look, were you presented to my acquaintance in your present style, or rather lack of style, with your hair and half your face hidden by plain caps my dresser would disdain to wear. I'm noted for taking the lead in matters of fashion; what must it do to my credit to send a person of so little elegance from my house?"

Vanora cared little for Lady Mary's consequence, but Eva's pleading face gave her pause. Vanora allowed herself the thought of putting off caps, putting on pretty gowns.

Memories of the way one held the head when it was dressed fashionably, the warmth lent a check when a color flattered one's complexion, teased Vanora. Silk should feel as luxurious in grey as in azure, but finding herself invisible during the holidays proved that premise false.

A spring of yearning gushed unbidden from beneath the rock of Vanora's resolve. To wear glowing colors was to encourage bright spirits; had she mourned long enough? To reexperience the whisper of flattering silks or muslins clinging to shoulders, caressing ankles, was to open herself to feeling again; could she order sentiment better this time?

Of a sudden, the hunger to appear attractively was stronger than cloves' taste. Vanora looked blindly toward the window, as though it were a glass on yesterday. The last time she had put on fashionable trappings, she had paid with her whole heart for the vanity.

Surely intent must enter into it, Vanora argued with herself. *I dressed then to attract gentlemen, and pain rewarded my efforts. If I assume elegance of dress and manner to assure Eva an appearance of* bon ton, *any benefit is sought for her. I shall want nothing for myself.*

Images of dressed hair, flushed cheeks, ribboned slippers, admiring male eyes, wafted over Vanora like fragrance recalled from lavender fields. She was overwhelmed with desire to experience the confidence, ease, anticipation of being in looks again.

Eva touched Vanora's sleeve, bringing her back to the discussion at hand. "Think how much pleasure we knew just in preparation for your come-out, Vanora," said Eva. "Were the two of us to shop and dress and dream together, think how much more pleasure we could find in town! Will you not share a season with me now, when we both can experience it, as you did then, when it was a child's game of pretend for me?"

Somewhere between heart and stomach, Vanora knew a flutter of fear and anticipation. "Do you truly wish it?"

"More than anything!" Eva declared. "If you'll enter into this season as a sister, not a chaperone, I shan't dread the highest stickler in the *ton* or the most top-lofty dancing partner. How much more comfortable to face society with you beside me rather than sitting amongst the chaperones!"

Vanora pressed Eva's hands. "How can I deny a request so prettily put! If it means so much, I shall put off my caps and have some new gowns as well." Vanora turned to Lady Mary. "I insist on dressing suitably for my age, however. I don't wish to parody a girl in her first season."

"Hardly suitable to your style!" agreed Lady Mary. "Sophistication better suits your unusual features and height. At least you hold yourself well up, so I need not bring out the backboard. Pull the bell, Eva," Lady Mary directed. "Lambern expects a summons."

As Eva flew to execute the order, Lady Mary continued. "My dresser is expert with hair and the application of lotions. Your woman waits as well, so she may be trained in my methods as Lambern and I decide on what suits you best."

"You were so certain of persuading me to this course?" Vanora asked, amused.

"No female alive can resist an opportunity to be made more presentable," Lady Mary assured her.

Vanora's ribs ached from forgetting to breathe. What kept her standing uneasily in Lady Mary's rose-and-white bed chamber was Eva's delight and her own mounting desires. During the past eight years, Vanora had lost the habit of hope. Now she felt the unrestrained neediness, even greediness, of nursery days. She yearned with the urgent intensity of a child to whom 'now' and 'this' were the world.

Vanora prayed to look presentable. She daren't hope for Eva's fresh beauty, but how gratifying to look into the glass and find a remnant of attractions she had carried to London in her first youth. It was entirely too cruel if, in losing heart and hope, she had lost all pretension to looks as well.

Vanora stared at her hands or out the window as four

females conferred and moved about her; she didn't wish to see her present self in the glass.

"Shall you put her into a divorce corset?" asked Eva, dodging round the room like a warble fly in excitement.

"Breathing and digestive portions of the body will be supported and restrained appropriately," said Lady Mary repressively. In a less strangled tone, she continued, "Little can be done about garments until we reach London, though a few simple gowns will give an improved outlook, a matter of vast concern. My sewing woman will take measurements directly, but just now I'll consider style."

"No fichus or tuckers," Eva decreed. "Vanora has a better chest than I."

Lady Mary ignored her to walk round Vanora in appraisal. "To minimize height, the opposite of my gowns is required. Where I use trims and openings down the center to form a longer line, Vanora's gowns must have deep flounces or rows of contrasting trim round the hem. This year's fashion for wider sleeves and pointed necklines also deceives the eye from the vertical. Bodices stop even higher than last year, but skirts gathered onto a wider band should shorten the figure. And fashionable, colored bodices with skirts of another tone will suit the purpose to admiration!"

General styles for gowns settled, Eva begged for the right to remove Vanora's cap, first pressing her onto a stool drawn away from a Hepplewhite inlaid mahogany dressing table.

"I've hated these spoilers since you set the first one on your head!" Eva declared. "Caps have hidden my true sister from me for eight long years, and I consider its removal a second come-out for you, Vanora."

The strings untied, Eva made a ceremony of lifting the cap away from Vanora's hair. "This time, you'll have the season you should have had eight years ago!"

Vanora smiled at Eva's fancy, allowing for youthful idealism. If only fate's blows could be set aside as easily as a cap. Vanora said, "Give the cap to Mysie, if you like."

Eva danced over to their maid with the despised article dangling from one finger. "Clear all Vanora's caps out of her room so she won't be tempted to wear one again, ever. You may have them all!"

Mysie accepted the discard with a bob. It was a mate for the cap the maid wore, Vanora admitted to herself. As Lady Mary's abigail worked behind her, Vanora felt tight coils of thick, straight hair loosen about her shoulders, pulling at her neck with their weight.

"Isn't it a lovely color!" exclaimed Eva, lifting handfuls of fair hair. "Vanora's hair is a softer tone than mine, but still golden, like ripened wheat fields bleached by sunlight. Shall it be scythed like a field of corn?"

"Who would have suspected," said Lady Mary, shaking her head at Eva and walking round Vanora. "How I envy you both length and thickness, for longer hair is gaining ascendency in style once more. I doubt my cropped head will reach half the required length to make a proper show this season, though I should have known that as soon as I was shorn, the fashion would turn about! We'll cut only enough for style."

After lifting side lengths experimentally, Lady Mary continued, "Current fashion is for the front hair to be divided, with ringlets on either side of the face, and the back hair to be worn low in the neck. Will it take a curl?"

Vanora began a reply, until she realized Lady Mary addressed her dresser, as though Vanora were a child to be prepared for public view without any say in the matter.

Lady Mary waved aside her dresser's quiet suggestion. "Certainly we can apply the curling tongs, but the first breath of humidity loosens set ringlets into dowdy strings. I wonder if I dare a more adventurous style?"

Lady Mary stepped in front of Vanora, delicate hands swooping about her face like pale moths. "Part the hair from the forehead half-way, then comb the back smoothly. On each side of the face, take the upper part of the hair and push it into a curve over the forehead, hiding its square-ness. Now, soften the angular jaw with similar swerves of hair below."

Vanora felt double wings forming on either side of her face as the dresser worked to her mistress' instructions.

"Catch the back hair into a low tail, then form it into myriad braids, looping them up in pear-shapes, to hang low on the neck in the manner of ringlets," Lady Mary directed. "Fullness at the back adds no inches to stature."

Eva skipped closer to survey the formation of Vanora's shining braids, setting them swinging with a playful finger.

"Child, you're as restless as a gadfly!" declared Lady Mary. "Sit on the bench at the end of my bed and don't move until I give you leave." Turning back to Vanora, she directed, "Show me your face."

Vanora looked up from clenched hands, feeling as if she might be chided along with Eva. How light-headed she felt without caps. She sat as though asleep, willing the outcome to be more dream than nightmare.

"Now that I've created a curving gilt frame for it, the face is more inviting," said Lady Mary. "However, the fashionable face clamors for attention, and your colorless features are mute! A pale complexion is most desirable, but not if one disappears into it. Let me consider."

While Lady Mary talked, her dresser folded out mar-quetry panels on each side of the dressing table, and Vanora admired the cunning design. A collection of pots and jars were revealed to Vanora's apprehensive notice.

Lambern held up a tiny pot suggestively. "That should do the trick," agreed Lady Mary. "Grey-blue eyes can be most intriguing, once attention is fixed there by darkening lashes and brows. Dark-rimmed irises appear remote, mysterious. Let's direct attention to the eyes, by all means!"

Vanora blinked as Lambern loomed in front of her, swooping toward her lashes with a dark substance on a stubby art brush. Vanora recalled her cousin's dresser applying crushed elderberries in this manner to her lashes and brows, cotton wool held underneath the eyes to keep stains off the cheeks, and decided this treatment was similar.

The application completed, Vanora opened her eyes to find reddened cotton wool threatening her cheeks. "Please!" she objected, putting up a hand to halt the dresser. "This is clearly paint, and Mama warned that tonish ladies ruin the health by dangerous painting."

Lady Mary drew her short stature into a haughty stance. "I'd as soon be seen on the street in my shift as to appear publicly with a naked face! It isn't healthful! London's air is laden with smuts, and mixtures for the complexion help to protect it."

Vanora expressed suitable apology, and Lady Mary continued, "Painting is a thing I should never tolerate for one instant. The females to whom you allude coat their faces with white and red lead paints, doing great harm, as your mama fears. Your fair skin needs no more than a light dust of rice powder, and rice is as healthful for the external body as for the internal. This pomatum with the faintest tinge of carmine enhances the structure of cheek bones, drawing attention away from a prominent jaw line. You may be equally certain that the pomatum for your lips, touched with alkanet, does little more than protect from dryness, with no ill consequences."

Vanora opened her lips to object, but Lambern silenced her by smoothing a red salve from another tiny pot onto them. Vanora had to admit that her mouth immediately felt more moist, so she stifled further argument.

At last Lambern and Lady Mary stood in appraisal, as though she were a glazed chicken that might not serve for supper, Vanora thought.

"May I see now?" Eva asked, like a good child waiting a turn at a book of engravings. "Vanora's hair looks lovely from the back in golden swags."

Lady Mary and Lambern exchanged a look. Lady Mary stretched out a hand as though assisting a duchess to rise, then turned Vanora toward her sister.

Eva's hands flew to cover her mouth, and her eyes showed the whole of gentian blue orbs. When she finally lifted her hands away to speak, her voice hinted tears. "I never doubted that you could be pretty again, but— Vanora! You're more lovely now than eight years since!"

Vanora felt her shoulders relax and her whole pose form into another posture. Her chin lifted as she saw admiration suffuse Eva's face. When Vanora spoke, she heard in her own voice a more musical tone, lower and richer, as though even her vocal cords entered into a new pattern of behavior with the proud posture. "If you're pleased, I need not even look into the glass to know I approve the transformation."

But Vanora couldn't stop a move to the cheval glass to survey the changes for herself. For a moment the reflection seemed a stranger's, for face, hair, expression, posture were hardly the accustomed view of the past eight years. Neither did the eager young Vanora of her own season look back in appraisal. This lady appeared assured, elegant even in the plain brown round gown she wore.

Vanora folded her hands at the waist and marveled at how graceful even the simplest movement felt of a sudden. *This must be the way a caterpillar feels when it awakens to discover it's a butterfly,* she thought whimsically.

Turning to her hostess, Vanora exclaimed, "You practice white magic, Lady Mary, for I'm hardly sensible of being the same person who walked into your rooms not an hour since."

"You most assuredly are not," said Lady Mary smugly. "My health preparations do wonders for the hair and complexion, but further, they constrain you to create magic within yourself. Fix in mind that you're a lady of presence, and no one will ever doubt it." Lady Mary looked like a cat that had been at the cream. "I scarce can wait to see you reunited with a former acquaintance in town."

Vanora felt color that owed nothing to carmine rising in her cheeks as a dandy's face filled her head. Holton made an art of the outward aspect. One naturally wondered what the dandy might make of her changed appearance when they came together once more in London.

8

Lady Darnley's balls could be counted on to start as squeezes and deteriorate into romps these days, Holton thought, perhaps due to the influence of a son nearing his majority. For that reason, Holton had dropped in on a Berkley Square rout before coming on to the Darnley ball.

The Berkley Square mansion housing the fourth earl's family attracted eligible *partis* like its heir and his set. Holton hadn't spoken with Lady Fenmore about specific plans for the evening, but he could guess that if she escorted the Scotch sisters tonight, this house would draw them.

Odd that he hadn't caught a glimpse of the Scotch sisters since their arrival in town with the Pleweses in mid-February. Each time he had called nearly two weeks since, he was told that the ladies were not at home. They must have indulged in an orgy of fittings and fripperies to have shopped so assiduously, he mused.

Mama had been curiously reticent on her plans for the

sisters, Holton thought as he stood in a throng on the stairs leading to the first floor, exchanging bows with acquaintances. More people came down than ascended, which indicated that he had timed his arrival perfectly to miss those merely putting in an appearance.

Holton had expected Mama to consult with him on a campaign to present Miss Eva, since he had expressed his interest in that direction to her. Naturally, Mama knew Society's hostesses as well as he, but Holton had thought to be taken into account. He had something of a reputation for encouraging young ladies' come-outs and could be expected to forward Eva's acceptance into Society.

Instead, Mama had said that his escort wasn't required and that they should no doubt see him everywhere in any case. Holton had hardly thought to find himself guessing where he might find Mama and her charges this evening.

Finally attaining the first floor, Holton continued to nod and chat as he made his way past rooms set up for cards, through an antechamber with a supper room opening off it, and into the ballroom. Occupying the whole of the west wing, the long room rose two floors to an ornate rococo ceiling, with a balcony along three sides for flirtatious promenades and a gilded box for the orchestra on the fourth. Holton entered the ballroom on the balcony and descended crimson-carpeted steps leading to the dancing floor.

From the stairs, Holton searched spindly gilt chairs set out on strips of carpet along the walls for chaperones and their charges. Mama sat conversing with a lady who must be Vanora, though he saw only her back. The somber brown gown and lace cap identified her sufficiently to Holton, and, in spite of the drab gown, he felt an urge to go greet her.

Quelling it, Holton looked about for Miss Eva. That

young lady should be under escort within Mama's eye, Holton thought, searching the long room avidly without show of interest. Mildmay stopped him for speech near the bottom of the stairs, and Holton exchanged words with every indication of interest in a tale of prodigious luck at cards. Holton's glance probed the room in brief flights from Mildmay's face.

Colorful patterns flitted restlessly as fish in a pool under three chandeliers centering the room. Wall sconces lit balconies, above and below, with lesser brilliance. Couples postured in recurring formations on the polished floor, and ceaseless movement throughout the room's crowded perimeter confused the eye. Balls promised dancing, but far more people conversed than pointed a toe, Holton thought.

At the far end of the room, a knot of men stood out the new quadrille. Holton recognized a few intimates at first glance, then, as the group reformed, still other particular friends came into view. Just as he caught a glint of candlelight on fair feminine hair among male heads and shoulders, it occurred to Holton that this was a congregation of bachelors. If these men flocked to a female, the attraction was beauty or fortune, he thought cynically.

Holton took leave of Mildmay at first opportunity and wove a slow progress toward the cluster that drew his attention. Halfway down the ballroom, Holton knew satisfaction as shifting forms in the group under his scrutiny revealed Miss Eva Chalmers in the briefest glimpse. Golden ringlets and a laughing face above a white-gowned shoulder were all he made out. Holton redoubled efforts to thrust through the throng.

Several paces away from his objective, Lady Hertford stopped Holton, asking if she would see him at her house the following night. Holton assured her of his pleasure in waiting upon her as the group he watched rearranged itself. Miss Eva stood next a taller lady.

Holton knew he stared, though the vision had been but momentary. Burned into his mind was an image of a lady beyond her first youth, but none the worst for that. Indeed, he could only admire Miss Eva Chalmers's poise in placing herself so near such an elegant creature. Most green girls would shy away from such comparison as must be brought to mind, but Miss Eva had laughed as confidently as though the elegant unknown were her best friend.

Holton said to Lady Hertford, "Two fair-haired beauties stand in a group beyond us. Perhaps you know whom I mean?"

"I'm little more than arrived myself," said Lady Hertford, "and I haven't learned the particulars of the latest incomparables as yet. I understand that the gentlemen have made it difficult for the ladies to meet the new toasts, however, for one can hardly come near them. Why don't you go along and learn what you may, on my behalf as well as your own? I may be required to issue invitations, if I haven't already sent cards to their sponsors."

Bowing, Holton drawled, "I'll accept your commission, as it accords with my own inclinations."

Lady Hertford laughed and waved Holton away. Holton found himself regretting a late arrival at the ball, when he might have met the fair unknown before his cronies crowded round. However, he normally set these gentlemen in the shade when he put his mind to charming a lady's company from them.

Holton had long since perfected a polite method of reaching the sweet center of such groups as surrounded the elegant unknown without giving offense. He laid a hand on a friend's shoulder at the group's outer edge, speaking to the acquaintance jovially and moving alongside him when the friend turned to return the greeting. Soon Holton was speaking to gentlemen farther into the group in the same manner, until he had attained the inner circle where Miss Eva Chalmers stood beside the elegant lady of mystery.

Holton stood for a moment, assuring himself that this vision bore up under closer inspection. The two ladies held court near a wall sconce, and in its flickering light he knew that his eye wasn't out. The lady was indeed a diamond of the first water, though not just in the usual style. Perhaps a citrine was more the jewel he meant, for candlelight gilded hair and complexion with a luminous, golden glow.

The elegant unknown turned briefly, not looking at him, before her attention was drawn in another direction. Holton felt a tug of memory, as though he should know her, much as one searches to name an echo of music in the mind.

Even though she stood in a half circle of prime bucks, the unknown seemed in total command. Her serene face was perfectly amiable; a half smile changed places from time to time with full-lipped laughter that showed perfect teeth and hinted at a dimple.

Holton knew an odd urge to take the pointed chin in his hand, as though it belonged there. The lady turned a glowing face away to answer a jest and he felt bereft. He consoled himself with the view of the golden head and long neck, arched as gracefully as any swan's. Shimmering golden chains of hair against a white throat and shoulders made every ringlet in the room appear childish.

Holton noted that distance was carefully maintained between these ladies and their eager admirers, not all of them known for holding the line. No male fingers reached for curving arms, no male bodies intruded across an unseen moat. Holton, too, felt the unspoken distance the elegant unknown projected without acting off-putting in the least. Here was a lady who knew her worth and wouldn't give herself easily, even to social touches. His fingers yearned toward her.

Suddenly, small, gloved hands were offered him, no insignificant attention from a lady. Eva's merry voice cried, "Holton! Lady Fenmore said you would no doubt put in an appearance this evening, and how happy I am to see you!"

Holton bowed and took her hands. "I'm fortunate to have drawn close enough to come to your notice, for you seem to have collected half the gentlemen in the room to yourself. And no wonder, for you look charmingly!"

A friend behind Holton groaned at this display of intimacy. "Should have known the old dog would have made the acquaintance of such out-and-outers before we might even catch the scent!"

Holton glanced back to say, "It takes an old dog to teach young pups tricks!" before returning to Eva. "This lady is a connection by marriage, so I may presume upon our acquaintance to ask to be presented to your companion."

Holton looked toward the elegant unknown on the last word, and she gave him her attention at last. The face was striking rather than conventionally beautiful, he decided, and when he had a few years to debate it with himself, he would determine exactly what struck him most about the lady.

For the moment, he was caught by her eyes like a rabbit in a snare. The unknown's eyes glittered silver in flickering candlelight, darker edges to the irises drawing him into their depths.

The elegant unknown awarded him an intimate smile as though they already enjoyed a long acquaintance. She spoke, and her tone was a caress, so that a delay ensued before the words' meaning penetrated Holton's bemusement.

"How quickly you forget a lady," she said, "and you vowed to remember me always as the Snapdragon!"

Holton felt as though a branch had just swept him off his mount, depositing him hard on his backside. He had never before experienced a moment in his social career when he had no reply. Laughter and slaps on the back from cronies hardly registered; he felt his mouth open and close again.

Reflexively, Holton took the gloved hand extended him. This couldn't be Vanora! Had Mama served up a jest?

The hair was the right color, recalled from a glimpse by other candlelight in a dark passage, but he had never envisioned it so artfully arranged. The eyes were familiar; he had once thought such eyes could be quite taking, were the face less frosty. This face was far from cold or colorless, and if Mama had arranged its transformation, he was well paid for wishing her to find Vanora a widower.

Coming to full awareness of jibes at his expense from the circle of bucks, Holton pressed Vanora's gloved fingers, which he couldn't seem to let go, and bowed over them.

Holton spoke for the benefit of his tormentors, chief of whom was the lovely Snapdragon. "Finding so rare a wildflower blooming amongst weeds threw me off my stride. Allow me to rescue you from such rude company by persuading you to a turn upon the floor." If he could take her off for a dance under their noses, his credit would be reestablished before jeering cronies. He would settle with Vanora for this discomfiture at his leisure.

The orchestra struck up an introduction to the waltz while couples began to take up places in a grand circle, ladies to the outside. Vanora indicated her sister. "Eva hasn't permission to waltz as yet. I hardly require it, having been out so long, but I can't abandon her here!"

Holton took the Darnley heir by the arm. "Do your duty, young fellow, and see Miss Eva Chalmers safely to my mama's side. Come along, Miss Chalmers." He placed a hand under Vanora's elbow and pressed a way for her through the protesting group of gentlemen, who declared that they would convoy Miss Eva Chalmers to her chaperone.

Stopping him just beyond the group, Vanora said, "I must warn you, sir, that I've pled lack of recent practice as an excuse to dance only the simplest figures tonight. My waltzing is as uncertain as the weather! I've performed the steps mainly with my sister, for the waltz was far too scandalous for much polite performance during my come-out."

"This closed waltz is a simple dance, and I promise not to allemande just as we reach nosy-parker row." When Vanora still hung back, Holton challenged. "You can't refuse a dance that's become all the go since Czar Alexander's visit to Almack's last summer. Think of it as a test, so you'll know better whether to allow Miss Eva to dance it." This was the right tactic; he felt Vanora yield to his hand's urging and wished he dared take her out into the garden. Silver eyes belonged to moonlight.

Vanora moved onto the floor, speaking over one amaranth-colored, melon-cut sleeve. "Very well, Holton, we shall waltz. But I warn you that I'm accustomed to lead Eva and may not be able to force myself to follow."

Holton laughed, partly to cover an increasing pressure in the chest upon clasping Vanora's left hand and setting his right between her bare shoulders. He naturally felt tension, from finding himself the butt of a jape, no doubt. His cronies wouldn't soon let him forget the stunner he had failed to recognize. He could hardly explain that she had changed past all possible recognition since their last meeting, leaving him as disoriented and embarrassed as though he had gone home to the wrong rooms in his cups.

Holton and Vanora stepped into slow triplets of music, not quite in concert.

"Listen more to the message from my hands, Miss Chalmers, and we shall proceed more smoothly," Holton instructed, as she seemed set on going her own way.

"I beg your pardon," she said with a spark from silver eyes, "but I warned you that I'm accustomed to lead. Hearing the strains of the valse swirling down upon us from an orchestra is far more inspiring than the keening of one violin in a music room. My attention is too taken with the music to concentrate entirely on your lead."

"Perhaps we shall deal better together once we reach the far end of the floor, out from under the immediate influence of such engrossing music," Holton said. Shifting his right hand to contain Vanora's tendency to lead, Holton slipped one finger along smooth skin, stopped only by equally smooth silk at the fashionably low, pointed back of Vanora's bewitching gown. He liked the way her eyes widened as he traced the boundary of her exposed back as far as his finger reached.

Could it be wise, he chided himself, to flirt so outrageously with an unmarried lady? Married flirts at her age knew the rules of such games. Since Vanora seemed inclined to dance him into the bystanders in reaction, he reluctantly gave up the daring caress.

Resettled against his arm, Vanora said with a hint of outrage in her voice, "You may only waltz with my sister when she wears a gown with a decent back to it!"

Laughing, Holton teased, "The Snapdragon's animadversion is less scorching when she confesses to wearing an improper gown."

He was both rewarded and punished for this devilment. Vanora flushed faintly, reminding him of rose-colored gold in the pink-touched lavender gown. She also forgot to follow his lead once more. Perhaps he should flirt with this lady only when they weren't waltzing, Holton thought.

"Your mama assured me that this fashion is bang up to the mark," Vanora said defensively.

"Has Mama taught you slang, or do you repeat compliments from the rackety crowd we just left?" Holton asked with a great show of interest. He recognized the lift of the lovely chin as a familiar action of the capped biddy she could never have been. "The gown is perfection," Holton continued, firming his hold on Vanora to prevent her taking her own direction. "It very nearly does the wearer justice."

"How kind of you to compliment my appearance, for you certainly can't commend my dancing with any degree of veracity," said Vanora. Laughing, silver-foil eyes enthralled him once more.

Holton had never realized the torment of seeing a lady's eyes nearly on a level with his own, not to mention the invitation of her lips. This must be the reason he had never cared for Long Megs. He must set her at a distance, before he forgot that the younger sister was just in his style.

"Somehow, Miss Chalmers," he rallied her as they swirled with the music's rhythm, still slightly out of step, "It comes as no surprise that you're inclined to lead!" As the closing strains sounded and he unhanded Vanora to bow, Holton knew regret at allowing her out of his arms, despite smudges to his pumps' polish.

A few sets later, Vanora considered how intervals of relative inactivity allowed one convenient glances about. The dance's figures didn't require her full attention as in her first season. Country dance patterns returned easily to mind with the lessons Lady Fenmore had insisted upon for the sisters. While she stepped the figures, Vanora watched Eva as closely as if she had sat by the wall, and she knew Holton's precise location at all times.

Vanora smiled at her plump partner as she faced up and advanced a double.

Clearly, Holton hadn't recognized her until she spoke to him. This both gratified and infuriated Vanora. While the admiration on his face even before he knew her had been most satisfactory, it galled that the man found her looks changed beyond all recognition. Why must he recollect, instead of her face, her unfortunate strong-mindedness? She had marked him clearly as a man who saw only externals.

Vanora concentrated on retiring a double.

Waltzing with the dandy had been nothing like frolicking with Eva. Vanora had thought as Holton clasped her that a gentleman's hand on one's person felt nothing like a dancing master's, either. She had hardly known where to look. She had forgotten to follow his lead as an urge to escape his compelling touch overset her.

When his fingers had slipped along the bareness exposed by this gown's deep point in back, Vanora had known her worst fears about both gown and dance were well founded. Her views on the dangers of dandies were confirmed as well.

Vanora gave her partner both hands to chassé up.

Obviously, Holton flirted as naturally as he breathed, like the other dandy who haunted her memory. She must guard against Holton's attentions bringing Eva pain. At first opportunity, she would inform the rake that he must change his ways, if he continued to make his attentions to Eva as particular in town as they had been in the country. If he were sincerely attached, Holton should be open to reform.

Country dances never heated one in just the way of that waltz with Holton, Vanora thought as she smiled at her perspiring partner, though this dance was far more athletic in performance than the waltz's slow glide.

Not that she could lay claim to grace, for as she had warned Holton, their steps didn't quite match. She couldn't imagine why she had agreed to take the floor, with so little experience of the waltz. But mismatched steps were of no consequence, for she meant to keep out of Holton's arms in future.

Vanora changed places on the first diagonal.

Holton partnered another fresh-faced young miss, Vanora noted in a quick glance at the other set during a back-to-back. She was both intrigued and irritated by Holton's ballroom performance. After the waltz in which they never achieved perfect harmony, Holton had captured Eva's hand for the country dance forming next. He had distinguished neither of the Scotch sisters with a second request to stand up, not that they lacked for partners, Vanora thought quickly.

Instead, the provoking man had approached one after another of the season's new faces, many of whom hadn't moved from among the chaperones. He was like a humming bee, busy amongst the freshest blooms of the season, Vanora thought. No doubt he rated each partner by some measure of pretentious judgment, for she saw that he exchanged words with various gentlemen after returning each girl to her duenna.

Vanora resented Holton's setting himself up as a connoisseur of young ladies in their come-outs. What gave him the right to blight hopes forever, she wondered. He could be condemning girls to obscurity on some whim of taste.

As the dance came to an end, Vanora thanked her panting partner prettily and accepted escort to Lady Fenmore. The gentleman was perfectly civil, if a trifle out of breath for so little exercise, and she was well suited to see the back of him after facing his red-faced front for half an hour.

"Do you mean to sit out a dance?" asked Lady Fenmore,

when Vanora refused Sir Gore Radford for the quadrille, and accepted his company for a breather instead.

"Eva shall carry the honor of Scotland upon the floor this time," said Vanora. "Lady Jersey's quadrille might have stayed in France, for my part." She smiled up at Sir Gore, leaning above her, whom she suspected of lingering to solicit Eva's hand immediately she was returned to her chaperone.

Vanora quizzed Lady Fenmore and Sir Gore, a youthful baronet, on names to join with faces of consequence to Eva's season. Reference to dancers gave her an excuse to watch Holton, as well. The second time Holton cast off before their eyes with a blushing chit just a bit too plump for the high-waisted gowns to hide it, Vanora frowned.

"You don't find Holton graceful?" Lady Fenmore asked.

"He's far superior in the dance to myself," Vanora answered. "I'm rudely curious, however. May I enquire why Holton seems to dance only with the youngest misses?"

Sir Gore laughed as Lady Fenmore responded. "It's a conceit he's devised for his own amusement. He says it proves what sheep his friends are. First he asks a young lady to dance, then he drops a favorable word to her account in friends' ears. He vows it never fails that young ladies dance more after he stands up with them than before."

Vanora fiddled with her fan, smaller than those unfurled in her own come-out, to mask surprise. "Does his praise raise false expectations in the gentlemen?"

"Holton assures me that it's never necessary to offer false coin in praise of a lady, for he declares that each has some individual charm to set her apart from the ordinary," said Lady Fenmore.

"Holton has a knack of discovering more about ladies

than they ever reveal to the rest of us," Sir Gore said, leaning between the ladies to share his observations equally. "His present partner may have perfectly shaped ears or sprightly conversation. Whatever he espies, his friends generally notice as well, once he draws it to our attention."

How like a rake to teach other men what to appreciate in ladies! Vanora thought, unconvinced of Holton's charitable intent. "I must ask him what he found to praise that brought gentlemen to my side," she said lightly, feeling aggrieved.

Sir Gore said bashfully, "In truth, you require no recommendation beyond yourself!"

Lady Fenmore added, "Since you and Eva had drawn much of Holton's acquaintance to you before he arrived, you can't credit my son with your success."

Distrust of Holton's motives still teased Vanora. Hadn't Lady Jersey said more than once that older bachelors always sought younger girls? Why must Holton, as well?

Lady Fenmore continued, "You may also enjoy to know that Holton suits himself entirely in the first duty-free dance of any evening, standing up with the lady in the room he deems loveliest."

Vanora endeavored to look unaffected by the compliment. "I should have expected he would stand up first with Eva, in that case," she blurted, guilt following closely upon heady gladness that he had chosen her above her sister for his first dance of the evening.

Supper was nearly forgotten and cravats wilted when Lord Fenmore put in an appearance at the Darnley's ball. He found his wife among the chaperones and occasioned derisive comments and envious thoughts from other ladies of the *ton* by sitting beside her for quite twenty minutes in conversation.

After bows and curtsies at music's end, Lord Fenmore watched his son return a young miss to her mama, near-by. "Still playing among the nursery set, I see," said Lord Fenmore grimly. Begging his lady to excuse him, Lord Fenmore followed Holton down the ballroom.

Catching up with Holton, Lord Fenmore laid a hand on the black Bath-cloth coat cut as precisely as the one he wore. "Walk with me, Holton, if you please," he said. Lord Fenmore noted the cool civility on the face so like his own as Holton acceded to his request.

"Keep me company in a glass of wine," Lord Fenmore urged, heading abovestairs to the supper room, certain to be nearly deserted so many hours past midnight.

Lord Fenmore continued, as Holton remained impassive. "A new season and crop of chits entertain your fancy, I perceive. Did you find another of your friends a mate with your dance-and-whisper *divertissement* this evening?" He saw Holton's jaw firm and realized his words had offended again.

In the supper room, Holton secured them both glasses before answering his father. "If I thought you truly interested in the reply, I should make you one. Perhaps you prefer to reveal why you've called me aside instead."

Lord Fenmore regretted the tide of emptiness between them upon which this arrogant son retreated. "Must I have an agenda to speak with my heir? I've enjoyed a chat with your mother; why must a desire for a few moments of your company require more purpose?"

"Purpose seems essential to your nature, Pater. I thought its absence was the element you found most lacking in my character," Holton returned.

Lord Fenmore swallowed the sharp retort that came to mind, his purpose not best suited by setting up Holton's back. "I merely seek your opinion on how the Scotch sisters go on thus far, society being your element as it is."

Holton looked utterly bored. "Exceedingly well, I should say. I arrived to find them nearly invisible amongst eligible men. Mama should have no trouble splicing the pair of them before summer. Don't pretend she hasn't told you the same, if you sat by her side as much as two minutes."

Lord Fenmore knew he handled the business badly, but he was too tired to search for subtleties. "The elder sister surprised me as a demmed fine figure of a lady, once out from under those caps, I must allow."

Holton drained his glass and set it on a small supper table nearby. "Is this the message you wish me to drink in with the wine? You should have arrived to watch me lead out that demmed fine figure, Pater, for Miss Chalmers can't even partner a man in a waltz without calling the steps. You make it perfectly clear that you expect me to marry. May I make myself equally clear that, when I wed, my choice won't be a lady as eager to direct my steps as are you?"

9

Bouquets began arriving early at the Plewes's townhouse the morning after the Darnley's ball, and the hour for morning visits brought the Scotch sisters' dancing partners on duty calls. Vanora suspected that more than duty kept young men languishing in the drawing room beyond the proper stay for a visit, and she considered how to hint them away. As Vanora had expected, Eva had forgotten rural beaux, with society gentleman to pay her attentions.

Vanora had danced with many of the same gentlemen as Eva, so she sat with her sister to receive callers, freeing Lady Mary. The gentlemen struck Vanora as younger than Holton, who still hadn't put in an appearance by half past two. Perhaps his particular attentions to Eva at Keathley Manor meant no more than she had feared at the time.

Vanora surveyed Eva anxiously as she sat on a brocade sofa, eager gentlemen bending toward her. Holton must not be permitted to break Eva's heart, Vanora thought, after pursuing her so ardently during the holidays.

At last Vanora's ears caught the male voice she awaited, from outside the door. Vanora gave Sir Gore Radford, seated beside her, the most attentive smile she had bestowed on him. Vanora allowed the door to open and close again while she pretended close attention to Sir Gore's muddled account of a curricle race.

Just before lack of notice could be deemed rude, Vanora looked up to greet the new arrival. Holton stood negligently posed inside the door, glass up to survey the room's occupants. Vanora surveyed him.

The dandy was quietly dressed in a coat of Spanish blue, over buff waistcoat and knitted pantaloons strapped into polished pumps. The crisp folds of cravat tied in a perfect Oriental style supported the cleft chin, and fair curls barely kissed brow and temples.

In no way did Holton's clothing draw attention to itself beyond quality of cut and materials. Remembering Lady Mary's strictures on fashion, Vanora realized that Holton gave himself an appearance of more stature by wearing pantaloons and waistcoat of the same color. His subterfuge pleased her, making her easier about using Lady Mary's health preparations for her face. Indeed, his entire appearance pleased her.

"Won't you take a seat?" Vanora said to Holton politely, indicating a chair on the fringes of the group near Eva.

Holton gave her a wicked smile and an elegant leg, continuing to stand as he ascertained how both sisters went on after the rigors of their first ball of the season. This pleasantry out of the way, Holton addressed the young fellow seated on the sofa beside Eva. "Fotheringay! I thought those were your chestnuts being led about the square. The leader seems to be favoring the front off-side."

The young man leaped from his seat, hurrying to the

window which permitted a view of Cavendish Square. Holton flicked aside the tails to his cutaway coat and seated himself gracefully in the newly-vacant space beside Eva.

He complimented her on the French washing-silk morning gown she wore.

Fotheringay turned from the window to find his place usurped. "I say, Holton, I should call you out for that trick, were you not such a famous wafer-splitter! Naught's amiss with my cattle, and well you knew it."

Holton lounged at his ease on the sofa. "Aiming at wafers at Manton's gallery, rather than ladies above your touch, is much the better notion, old man," Holton twitted.

The young bucks rallied both men in the same vein, and Vanora listened in consternation to a catalog of Holton's excesses, particularly where pursuit of ladies was concerned. A queer pain jabbed under her corset's center point.

Fotheringay held up his hands at last, crying pax. "I confess Holton bests me at shooting, but not at gaming or dancing. We can hardly compare charms for ladies in this company fully, so I plead a continuance to another time. Having lost one of the best seats in the room," he bowed to Vanora, "I refuse to have abuse heaped upon me as well."

Taking pity on the stripling, Vanora intervened. "Perhaps you would show Lord Fotheringay the prints Lady Mary recently purchased, Eva, to console him for loss of his seat." Smiling benignly on the gratified young man, Vanora refrained from looking at Holton.

The other callers immediately discovered a passion for prints. Even Vanora's companion, no longer eager to finish a race he had prosed about for ten minutes, moved to the far end of the room with alacrity. Holton took the sofa beside Vanora as the younger men excused themselves to join Eva, clustering round the print stand down the long drawing room.

As Vanora half turned on the sofa to keep Eva under her eye, Holton said, "I shouldn't worry about your sister. None of the young bucks is about to permit another to gain an inch with her; she couldn't be safer at your side."

"I should send them away," Vanora said. "Most have stayed twice the polite fifteen-minute call already."

"Let me make note of the time," said Holton with a droll look, craning past her to observe the porcelain mantle clock. "I shouldn't like to get on the wrong side of the Snapdragon by outstaying my welcome."

"Do you truly think me a dragon?" asked Vanora.

"Perhaps overly protective," he answered.

Vanora frowned. "Seeing a young girl through a season is an enormous responsibility, not to be taken lightly."

"I should like to see you learn to take life more lightly," Holton responded. "You sound far too much like my father when you speak of responsibility."

"I shall take that as a compliment, as I couldn't accept that you would insult a lady in her own drawing room. Lord Fenmore is most kind to Eva and myself, though I perceive that we take his lady's attention away to a shocking extent."

"Pater's pleased for Mama to have the distraction of presenting you, I don't doubt," said Holton with a curl to his lip. "He's far too busy with his duties in the House of Lords to require much attention from anyone."

"The Lords considers such weighty matters this spring that he must be exceedingly occupied. Besides rumblings from estates for repeal of the war's taxes, unrest since introduction of the Corn Bill last month makes action vastly expedient," Vanora said. Holton's tone sounded bitter, she thought, curious about relations between father and son.

"The issues are heavy enough that I'm relieved to have

no vote in deciding them," Holton said, looking toward the window, where budding trees in the square's garden raised slender wands of spring magic, hazed with green.

"But you're a landowner," Vanora said. "The matter should be simple for you to decide. Are you not obliged to support restrictions on importation of foreign grain? You must wish your tenants to get the best price possible on their crops so they're able to pay you rents."

Holton shrugged. "The land is my father's. I know the tenants on the estate I manage for him well enough to perceive their needs. Far more than the rent is at stake, for tenants have families to provide with life's essentials. Allowing import of grain reduces wherewithal to do so."

Holton raised both hands, palms upward. "But I see two sides to the issue too clearly for a decision to seem easy. The British poor consider the price of a loaf more vital than what's earned on a measure of British grain when it sells. I don't envy Pater his vote on the question."

Silence fell between them, and Vanora watched Holton study a painting through his glass as though the answer to the matter of the Corn Bill might be found there. She hadn't considered what a grown man waiting to inherit his father's responsibilities should do with his time. Perhaps society's dandies disported themselves in lieu of better occupation.

Vanora said, "I should hope lawmakers see the needs of all people affected by their votes, not just those in similar circumstances to themselves. Making decisions ought to be difficult when the best way isn't clear-cut. Might not your dual empathy lead you to more fair decisions when you must take up your seat in the Lords?"

"You don't find vacillation indecisive?" Holton asked lightly, but his expression showed interest.

"I think it the natural response of a concerned mind," said Vanora. "Recognizing needs on both sides of issues won't bring you to quicker decisions or even to the best ones in every case, but surely John Bull feels that the ordinary person is taken more into account by such government."

Warming to an opportunity both to press her views and encourage Holton in worthy goals, Vanora continued. "The French peasant and American colonist might not have needed bloody revolutions if they had felt themselves heard by lawmakers such as you can become."

"Your notions reflect the Scots' old French ties, no doubt, but I'm flattered that you find me up to the weight of a seat in the Lords when I must assume it," Holton replied, sensible of Vanora's encouragement.

Vanora found no trace of banter in Holton's voice or demeanor as he gave her a smile quite unlike the usual teasing ones that tilted shapely lips. Perhaps he would make a suitable husband after all. Holton's serious side boded well for her intentions to reform the dandy—for Eva's sake, she reminded herself quickly. A tiny pain twinged again under her corset top; Mysie must have mislaced her.

Vanora pushed away chagrin at forgetting that Holton was Eva's beau in their intimacy of shared thoughts. She challenged, "You pursue political topics far more deeply than you let on to your father, I perceive."

Holton's pose instantly changed to convey ennui. "One can't avoid doing so if he mixes with men of reasonable intelligence," he drawled. "Flaunting opinions hardly makes one a politician, for they trip so easily off the tongue."

"Don't think to hide behind a dandy's indifference now, for you've shown me that you care deeply about tenants and the poor. How can you pretend to think only of your coats, when your mind obviously harbors matters of far greater consequence?" scolded Vanora, determined to persuade Holton to more responsible behavior matching his self-revelations. The change must work to his own good, as well as to Eva's.

"But I think of far more than my coats," objected Holton languidly, taking out an enameled snuff box and opening it with a flick of one white-fingered hand. "Waistcoats are far more challenging to design, and their fit affects that of the coat profoundly."

Holton stopped to partake of an invisible pinch, and Vanora was faintly disgusted. *Snush* was a fashionable affectation in her opinion, just another way for fops to waste energy in the perfection of useless arts.

Holton brushed his immaculate buff waistcoat with a lace-trimmed handkerchief after tucking away the snuff box. "Further, my time is consumed with drawing, practicing the guitar, and making translations from the Greek. By the time I've read the current novels, I hardly have any mind left for the ladies, the reason I'm so much at your mercies."

Vanora was diverted from his evasions by memory of Holton's attentions to young ladies the previous evening, another behavior which required alteration. "You appear to have entirely too much of a mind for the ladies! Certainly you spent the whole of last night going from one Miss to another, flirting in the most shocking way. What if young, inexperienced ladies take your attentions to heart?"

"Your interest in my actions is most flattering!" Holton said in a mocking way. "How can you call it flirtation, when I merely fulfill the purpose of social occasions, that of becoming acquainted with as many amusing people as possible? Choosing to welcome young ladies into society is a social duty which makes the evening more pleasant for them and for me. Acquit me of making love to them, for my attentions merely add to an appreciation of themselves."

"Do you say that your attentions to young ladies mean nothing?" asked Vanora, hating Holton's foppish pose.

"Exactly!" Holton paused. "No! Yes!" He looked down the room toward Eva, then back to Vanora ruefully.

Vanora folded her hands primly. Clearly, Holton meant to support whichever response put him in the best light, proving the insincerity she had suspected all along. Vanora's temper spilled like an overfilled teacup. "I must warn my sister to view your attentions just as I expected of dandies!"

Holton said in irritation, "Confound it, you know my attentions to Miss Eva are an entirely different matter from casual dances with girls in their come-outs!"

"Just how do your attentions differ?" Vanora asked sweetly, hating every simpering Miss that Holton had ever partnered. "Perhaps you'll explain so I may discern just when your attentions become distinguishing!"

Holton's chin rose in hauteur above his starched cravat, "If this is your sisterly way of asking my intentions toward Miss Eva, I must say they're entirely honorable."

Vanora found herself more provoked than reassured by his words. "A dandy is so intent upon himself that he may never notice how much a young lady has come to count upon his professions of affection," she said, wishing to scour the arrogance and complacency from the handsome face before her.

Experiences from her own come-out crowded Holton from Vanora's mind. Control of tongue and temper began to slip away like a greased pig at a fair. "The dandy searches for the most graceful expression of lovely thoughts, while a lady's untried heart believes them genuinely loving ones!"

Searing memory of another gentleman with teasing eyes, a too-ready tongue, and exquisitely tailored coats blotted out Vanora's earlier impression of Holton as a thoughtful person. She gave in to the urge to tongue-lash a dandy.

"You may be certain that I shan't allow Eva to fix her interest on a man who finds it easy to flatter every lady he meets, never fastening on one with a sincere regard!" Vanora said, almost seeing another face than Holton's. "You must reform your reputation for easy dalliance, spoken of by the young men visiting here today, before you deal with Eva!"

Holton no longer lounged negligently on the sofa, and a muscle worked in his lean cheek. A change in Vanora's posture and expression, as well as her tone, made it seem as though a different lady addressed him from the one who had spoken with such understanding earlier. He had been lulled into revealing opinions not generally discussed, only to have the lady turn on him unreasonably, like a pecking pigeon.

"Obviously, you've associated with quite the wrong gentlemen in the past, Miss Chalmers, for you confuse the dandy with the rake, doing yourself and me a disservice." Holton strove to hold his temper in check and his voice low, glancing down the room to the print stand.

"My understanding doesn't preclude the dandy from being a rake as well, sir," said Vanora more quietly, following his look. She had never meant to become so heated that her voice quavered. Where was her avowed control? "There's little difference in the two, to my mind."

"You've displayed an unusual level of mental acuity on other topics for a lady, Miss Chalmers," Holton said in a voice so controlled that it maddened Vanora further. "Surely you comprehend that a dandy raises appreciation of ladies to an art, while a rake exploits them. The difference is that of a person who values every nuance of a beautiful painting, rather than simply lusting to possess himself of its charms!"

"You go too far in expressing yourself, sir!" Vanora

clenched hands and mind against the disquieting picture suggested. The dandy's words were too warm, and she had vowed never to consider heated passions again. The love she cherished from the past was pure, the highest form of the platonic. "Take care to leave such improper speech out of conversations with my sister!"

"Please accept that I'm known for adroit address to young ladies in their first seasons," Holton said stiffly.

"My point exactly, sir," said Vanora, coming to the boil at the reminder. "I should prefer that Eva's affections fasten upon a gentleman who's less proficient in excesses and dalliance than your own cronies brand you! You must show me that you can conduct yourself more temperately if you wish to secure Eva's affections!"

Holton rose from the sofa in one easy motion, regarding Vanora down the length of a classical nose. Chiseled lips barely moved as he said softly, "No doubt your sister inherited some part of your strength of mind, Miss Chalmers. Her affections may not be at your disposal. You will excuse me, I don't doubt, for I've stayed quite three minutes beyond the proper time for a call!"

Holton strode down the room to take his leave of Eva, answering the noisy jests of cronies still crowded round her at the print stand. He quitted the room without another glance in Vanora's direction.

Vanora sat mumchance on the sofa. *What have I done,* she asked herself uselessly, hands trembling together in her lap.

We talked so agreeably, until I heard myself scolding like a fishwife, Vanora thought. *I was furious for no reason, and the anger spewed onto Holton. How can I demand that he control his behavior, when I don't understand my own?*

*   *   *

Holton set his high-crowned beaver on his head precisely to avoid throwing it in the street and stomping it
flat as a paving stone. The dragon had changed scales,
but she breathed fire in just the same fashion. He wouldn't
countenance Vanora throwing high-handed twaddle in
his face.

Setting off down the square, Holton was hailed by his
groom, driving alongside in the phaeton. Holton had forgotten that he drove to Cavendish Square, and no wonder.
"Walk them; I'm calling on Mama," he ordered shortly.

"You're never going to walk round the garden," said
the man, making to hand him the reins.

"Don't tell me what I shall do!" Holton roared. Embarrassed by this lapse of control, he grimaced. "Sorry, Jem.
Guess my dander's up, but that's no reason to take it out
on you. Just walk 'em for me."

As he set off across the wide street between houses on
this side of the square and the garden at its center,
Holton wondered if something in the atmosphere
accounted for Vanora's brainstorm and his own. The
visit had gone quite well at first; he had actually begun to
feel close to Vanora, to think her sympathetic and understanding. Just when he was deciding she would fit into
his family admirably, Vanora cut up rough at him in that
inexplicable way.

How dare Vanora imply that he deliberately encouraged chits to fall in love with him! He prided himself on
knowing to a word how to puff up a young lady's faltering
self-opinion without taking one step beyond the boundary
that raised expectations in either a girl or her guardians.

Were Vanora a man, he had ample grounds to call her
out, for she challenged his very honor. In fancy, Holton
saw Vanora in the sights of a chased steel barrel, twenty
paces away. He took aim at the point of the amaranth-
colored ball gown's neckline, close enough to the heart.

Holton recalled the silky feel of her back as they danced. He raised his arm and deloped. Perhaps she didn't deserve shooting, but a spanking wouldn't come amiss. His mind veered away from the vision that thought inspired.

Jem had stopped beside him again. "What is it now?" Holton snarled.

Touching his cap, the groom said tentatively, "Thought you might not have noticed, guv. You've passed Lady Fenmore's house clean by."

Holton looked round with an oath. He had navigated round the square's garden, crossed the other street, and walked past Mama's house while his thoughts boiled. Holton turned about to retrace his steps, suppressing consideration of the Snapdragon until he was safely in Mama's company. She might know what to make of this bumble-broth.

Shortly, he was pacing Lady Fenmore's sitting room in the house across Cavendish Square from the source of his troubles. Even the room itself was calming, for it was papered and painted in blue and white, and tones of blue upholstered the sofa and chairs set in cozy proximity on a Brussels carpet. Needlepoint cushions in bright patterns welcomed attention without insisting on it, and watercolor likenesses of her three sons as boys hung above a china table. Holton felt comforted by familiar surroundings.

Lady Fenmore rang for wine immediately, seeing Holton's agitation in his first restlessness on entering the room. She let him walk about without comment while the wine was brought and he tossed down a glass. When he poured another and flung himself upon her cut-velvet sofa, she ventured to speak. "Were you visiting in the square?"

"Witch!" Holton said affectionately. "You often seem to have second sight!"

"Most mothers do," Lady Fenmore said with a smile.

"Few unmarried ladies have even ordinary insight," Holton said with a return to his grievance.

"What Miss misunderstands you?" Lady Fenmore asked gently, feeling she knew the answer quite well.

Holton explained his call on Eva and the Snapdragon, describing the pleasant accord of his talk with Vanora about politics, then the conversation's descent into accusations about his way of life. As he relived the exchanges, Holton's fury mounted once more until he was well up in the boughs.

"She's confused the dandy with rakes, and persuading her the two are no more alike than chalk and cheese is beyond my powers!" Holton sputtered. "I can't conceive how I avoided giving her the severest setdown!"

When he had talked himself into frowning silence, Lady Fenmore considered. "Most people find politics a volatile subject, but it seems that you and Vanora agree well enough there. Does she actually forbid you to woo Eva?"

"Not in so many words," Holton admitted grudgingly. "She finds my attentions to young ladies some cruel kindness, likely to pitch every dancing partner into mad love with me."

Lady Fenmore raised her brows, careful not to laugh aloud. "This topic seems to occupy her thinking, indeed, for Vanora asked me at the Darnley's ball why you danced only with the youngest ladies."

"Does she see me as an evil cradle robber?" raged Holton. "If I intended to do one of the chits damage, I've had a surfeit of years to contrive it! How dare she order me to reform my way of life!"

"Do you doubt your ability to do so?" asked his mama.

Holton glowered. "Never say you'll turn your coat on me, Mama. Nothing in my life requires reform! Miss Chalmers's scolding won't move me from my purpose. I mean to court Miss Eva as assiduously as ever."

"As you did last evening," Lady Fenmore said agreeably.

"Exactly!" Holton insisted. Silence stretched between son and mother. "You may not have realized how I intend to proceed, since you haven't seen fit to consult me on your plans to fire off the sisters. I have no intention of making Miss Eva conspicuous by unusual attendance upon her so early in the season. I mean to allow her a period to try her powers, to find her own level on society's seas. Gradually, I shall increase my attentions to her until she realizes that her happiness lies with me."

"You aren't concerned that Eva might pledge her affections where she wields those powers?" asked Lady Fenmore politely.

"I mean to dance close enough attendance upon Eva to prevent her fixing her interest with any one of the young bucks so eager for her smiles," Holton said. "If Vanora thinks she has more influence with her sister than I can gain, she's welcome to wield it."

"And what of Vanora's influence with her father?" Lady Fenmore asked quietly.

Holton sprang up to set his wine glass on the tray beside a matched decanter. "You're right, Mama. I must control the slightest display of ill feeling toward the Snapdragon's interference in my life. She may think to lead me by the nose, but I shall be outflanking her the while! The most successful attack is the one you don't see coming."

Lady Fenmore smiled complacently.

"Miss Chalmers obviously has some bee in her bonnet concerning the dandy set, Mama, and it's becoming a curst nuisance!" said Holton. "I'm more determined than ever to learn who she knew in her come-out to give her this unreasonable disgust of dandies!"

10

Vanora peeked through a slit in her chamber's drape, hardly enjoying this view of the square. Eva had insisted on accepting Holton's invitation to go driving, despite Vanora's offer to take her shopping instead. Now Holton and Eva prepared to depart for Hyde Park, under her very nose.

Vanora wished it would come on suddenly to rain.

Holton handed Miss Eva Chalmers up the step of his curricle and onto the leather-upholstered seat for two. Eva clung to his hand prettily, while her strong-headed sister would no doubt spring onto the seat unaided, if she didn't insist on fiddling the ribbons herself, Holton thought.

Though two days had passed since he had called in Cavendish Square, Holton still felt a strong sense of grievance against Vanora. He hadn't cared a fig that he was left alone to cool his heels while a footman went above stairs to inform Eva that he waited to take her driving. He had no desire to see Vanora, though he was perfectly capable of showing her every observance when he must do so.

The groom swung onto the back perch as Holton flicked the reins over his greys. The curricle gleamed like Chinese lacquer, its trim and wheels picked out in silver to give the black equipage an air of quiet elegance.

Holton wondered if Vanora watched from an upstairs window as his rig swung smartly out of the square.

Taking Holles Street to the south for one block, Holton paused briefly at its intersection with Oxford Street.

"Half London must be shopping or heading for the park," Eva commented, watching the steady flow of vehicles.

Holton inserted the greys neatly ahead of a phaeton-and-pair, resigning himself to a slow crawl along London's most fashionable shopping street. "Surely you prefer the park to fusty shops," he teased, noticing that Eva's celestial blue bonnet, ruched in the same way as the puffed tops to the long sleeves of her carriage dress, turned from side to side.

"At present I prefer a drive to Hyde Park because it's the fashionable thing to do at five o'clock, and I mean to be all the crack," confided Eva. "But this street is quite the most engrossing place in London."

Holton took his eyes off traffic an instant to smile into Eva's ingenuous face. How could such a darling have a shrew as a sister? "Do you and your sister come here daily?"

"Not every day," Eva said wistfully. "Vanora calls it a waste of time to be dawdling in and out of shops with no specific purchase in mind. I enjoy to have men dressed fine as butlers bow me in, just as though I were a duchess!"

Holton smiled. What a dear child she was, to be sure. London was a May game to her, and, in her company, he could experience his familiar world anew. As they passed establishments catering to the carriage trade, Eva confided her opinions of the merchandise to be found in most of them. How pleasant to chat without censorious comments, Holton thought, turning left onto Park Lane at last.

Eva looked eagerly past his hands at the bare grounds of Hyde Park to the right. She sighed and observed, "If the park were a farm, I'd have to commiserate on the pasturage."

Holton laughed as a breeze stirred curls under Eva's French bonnet. A lighter blue lining directed attention to eyes that never took one to task, unlike Vanora's.

"The park isn't recovered from the peace celebrations last August," he said. "At least bare brown earth begins to give way to green in spots, so grass promises to grow again."

"Vanora warned me that one comes here to be on display, so I hadn't set my heart on viewing nature," said Eva.

Holton guided his greys to the right just before Piccadilly, into the main entrance at Hyde Park Corner. "Perhaps a daffodil has raised its head for your pleasure," he said, noting that heads turned their way already. "But the loveliest flowers in Hyde Park are to be found in carriages, and I have the pick of the blossoms in mine."

Eva nodded to a friend in a passing carriage. "You pay by far the prettiest compliments of any gentleman I've met," she said at the same time.

"Since you no doubt hear encomiums by the dozens, I must consider myself highly flattered," Holton answered, noting that Eva's acceptance of his tribute was decidedly offhand.

"I doubt you are moved by flattery any more than Vanora," said Eva, "for you have been on the town forever."

Holton held his pair to the sedate walk set by throngs of riders and carriages on Rotten Row's mile-and-a-half drive. "I'm gratified that you don't take me for a flat. Does Miss Chalmers enjoy this season more than her first?"

"I should hope so," said Eva, peeping past her bonnet brim like an accomplished flirt at a gentleman on horseback. "If she found pleasure in the first, I'm not sensible of it."

"Why do you think that was?" Holton asked, wondering if it were strictly honorable to quiz this child, but set on learning the lovely Miss Chalmers's secret.

Giving Holton her full attention, Eva settled onto the seat with an air of satisfaction. "I've given the matter the greatest consideration, for you must know that, on this topic, Vanora won't utter. I couldn't continue to tease her about it once I saw the agitation of spirits it cast her into, but one can't help forming opinions from what one observes."

"A sister's opinions must be of the first consideration," Holton assured her, glad that Eva was too taken with their subject to make it necessary to draw up constantly for conversation with admirers.

"Our cousin, with whom Vanora came out, continues a correspondence with her," Eva confided, "so I collect there was no falling out between the two of them. And my aunt Lauder still declares Vanora the most sensible female she knows, so I doubt they pulled caps either."

"You speak as though Miss Chalmers often has a difference of opinion with her acquaintances," said Holton, thinking how politely he put the point.

"Vanora doesn't keep her tongue between her teeth when she believes a thing needs saying, which can ruffle feathers in those who don't perfectly understand her," Eva said. "Fortunately, she's most outspoken with people she cares for deeply, and we have learned how to hear her."

"Hear her?" Holton nodded to Fotheringay and passed him by, unwilling to stop at this interesting juncture.

"Surely you have intimates whom you allow to speak freely, when you might take the greatest offense at the same words from anyone else. A person may cut up rough at you and be excused, when you know he would stand staunchly in your corner were anyone else to cast aspersions."

Holton visualized Vanora bricking him into any corner in which she discovered him. "Your tolerance is commendable."

"Having Vanora for a sister is well worth a scold now and again, for she's the greatest comfort when one requires support," Eva said. "She must have known heartache of enormous proportion, for she feels so compassionately with others in tribulation."

"Some occurrence in her come-out, do you suppose?" Holton queried quickly, glancing at Eva. One of Brummell's famous set-downs might have left a poor opinion of dandies.

"Indeed!" Eva agreed, returning his gaze with a nod. "No doubt her heart was broken, for she often refers to herself as a raingoose, which lives out life alone if its mate is lost. Isn't it the most romantic thing?"

"Surely a sensible lady would put such an experience behind her after a period and look about for another worthy object for her affections," Holton protested, thinking Vanora's past attachment a serious one indeed to be equated with a mate. The notion displeased him. "You assured me that your aunt finds Miss Chalmers imminently sensible."

"But ladies can be quite totty-headed where their affections are concerned," said Eva dolefully. "Is the same not true for gentlemen? Perhaps not, for Papa says that's the reason he must approve before we may bestow our hearts. Vanora talks a great deal about using one's head in matters of the heart, as well, for she insists that a lady can only love once. I apprehend that she doesn't wish me to waste my single opportunity to love." Eva flirted with long lashes.

"Do you fear you love unwisely?" Holton asked absently, wondering how Vanora's loss led to an aversion to dandies, unless she had an unfortunate experience with one.

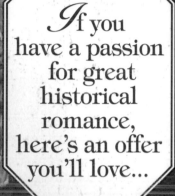

If you have a passion for great historical romance, here's an offer you'll love...

Yes! I want to join the Timeless Romance Reader Service. Please send me my 4 FREE HarperMonogram historical romances. Then each month send me 4 new historical romances to preview without obligation for 10 days. I'll pay the low subscription price of $4.00 for every book I choose to keep—a total savings of at least $2.00 each month—and home delivery is free! I understand that I may return any title within 10 days and receive a full credit. I may cancel this subscription at any time without obligation by simply writing "Canceled" on any invoice and mailing it to Timeless Romance. There is no minimum number of books to purchase.

NAME

ADDRESS

CITY   STATE   ZIP

TELEPHONE

SIGNATURE

(If under 18, parent or guardian must sign. Program, price, terms, and conditions subject to cancellation and change. Orders subject to acceptance by HarperMonogram.)

"Surely you don't expect me to divulge that to you," Eva said reprovingly. "One only tells a sister that sort of thing. Besides, I've come to London to enjoy the season to the fullest, since Vanora insisted I must come, and falling in love isn't part of my plan!"

"Perhaps your sister's sensibilities are greater than your own," Holton teased. "While she's merely mistaken to believe a lady capable of loving just once, you think love comes at your bidding like a tame pug. How can you speak of falling in love, yet plan when, or when it will not, occur?"

"Do you truly believe Vanora could love again?" Eva asked, responding only to part of his statement.

"As surely as grass greens again here in Hyde Park!" Holton declaimed with a flourish of his whip. The challenge to prove Vanora wrong on this subject appealed to him, but the younger sister was far more in his usual style. "Anyone might love more than once, given the proper circumstances and object for affections."

"I've observed that you encourage your acquaintance to notice young ladies," Eva said, responding to bows from a passing rider. "Perhaps you might help with my plan to bring Vanora to the notice of specially kind gentlemen."

"You wish me to play matchmaker to your sister?" Holton asked, feeling both intrigued by and resistant to the idea.

"You do the thing quite well," said Eva coaxingly.

Holton considered, as he drew in to allow Eva speech with a riding party of young sprigs and their ladies who signalled for her attention. Find the Snapdragon a suitor himself? What poor soul would he bring under the cat's paw? But Eva seemed convinced that Vanora had suffered heartbreak during her come-out, and Mama had suspected the same.

What a shame for so attractive a lady to waste her life alone because she had fallen prey to a bounder or bad luck, Holton thought as young voices prattled about him. He felt incensed at any soldier who could leave her behind, to go die in battle. Rage rose against a rake who could abuse the trust of a lady of such obvious character.

As he eased his rig back into the passing parade, Holton returned to the interrupted subject. "Were I to put fellows in the way of bettering acquaintance with Miss Chalmers, how would I judge who might recommend himself most to her?"

Eva looked as thoughtful as one could in such a fetching bonnet. "A gentleman very like yourself should do nicely."

Holton let his hands fall in momentary distraction and had to bring his pair to order once more. "You can't be unaware that your sister finds dandies most objectionable!"

"Indeed I am! But no doubt she's by dandies as she is by bannocks," said Eva earnestly.

Holton heard the crunch of gravel and sand under the curricle's two wheels clearly, so there was no reason to suppose that his auditory system was at fault. "What can bannocks possibly have to do with dandies?" he asked, thinking that neither sister had the least idea of the type, since Vanora had likened dandies to rakes.

"Bannocks are Vanora's favored treat for tea, you see. Yet when there's only one left on the plate, she denies any partiality, unwilling to admit that she desires it in the least. Indeed, I decide whether to leave cakes to her, depending on how strongly she denies wanting them!"

Holton laughed at himself and this absurd child. For one heartbeat, he had found himself wondering if Vanora could be more kindly disposed toward himself than he had reason to suppose. "I can assure you that your sister's common politeness over teacakes has nothing in common with her repudiation of dandies!" He was startled to note a set to Eva's jaw very like Vanora's most mulish look.

"You may think I'm too young to understand these

things, which is just what Vanora says when I tease her about a dancing partner; but I remind you that I've observed my sister far longer than have you," Eva insisted. "When she's in society, she shines sedately like a wax taper; but when a man of particular interest is by her, Vanora glows like an Argand lamp, ten times brighter than a candle."

"Tell me who makes her light up so spectacularly, for it sounds as though I need waste no effort on introducing her to further gentlemen," said Holton lightly. Naturally he cared who the fop was, he thought. Too many gallants on the town were the merest triflers, and the Scotch sisters were under his mama's protection, socially speaking. It wouldn't do to allow Vanora to become enamored of an unworthy bounder.

Eva wore an expression that recalled his youngest brother in mischief. "You must know I could never betray my sister, were there one gentleman who animated her more than another. You must simply watch her for yourself to see if I'm correct in my assessment."

"What if the man's a rapscallion?" asked Holton reasonably. Vanora was so busy looking out for her sister's interests that she might never notice the undesirable qualities of men hanging out for herself. "Couldn't I be of more assistance to Miss Chalmers if I knew the identity of this gentleman who already enjoys her good opinion?"

The rutched bonnet dipped, hiding the rosy face. "Honor forbids speaking mere guesses, sir," Eva said demurely. "Fotheringay assures me you're a downy one, so I don't doubt that your own powers of observation will inform you of any preference Vanora may be forming. And perhaps if you know a suitable gentleman to bring to her notice, you may turn her from an unworthy inclination before it's fully formed."

By the time they turned out of Hyde Park again, Holton had given up the notion of gaining further hints from Miss

Eva as to what gentleman might have caught Vanora's fancy. Of a certainty, he would keep the Snapdragon in his eye.

He's here! thought Vanora in delight and despair, spotting Holton from a sofa in Lady Saulton's music room as he entered. Not that it made any difference to her participation in the occasion, for she attended merely to chaperone Eva at this waltzing party.

As Holton bowed to one of Lady Saulton's daughters, standing beside Eva, Vanora wondered why he attended a waltzing party in the first place. Such parties were formed to allow practice of the figures in the dance, and Holton's superior skill placed him above the need for rehearsal.

Eva led Holton toward her. She wouldn't touch hair or dress, Vanora told herself sternly. If she looked presentable enough to escort Eva to this romp, her appearance must do for Holton as well.

Vanora felt trepidation at the encounter, for Holton had spoken no more than civilly when he brought Eva in after yesterday's drive in Hyde Park. Vanora could hardly blame him, for she knew she owed Holton an apology for overly plain speaking. Not that she could renounce her opinion that the dandy must behave more temperately, but expressing it so heatedly to his head had been inexcusable.

Holton made her an elegant leg and turned to present a gentleman close behind him, whom she hadn't noticed. "May I commend Sir Edward Bennet to your attention? Sir Edward lives next the estate I manage for my father in Berkshire, and we've hunted the Old Berks together since we were lads."

Vanora made the proper responses, forming what opinion one might on no more than a glance at Sir Edward. A bit taller and somewhat broader than Holton, the man seemed to have most of his hair and teeth, though she would place him near forty in age. Perfectly amiable, no doubt, with that anxiously pleasant expression, but his figure lacked Holton's elegance. And she'd wager they used different tailors. Sir Edward was too long in the tooth for Eva, she concluded.

"Sir Edward doesn't care to waltz, Miss Chalmers," Holton said. "I enticed him here today with the promise of meeting a lady whose conversation is more sensible than the dance. If you'll sound his opinions on taxation and the Corn Bill, you'll discover them worthy of a responsible man."

Did she hear the faintest emphasis on the concluding phrase, Vanora wondered guiltily, inviting Sir Edward to sit beside her. She could do little else without looking nohow, which Holton must realize. How high-handed of Holton to assume that she had no wish to participate in the waltzing lessons! He couldn't dispute that she needed them.

Holton turned to offer Eva his arm. "Will you do me the honor of showing me the way the waltz should be done? I've every hope that we may dance so exquisitely that word of it will reach Almack's patronesses, one of whom will immediately confer permission to waltz upon you at the next assembly."

Eva agreed absently, Vanora noted, when she should be in alt to receive Holton's flattering invitation. This country baronet fixed her sister's attention more than the elegant Holton. She had best pay Sir Edward mind, Vanora decided, if Eva could be interested in him despite his age.

Before Vanora could offer a topic, Sir Edward spoke. "Delighted to meet a woman of sense, sitting out the waltz, for the dance is no more than an excuse for hugging to music, and in public at that! My dear wife never countenanced it."

Married, and no dancer; the man wouldn't do for Eva,

Vanora thought. "Yet you permit Holton to bring you to a waltzing party, when you and your wife have no desire to dance it. Is he so close a friend?"

"Just myself who won't dance it now," he said hastily. "Wife passed on these two years since, rest her soul."

Vanora murmured expressions of sympathy.

"A dangerous dance," Sir Edward warned, "decried by moralists, led by no less a personage than her grace the Duchess of Gordon! Consider your sister's welfare!"

Vanora considered Eva's whoops when this conversation came to her ears and distracted the baronet by inquiring into the nature of his family.

Sir Edward named his three children to her with pride. Two daughters had first graced his union, then producing an heir had deprived him of sweet Cornelia.

Memory stirred from the season Vanora strove to forget. Sir Edward looked somewhat familiar, now that she studied his long face. "Cornelia Debenham, who came out the same year as myself, lived in Berkshire," said Vanora.

Sir Edward beamed at the name. "That's my Cornelia! Fancy you knowing her those eight long years past, and now my being presented to you within a week of reaching London! Thought you looked familiar. An omen of a good outcome to my purpose, I dare hope! Holton called you Miss Chalmers; I can scarce believe that a lady of your countenance was permitted to leave London without making a match."

"We weren't all so fortunate as Cornelia," Vanora said, turning to watch the dancers and finding Holton at once. She dimly recalled chats with a diffident girl as they tucked up curls in chambers set aside for ladies.

Cornelia had married, produced a family, and died in the last eight brief years. But Cornelia had at least lived before she died. Vanora felt a sense of kinship for this man, who had also lost his love, as they spoke of Cornelia.

"You chaperone your sister through a season, I take it," observed Sir Edward, nodding to the cleared center of the room where open waltz figures were under rehearsal, led by the noted dancing master Thomas Wilson. "A grave responsibility for one just past Society's frivolities."

This respectful recognition of her age and of the role she had assumed struck Vanora as less than gratifying. "My sister wishes me to share the pleasures of the season with her," Vanora felt compelled to explain, unwilling to be seen in the light of gooseberry, as Holton had first thought her.

"I'm delighted to hear it," said Sir Edward. "Perhaps you will allow me to partner you in a more seemly country dance upon the first possible occasion."

"I shall be pleased," said Vanora, thinking Sir Edward a far safer dancing partner than Holton. "Won't you tell me more about your Berkshire home? Did Holton say that your estate is close upon his father's?"

"Indeed, some of our fields march together," Sir Edward said. "Holton seldom visits the estate in his charge without taking his meat in my house, unless he has a party with him."

"He entertains in the country?" Vanora asked idly, watching the graceful curve to the attitude of Holton's arm as he separated from Eva to chassé.

"Perhaps entertaining isn't quite the word," Sir Edward said uneasily. "He brings gentlemen for the hunt, you see, and naturally some of the party can't be taken about to neighbors. But I apologize! This topic is too warm for a lady's ears! I'm out of practice at conversing with ladies."

More informed than Sir Edward liked to think, Vanora knew that men often took bits of muslin on hunts to the country when the host was a bachelor. No doubt lady-birds were the main sport of hunts for a dandy, she thought grimly.

Vanora observed Holton, side by side with Eva, his

hand familiarly upon her waist and hers trustingly on his. Holton had disputed that the dandy was synonymous with the rake, but his neighbor described rakish behavior to her. He must be brought to modify such inclinations, for Eva's sake.

Sir Edward bent toward her with an expression of concern. "Mustn't give you a bad impression of Holton, you know. His tenants think the world of him, and his father would never leave them in his charge, were it otherwise. Tries all the latest agricultural methods and has the land in better heart than it's been in generations!"

"No doubt Holton's heart is as much in visits during the planting as the hunting seasons!" Vanora observed tartly.

"You'll think well of him when I tell you that the best horse is sent for the doctor to attend rustics on that estate, while most cottagers must make do with the services of the parish medical officer. Kindest fellow of my acquaintance, I assure you!" Sir Edward said eagerly.

"Tell me about your children," said Vanora, to switch the subject. No doubt Sir Edward was too nice in his views to realize that Holton was a libertine. Even the way the man danced was enough to heat an observer's cheeks!

The baronet quite doted on his offspring, Vanora soon discovered, for tales of their beauty and cleverness carried them easily to the rest period the dancers at last demanded. Holton brought Eva to them, and Sir Edward insisted that she take his seat beside Vanora.

"Let me place a chair so you may sit upon Miss Chalmers's other side," said Holton to Sir Edward, turning to draw a decorated black-and-gold side chair to the sofa.

Vanora stiffened as realization struck. The dandy had presented his friend to her in the same spirit he introduced young ladies to his cronies' notice at balls. Holton had fobbed her off onto Sir Edward! While the baronet was entirely unexceptionable, she hotly resented an implication that, like a chit with a squint, she required Holton's good offices in order to attract a gentleman's attentions.

How foolish to interpret Holton's compliments to her at the Darnley ball as an indication that he found her altered appearance personally pleasing! Vanora had allowed herself to be taken in by a dandy once more.

It was bad enough that Holton believed she required assistance to gain notice. Worse, his choice on her behalf indicated where he believed Vanora could hope to look for a suitor—to a widower! She would as soon eat warmed-over oatcake as settle for a widower, not that she had the slightest wish to marry any man. And she could choose for herself, should she decide she would wed!

"May I drop you somewhere?" Holton asked Sir Edward outside Lady Saulton's house after the waltzing party. If he kept the baronet in company, he might form an impression of Sir Edward's reception of Vanora.

"I had thought to call on my mama in Brook Street near Hanover Square. Don't care to take you out of your way, old man, for unlike the dandy set, we country men don't fear to scuff our boot leather by walking."

"No need to wear it out, either," said Holton, indicating the approach of his curricle. "Climb in."

Holton took an indirect route toward Lady Bennet's house but decided on a direct path to the information he sought. "Did you find Miss Chalmers just as I said?" he asked.

Sir Edward shuffled his feet in the box. "Lovely lady, indeed. Seems to think just as she ought. Discovered that she recalls my Cornelia, and demmed if I didn't have some vague recollection of Miss Chalmers! Came out the same season as my Cornelia, don't you know."

Holton's interest rose like a hound nosing the first faint

whiff of fox. "You knew her in her come-out? What was she like? Did anyone in particular show her attentions?"

Sir Edward frowned up at three- and four-story town-houses as though vetting the neighborhood. "Can't say that I recall much about Miss Chalmers; probably too much the dasher for me to believe a suit could prosper. But some odd story about the lady—" he appeared to search his mind. "No, I can't dredge it up."

Holton slowed his pair to a walk. "Think, man! Do you mean scandal, or just a green girl's silliness? Surely you retain some impression."

Sir Edward obliged, creasing his brow in further efforts at thought. "Sorry," he announced at last. "Recall there was talk, but you must know that my whole attention was fixed on my Cornelia, and had not Miss Chalmers been her acquaintance, I shouldn't remember the lady at all. Tell you what, though," he added, as Holton loosed an oath, "my mama might bring something to mind. She watched that year's crop of ladies right closely on my behalf, as you might guess."

"But of course!" said Holton, bringing his pair to a brisk trot. "I'm charmed to wait on her now."

Moments later, the two gentlemen were seated in the dowager Lady Bennet's crowded drawing room. Looking about, Holton believed that Lady Bennet had never relegated furniture to other chambers as she acquired new pieces, as was the custom. Perhaps her mind housed each item it had ever acquired, as did her drawing room.

A footman threaded his way through chairs, tables, and sofas standing cheek by jowl to deliver a tea tray to his mistress. Holton steeled himself to drink cat-lap and like it, if the lady's memory could be made to serve.

Holton complimented Lady Bennet on her furnishings, since keeping so many about her indicated that she valued them. When ready words and teasing glances had warmed her to the point that she urged another macaroon on him, he judged the time auspicious for his query. "On the drive here, Bennet and I discussed a lady in attendance at Lady Saulton's waltzing party. He recalls her as a friend to his Cornelia in her come-out, but we can bring nothing more about her to mind. We feel certain that your memory of that season is superior to ours."

Lady Bennet looked gratified. "Naturally, any matter relating to my Edward must remain uppermost in my mind," she said, reaching over to pat her son's knee possessively. "What is the lady's name?"

"Miss Vanora Chalmers. She's niece to Lord Lauder, you might recall," Holton supplied casually, his inner ear straining for the least nuance of information.

"Miss Chalmers!" said Lady Bennet, with a worried look toward her son. "Yes, indeed! Came out with her cousin, I recollect, and Lady Lauder had her hands full, with both girls attracting the gentlemen like ants to a picnic. Both were lovely, definite favorites with the beaux. Lady Lauder's daughter was perhaps the more favored, as Miss Chalmers' portion was certain to be less."

"Do you recall anything out of the ordinary about the girls, beyond their powers of attraction?" asked Holton.

"Not to put a name to," mused Lady Bennet, eyes seeking her son's face as though to gauge his interest in the matter. "Lady Lauder's gel was engaged to George Hartlebury near the end of May; Lady Lauder held a dress ball to announce it before they returned to Scotland late in June, I recall. But even before her cousin's engagement was generally known, Miss Chalmers seemed to lose interest in the season."

"How do you mean, 'lose interest?'" Holton asked, wishing he could remove the dowager's cap and poke inside her head to seize what he needed without roundaboutation.

"It's difficult to put into words. With her golden hair and skin, the chit seemed to glow from within." The dowager frowned toward her son. "Then, as spring warmed to summer, it was quite as though the light had gone out."

Holton let out the breath he had been holding without realizing that he did so. "We both apprehend how the *ton* enjoys speculation, Lady Bennet. Do you recall talk about Miss Chalmers and a particular gentleman, which might account for the change in her? A disappointment of hopes, perhaps?"

"Naturally one hears things, Mr. Holton, though one never gossips!" Lady Bennet looked at her son again, who seemed to be listening as avidly as Holton himself, and she appeared to come to a decision. "No one knew the straight of it, for the girl was as closemouthed as her Lauder connections. Various theories were bruited about, some not quite nice. Tame versions had her lover lost in the war, though even there one heard speculation about how involved they must have become. Surely one would be less overcome by the loss of a person one knew in a *proper* way!"

Lady Bennet addressed Sir Edward in a tone of warning. "Best not to fix one's interest where the least hint of uncertainty exists, surely!"

Multiplying one protective mama's reaction by the number of old cats in the *ton,* Holton was appalled. He might have no clear picture of what had occurred to darken Vanora's view, but he suspected that a dandy without scruples had soured her view of the type, if no worse.

Holton determined to be kinder to Vanora in future, while he endeavored to improve her opinion of dandies.

11

Two days after the waltzing party, Holton pulled his pair in before his parents' townhouse. Ready to surrender the ribbons to his groom, Holton paused as a recessed door opened across the square.

From this distance, he was unsure who pulled the door shut and descended the two steps to the pavement, but fashionable walking dress indicated that one of the Scotch sisters might have stepped out. Holton knew which sister was most likely to flout convention by leaving the house alone.

"Walk them, Jem," Holton ordered, shoving the reins into the waiting groom's hands and hastening across the street.

Scrutinizing the tall, trim figure as he hurried toward her, Holton knew the lady for Vanora, face obscured under a large Oldenburg bonnet. He hurried round the iron railing setting off Cavendish Square's circular garden to intercept her before she could disappear within.

Coming up with Vanora in the wide street's center,

Holton said, "Whatever do you mean, walking out alone? Surely Mama didn't neglect to warn you that ladies don't traverse London streets without a maid or footman!"

Vanora raised wide eyes from contemplation of her side-laced half boots. "Holton! You startled me! I hardly expected to meet anyone in the street at this hour of the morning. Why are you about so early?"

"You shan't distract me from ringing a peal so easily, my girl. What do you mean, coming out alone in this way?"

Recalling how recently she had tongue-lashed him, Vanora reflected that Holton stooped to scolds himself. "Surely one is perfectly safe taking the air in the square's garden, within view of the Plewes's house," she protested.

"You mustn't count on safety in any street, particularly at this time," Holton warned, brows coming together in concern. "Disquiet over the Corn Bill has led to street riots, and roving bands of disgruntled ruffians have attacked carriages and pedestrians throughout London."

Vanora objected to being instructed on conduct, but enjoyed Holton's concern for her well-being at the same time. "You don't mean in neighborhoods such as this!"

"No one can predict mob behavior," Holton assured her, "and agitators are well aware that creating havoc in their own poor neighborhoods will bring no attention from the proper quarter to their objections. Promise me that you won't come out alone again." In his fervor, Holton grasped Vanora by the elbow of her ruby *gros de naples* spencer.

Seeing the urgency in the blue-grey eyes entreating her, Vanora lost sight of the question. A sudden, rude bump in the back pushed her almost against Holton's chest, and her first panicked thought was of mob attack.

Heart galloping against her ribs, Vanora grasped Holton's arms to remain upright. Mobs were forgotten as contact with hard muscles through superfine sleeves threatened to finish the descent to her knees.

She smelled Holton's sharp, citric scent, as she had under the kissing ball at Keathley. Vanora thought wildly that she was nearly in position for an encore.

Holton set Vanora carefully back on her boots an undetermined time later, and both looked about to discover the source of the shove. A grey equine muzzle stretched toward them again as the groom eased Holton's cattle past.

"Didn't mean to give the leader his head," Jem apologized from the seat of the curricle as the greys arched graceful necks. "Beg your pardon! Thought I'd best mention that traffic may disturb you where you stand."

Holton still held Vanora by one arm, unwilling to break contact entirely. He drawled, gazing warmly upon her, "I can hardly reprove you in the circumstances, Jem."

Vanora pretended to admire the greys, aware at last that she and Holton stood exposed, under the windows of, and quite possibly interested eyes from, the square's residences.

"Never mind the rabble you threatened," Vanora rallied Holton, laughing to mask discomposure. "I was in less danger before you halted me in midstreet for a jaw me dead! No doubt I'll be safer strolling in the garden!"

Holton turned with Vanora toward the garden's entrance, tucking her grey-gloved hand close to his side as he placed it on his Spanish-blue sleeve. The colors looked well together. "I'll walk with you, my errand to Mama can wait. Tell me what brings you out on this lovely spring day," he said with a half smile and lazy hand toward the bleak sky.

Vanora thought of the Elgin marbles as she watched Holton's shapely mouth. "Don't roast me, for it's doubtful that the sun will show itself today! But if you wait on the weather for an airing, you'll stop inside indefinitely. Very likely, my outing will end in a dash from a downpour!"

"I'll race you, in that event," Holton promised, thinking how comfortable it was to walk with a lady near his own height. Matching one's steps to such a companion was far more natural than he had found it with shorter ladies.

Searching for the key to the garden's entrance in her ridicule, Vanora found her fingers inclined to fumble, perhaps from wearing gloves. When she wrestled out the heavy key, Holton took it from her to unfasten the iron gate, matched to the waist-high fencing that set aside the garden to residents' use.

As long as they kept to the path circling the garden, separated from the spiked railing only by cultivated low shrubberies, they would remain properly in view, Vanora decided. The looks the dandy bestowed upon her, though doubtless no more than reflexive flirtation, confirmed her intention to avoid a walk into the garden's center.

On the thought, Holton moved straight forward.

"I much prefer the perimeter to the center of the garden," Vanora said, hanging back. "The statue placed there to honor the Butcher of Culloden is hardly one I care to dignify with my attention."

"As you will," Holton said, wondering idly if Vanora truly objected to the memorial or merely insisted on her own way even in small matters. "You're a devout nationalist?"

"Calling attention to the Duke of Cumberland, who directed the slaughter of my ancestors a scant seventy years past, is an insult to Scots," Vanora assured him.

"I prefer to compliment you today," he said, smiling.

"I'm pleased we met privately," Vanora said as they stepped along the garden's perimeter path. "It's difficult to make amends publicly, and I must beg your pardon for inappropriate speech that may have offended you during your last morning call on us."

A brow quirked as Holton took in the unexpected apology. "I confess, learning that you held so poor an opinion of me was quite lowering. You seemed to base your opinion on a misinterpretation of terms, however, and I dare hope that you may not hold me in total disaffection."

Vanora's chin rose, and she feared that her color did as well, as she considered the recent sensations of finding herself nearly in Holton's arms. She avoided his eyes by facing forward as they strolled, her bonnet's deep brim isolating her while she made herself say, "It was unkind to call you a rake, for Lady Fenmore had already explained to me that the attentions you pay girls in their come-outs are well intentioned on your part. I'm truly sorry."

A sense of relief followed upon the necessary speech and receiving Holton's civil response. Vanora's standards wouldn't permit her to upbraid Holton for pushing Sir Edward at her while she owed him the guilty debt of apology.

Penitence didn't remove the memory of Sir Edward's revelations about Holton's house parties, which included ladybirds, either. She still had a few bones to pick with Holton on several points, at the appropriate time. The pleasure of his company this damp spring morning made it seem a shame to waste the encounter on brangles.

"You speak of misunderstandings on my part," she said. "Does a dandy not pay particular attention to his appearance in order to come to the notice of ladies?"

Holton covered the hand on his arm with his free one. "Naturally one is pleased to deserve your notice, but the dandy doesn't array himself like a peacock to parade about for ladies. The dandy philosophy compasses far more areas than niceness in dress. A dandy may undertake excellence in art, music, or literature, as well."

"Do you write poetry as well as play the guitar?" Vanora asked playfully, but experiencing real interest.

"I could versify with the right inspiration, no doubt," Holton said with a significant look into the dark-rimmed eyes fixed consideringly upon him. "Appreciation of others' work is more my strength in literature. As for music,

I've been known to strum quite soulfully on picnics."

Vanora imagined Holton's long, slender fingers playing over something other than the instrument's strings, from hints dropped in drawing room gossip. She said quickly, "Then the dandy is like the scripture's lily; it toils not, neither does it spin—except for intrigues!"

Holton gestured languidly, thinking that Vanora prodded the same spots as Pater, just more gently. "The Beau himself has said that 'A life of leisure is a most difficult art.'"

"But I've heard that the dandy's motto is '*Nil admirari*' wonder at nothing," said Vanora. "How can pursuit of impassivity and a life of elegant idleness be admirable?"

"To be impassive is to be in control," said Holton. "And can it be admirable to waste oneself on less than the best one may achieve? The dandy's aim isn't to *care* for nothing, but to attain such mastery that he's *surprised* by nothing because of his superior understanding."

In the distance, the iron gate clanged, and children's shrill calls swooped across the garden like birds set free from a cage. Vanora's spirits soared with them. Holton spoke genuinely, as he had in the Plewes's drawing room.

"I confess to believing the dandy both a rake and a coxcomb," Vanora teased, "who cares more for the knot of his cravat than the twists of his fate."

"Those two terms are not to be used indiscriminately," Holton said, wishing he were more certain of meeting this lady's surprises with impassivity. He must encourage her in this lighter mood; it suited her. "A dandy is neither a rake nor a coxcomb! The rake has no regard for a lady's feelings, and the coxcomb has no regard for anyone's sensibilities, to wear such exaggerations of fashion!"

"I wonder which you consider the greater sin!" Vanora said astringently. "However, I begin to see why you object to being labelled a rake, and I sincerely regret referring to your ballroom actions as such."

"How could I refuse to accept so handsome an apology?" Holton leaned forward to see Vanora's face past the bonnet's brim and received a smile that brightened the grey day.

Eager cries rode a chill breeze past them, and two boys appeared, running on the intersecting path ahead. The little fellow in the lead, looking back instead of ahead, swerved onto the perimeter path. Legs and arms toiling mightily, he set a course to collide with Vanora.

Holton quickly stepped ahead of her, catching the child and swinging him off his feet. Setting the racer down again, Holton stooped to the boy. "Swift on your feet, aren't you?" he said approvingly. "Best to check that the path is clear ahead when you travel at such great rates, you know."

Mumbling apology, the boy charged off again to join his companion, turning into the center of the garden once more. Watching Holton with the boy turned Vanora's heart into a bowl of warm pudding.

Dreamily, she asked, "Do you think them a pair of brothers, or friends?"

"Perhaps both," Holton said, approving the softened aspect to Vanora's face. "What of us; shall we cry friends?"

"A comfortable notion," Vanora said, welcoming closer connection between the two of them. "I was uncertain that London ladies and gentlemen could be anything but flirts to each other, from what I've observed thus far."

Holton laughed, pleased to find his standing with this lady more agreeable. "Flirting is a pastime, not a way of being on terms. Certainly it's a quite pleasurable game."

"And a dangerous one!" Vanora said, reminding herself of how often the man strolling at her side in chill spring air played the game. He flirted as easily with her this morning as with Eva, making his attentions to one, or both, meaningless. Could one ever trust a dandy's dalliance? She thrust away the thought for the present.

"Do you believe friendships between men and women safer than flirting?" Holton asked in teasing challenge as he took Vanora's hand on his arm again to help her along the perfectly smooth path.

"I'm doubtful such friendships are possible," Vanora returned, rising to one of Holton's mocking debates. "Not true friendships, at any rate, outside of those between brothers and sisters."

"Why would you believe unrelated ladies and gentlemen incapable of forming true friendships?" Vanora's unexpected pronouncements tickled Holton's fancy, and he was as ready to explore the paths of her thinking as to walk this gently curving path at her side. She might even let drop some inadvertent view into her past experience with dandies.

Vanora looked up through branches of half-dressed trees shivering against grey sky. "A female's fondest desire is to be understood, to have a friend empathize with every nuance of her sentiments, to know even the weaknesses of her character, but to love her in spite of them." She gave him a mischievous smile.

"Men, however, wish friends' views to confirm the illusion of self they present the world," Vanora continued. "One is expected to deny male weakness, to support the male notion of his supremacy in every situation. So the only honest friendship must exist between women, for only females wish to be accepted for faults as well as strengths."

Holton considered her words; had she suffered a grave disappointment of the heart? "What vain fools you make us sound!" he bantered. "It's just as fair to say that women support our illusions of strength to keep us chained into the role of Atlas, supporting a world women have no desire to shrug onto their own slight shoulders!"

"Women might share the burden, given the opportunity," Vanora returned swiftly.

"Some do," Holton replied, enjoying the surprise on her face. "I've watched Mama share Pater's burdens in many ways, seeming as much friend as wife."

Vanora put out her free hand to greet leafing limbs and rosy-purple mezereon blossoms reaching to passers-by. "My parents act friends as well, I confess. I don't comprehend why my parents and yours have achieved that standing when many married couples seem barely tolerant, even in company."

Challenged by Vanora's observation, Holton considered and replied, "One conjectures that such couples love each other, even after years of marriage."

Vanora swept the notion away with an impatient hand. "But marriages often begin in a fever of love and progress to frigid civility or none, even damage to the union and people concerned! Caro Lamb and Lord Melborne come to mind."

"Certainly they seemed fervently attached early on," Holton agreed, "but I'd hardly hold them up as examples." How like Vanora to speak of people other unmarried ladies only whispered about privately, thought Holton. She could hardly be called missish, and he found it refreshing.

With unwed ladies, Holton normally set a guard on his tongue, saving less innocent and more interesting conversation for chats with married flirts. Recognizing how he termed such female acquaintances, he wondered if Vanora's original premise on friendship between the sexes was more correct than he had first credited.

As they rounded the south curve of the garden, Holton heard a door close and glanced toward his parents' house. His father stood in the doorway, watching their progress instead of climbing into his carriage. How pleased Pater must be to see him with the elder Scotch sister, Holton thought sourly.

Vanora waved to Lord Fenmore, who tipped his tall beaver hat, displaying silver-gilt hair that gleamed even on a grey day. Vanora appeared on good terms with Pater, Holton reflected wryly as he returned his father's salute.

Continuing their conversation, Holton admitted, "I can't bring to mind a woman in the *ton* I might call 'friend,' apart from Mama and, now, you."

Vanora nodded. "Lady Fenmore accepts everyone so readily as they are, that all must think her a friend."

"Unlike Pater," Holton said grimly.

Vanora took up his words instantly, though he had spoken almost to himself. "I don't doubt that he loves you, but I've noticed less rapport between you and Lord Fenmore than between you and your mama. Even forms of address for your parents reflect that difference."

"So they do," Holton admitted, thinking that Vanora didn't hesitate to speak her piece on any subject, even quite personal ones. "No doubt Pater feels a dutiful affection, but he can hardly be said to approve much about me."

"But you hardly court his approval," Vanora pointed out. "It appears to me that you set out to vex him as much as possible by your manner."

"This is plain speaking!" Holton said, wondering if sight of his father had turned Vanora censorious. "I didn't realize you observed my family so closely as to expose our faults. Do you cry friends by offering criticism?"

"Not criticism, but friendly observations," Vanora said. "It pains me to see two men with much in common fail to value one another."

"I refuse to accept blame entirely for that situation," Holton said distantly, kicking at a pebble on the path in spite of his gleaming Hessian boots.

"Nor must you," Vanora said eagerly. "But you can change only your own behavior, so it does little good to lecture you on how your father might act."

"You might consider lecturing my father instead," Holton objected. Though he smiled, Holton felt that Vanora meddled without appreciating his situation in the least.

"Perhaps I shall do so, opportunity presenting itself," Vanora agreed. "For I collect that you each refuse to give the other what he desires in your dealings."

Curiosity won over Holton's sense of ill use. "How so?"

"Not being on hand at the start, I can't say how the round-robin began," Vanora admitted, "but it appears to me that your father doesn't give you what you want—his approval—so you refuse him what he desires—pursuing what he calls a responsible course of life. If one of you doesn't break the pattern, it goes round like a fowl on a spit until both your gooses are thoroughly cooked!"

Holton laughed in spite of himself. "I suspect that you but try another route to reform the rake to your own ideas, not my father's at all!"

The teasing charge of meddling dampened Vanora's enthusiasm no more than the cool, moist air. "I hardly agree with all your ways, but I don't address those concerns now," she assured him.

"What Pater desires is that I marry at once and get a nursery of brats!" Holton said with a curl to his lip. Vanora couldn't finish a conversation without poking her pretty nose into one's affairs, just like his father. Her step might match his more closely, but Eva was less provoking company, Holton reflected.

A vision of charming little scamps sired by Holton arrested Vanora's attention for the space of an indrawn breath. Recovering, she said, "I had in mind more your disavowal of any knowledge or interest in politics before your father. You choose a pose determined more by what draws his ire than by your real character. As long as you allow him to dictate your course by choosing it to vex him, you have no more independence than under a nanny!"

Unconvinced but uncomfortable, Holton determined to tease Vanora away from the subject. "Is this what your brother meant when he said that you demonstrate regard by gnawing on one? You must be greatly attached to me, if so!"

The cool breeze was suddenly welcome to Vanora's cheeks, which must surely match her ruby spencer. "I merely offer you observations in the same spirit as I do my brothers," she said in hasty mortification.

"How appropriate," Holton drawled, uncomfortable in view of her blushes with his jest about attachment, "for I cherish hopes of standing in that relationship to you one day."

As the speech left his lips, Holton doubted its meaning for the first time. Seeing Vanora's startled look before her bonnet hid further reactions from view, he wished that they could repeat the last circuit of the garden. Done over, he would allow nothing to dispel the camaraderie budding between them early in their walk, a herald of more to come, as the sloe blossom foreshadowed a blackthorne's leaves.

Holton's words acted as a mirror to Vanora, causing her to take stock of her deportment this morning. Vanora had totally forgotten, in the transports of a spring stroll with a handsome dandy, that Holton's intentions inclined toward Eva. She was stricken with guilt at the sweet pleasure she had savored in the company of her own beloved sister's beau. Vanora's sentiments on this occasion had hardly been suitable to a sister-in-law.

12

The *stroll with Holton* in Cavendish Square's garden sprang to mind, as it had many times, when Vanora spied Lord Fenmore at Hertford House a week later. In the interval, she had met Holton at a dozen different entertainments. They both had retreated into amiable but cautious civilities after the odd intimacy of that morning walk.

As Vanora stepped off the dancing floor with Sir Edward, she spotted Lord Fenmore in conversation with his wife and Lady Cockerell. She hadn't realized Holton's father was in attendance, but with the Prince Regent present for part of the evening, she might have expected to meet Lord Fenmore.

Curtseying to Sir Edward in polite dismissal, Vanora turned to find Lord Fenmore at her elbow. Speaking to him allowed her to present her back pointedly to the hovering baronet, so Vanora greeted Lord Fenmore warmly.

"You look as much a young lady in her first season as

your sister, with eyes dancing more prettily than your slippers," Lord Fenmore said warmly.

Seeing his appreciative twinkle, so like Holton's, Vanora replied, "You're as much a flirt as your son, sir!" The teasing warmth disappeared from his face at once.

"If you were indeed a green girl in your come-out," grumbled Lord Fenmore, "he would be doing the pretty to you instead of leaving it to an old man like me!"

With sudden resolve, Vanora stepped to Lord Fenmore's side and took his arm. She would set matters to rights for Holton by a word in his father's ear. Compelling him to walk off with her, she said, "You don't fool me with that crabbed tone, sir, for I know how proud of Holton you must be."

"Proud!" snapped Lord Fenmore.

"Just so," said Vanora. "Holton's support to you politically must be invaluable. I'm aware how much the right word from him to a young lady in her first season boosts her confidence to present herself well, and in addition, his interest attracts more partners to the girls. Fathers must own themselves indebted to you, because of your son's kindness to their daughters, and look kindly upon your approaches over matters in the Lords!"

Lord Fenmore turned his head quickly toward Vanora.

"Further," she said, noting the arrested look to his face and steering him out of the ballroom, "you must be gratified to see Holton such a leader in the *ton*."

"I hardly see why Holton's frivolity is a subject for self-congratulation," said Lord Fenmore severely.

Vanora gave him a teasing smile. "You shan't gammon me, sir, for I'm well aware that a man who sways thinking readily in the social world will lead opinion in the Lords when his turn comes to do so. He's very nearly as adept as you!"

Lord Fenmore looked ready to argue the issue, then

smiled. Patting hands Vanora had clamped purposefully to his sleeve, he said, "Tell me where you're taking my person, my dear, for it's quite clear where you've guided my thoughts!"

When Vanora and Lord Fenmore quitted the supper room for the ballroom, they found Lady Fenmore giving Eva leave to dance with a bashful young swain. Once Vanora was claimed as well, Lord Fenmore said to his wife, "Did you observe that remarkable young woman abduct me against my inclination?"

"You mean Vanora?" said Lady Fenmore. "I shouldn't put much beyond her, once she sets her mind to it, but I doubt you put up a fight against such a lovely lady."

Fenmore snorted. "You're a pair of flatterers, the two of you! Don't think I can't see that she's another such as you, for she handled me with all the aplomb you show yourself." He recounted Vanora's statements about Holton.

"She spoke no more than truth, my dear," Lady Fenmore said, "for you must admit that Holton is an admirable son."

"Holton will have her, if he has the judgment I showed in offering for you," Lord Fenmore said, taking his wife's hand in both his own. "Vanora has exactly your pleasant way of defending the boy; she points out his strengths without putting me in the wrong. Don't think I fail to appreciate that you can get round me without raising my dander, and I see that young Vanora's capable of the same trick!"

Lady Fenmore sighed. "I hope you may be right. You voice my own fears when you say that one's case must be presented without stirring up a hornet's nest. Vanora so often lets a strong will fly away with worthy aims!"

*   *   *

"Drury Lane!" said Eva with an unladylike bounce. "It's very nearly worth a season, simply to attend the theater!"

Vanora almost frowned repressively on this exuberance, then decided Eva's high spirits weren't out of line. As their party entered the theater, Sir Edward shared his solicitous attention between Lady Fenmore and herself, and Eva walked ahead under Holton's protection.

The evening's entertainment oppressed Vanora. Her last attendance at the Theater Royal was during her own come-out, and two years later that building burned down.

Vanora twitched her thoughts away from the last visit to Drury Lane. Like the old theater itself, that time was but ashes. Sagging spirits were no compliment to one's hostess, so she must repress memory and put a good face on her reluctance to attend tonight's performance.

Holton paused at the curved stairs to the left of the crowded vestibule, turning to give Vanora a smile that routed her phantom from the past. She was reminded of Holton's face in Cavendish Square's garden, as they walked and talked so comfortably, week before last.

Holton's eyes forecast a smile before shapely lips began their slow curve, much as light lit the eastern sky before sunrise. Seeing Holton smile now, with golden fingers of candlelight caressing the contours of his face, made Vanora realize that this expression was familiar as an old friend's.

"Our box is on the second tier," Holton said apologetically. "I hope an extra set of stairs won't tire you. We're in good time for the curtain and needn't hurry."

"As well as I've dined in London, I shall welcome the exercise," Vanora said warmly, then realized she had responded as though he spoke for her benefit alone. Lady Fenmore didn't appear to notice anything amiss, however, and Holton looked no more amused than usual.

Inside the box, Vanora found the upholstered seating much like any hostess's rout chairs. When Lady Fenmore urged her forward, Vanora demurred.

"I shall enjoy sitting here," she said, placing a hand on the nearest chair. Shadows in the back of the box suited her more than the chandeliers' lights on either side at the front. If Holton sat forward with Eva, as she expected, she could keep them in view without being obvious.

Holton's eyes glowed again, as though he read her motive. "We must do the other patrons a favor by placing the most ornamental occupants at the front of the box. Ladies, if you please!" He handed first his mama, then Eva and Vanora onto chairs.

Holton shifted the remaining chairs to seat Sir Edward and himself behind. Offering a seat positioned between Lady Fenmore and Eva, Holton invited, "Sit here, old man, where you can catch Mama up on neighborhood gossip from Berkshire."

As Sir Edward took his seat readily, Vanora reflected that the baronet must enjoy a good gossip above her company.

Then Holton moved a chair close behind Eva and herself. As he bent forward to ascertain their comfort, Vanora caught the clean scent of citrus. It wouldn't do to turn her head far, she thought fancifully, recalling the holiday's kiss.

Sitting in a mist of memory and Holton's scent, Vanora felt Holton's lips on hers as clearly as if Christmas Eve were yesterday. Contact hadn't lasted as long as a snowflake's touch, but it appeared that experience's length had little to do with memory's endurance.

Sternly, Vanora reminded herself of where and who she was. She attended the theater as Eva's companion. Holton's interest fixed on her sister.

Eva smiled over her shoulder at Holton, quite comfortable with the closeness. "How can you set Sir Edward to gossiping with Lady Fenmore, when the curtain goes up almost momentarily?" she asked, fanning herself and him.

"You'll find London audiences far less polite than those in private theatricals," Holton said, leaning closer again to speak, placing his arm along the back of Vanora's chair.

Hoping she appeared unconscious of Holton's heedless touch, Vanora felt his forearm's hard length press the expanse of back exposed by her dress' neckline. Vanora's mind spun out a thought that evening dress was well named "undress," for all the protection it afforded one.

While Holton informed Eva on rowdy conduct to be expected from those seated on benches in the pit, including howling down actors' speeches and pitching orange peel on stage, Vanora sat unmoving. Her thoughts bounced about like a hard tennis ball off the four walls of the court.

Being in this place, close by a dandy, made memories rise like specters from the past. The result was confused agitation. Vanora felt flashes of panic and longing, regret and anger, acceptance and denial. She could as easily cry as laugh. All she knew for a certainty was that she didn't care to refine upon the past, particularly not tonight.

Her agitation might well stem from Holton's heedless attentions, she thought. Vanora's gaze crossed the pit to the third tier of boxes as her mind fought off the past.

"Looking for acquaintance?" Holton inquired. "Some believe it more fashionable to arrive late, so you'll see more boxes occupied after the first act."

Both the theater and evening had dimmed for Vanora. "So I recall," she said without turning round. "This isn't my first visit to Drury Lane, though my last visit was to the previous structure."

"Audiences haven't changed, if the surroundings have. Do you enjoy the theater? You seemed less than enthusiastic about coming tonight," Holton said quietly, while Eva turned to answer a question put by Sir Edward.

"We're fortunate to have such a favorable view of the stage," Vanora evaded. "Last time I attended, we sat on the third tier across the way, toward the back. I don't doubt one takes in more of the performance from here."

Holton had felt Vanora stiffen when he first laid his arm along the back of her chair. Enjoying her response and his own, he had left it there. But when he asked innocently about her reluctance to come tonight, he felt Vanora go rigid in an entirely different way.

Holton discovered that he didn't care to have Vanora overset. "Indeed I hope that you'll find more pleasure in tonight's visit to the theater, and not just due to the agreeable location of this box," he said.

Vanora reminded herself that Holton wasn't the dandy whose memory reached over the years any more than this was the old Drury Lane Theater. "Both the box and the company are vastly agreeable tonight," she said, giving Holton a quick look from the corner of her eye. Close as he leaned, she didn't dare turn her head further to address him.

Holton felt Vanora relax and caught his breath as she cast a glance almost worthy of Eva upon him. He knew an urge to teach her further flirtation. Leaning closer, he murmured, "And you are no doubt quite different from the green girl who attended that past performance. No matter how pretty a miss in your come-out, you couldn't have compared to the elegance of person and mind you achieve now."

Vanora's spirits rose higher than the curtain as it lifted to display the stage, bright by comparison with the theater's lesser light. Perhaps her present could be brighter than the past, she dared to hope, without defining what she hoped for, or what in her past was dark.

"I shall use the play's start as an excuse not to answer such obvious flummery," she said, settling against the chair in a parody of concentration upon the stage.

Vanora's movement against his arm discomposed Holton. He knew a need to circle both arms round her while he traced the curve of white shoulder and throat with lips hungering for the taste of her pale skin.

His mind controlled the urge. Naturally, Holton had felt inexplicable attractions to ladies before, and he assured himself that the allure of Miss Eva's sister would fade.

Holton concentrated his attention upon Eva, naming the actors for her as they appeared. Vanora wondered if familiarity with the cast meant he was equally well known to them from visits to the Green Room.

The audience mostly ignored the actors until a small, swarthy man of wild demeanor literally took over the stage as Shylock. The crowd roared its approval of his performance, even insisting that he repeat a speech that struck its fancy.

Eva turned to Holton for edification.

"This isn't uncommon, especially with Edmund Kean's performances," he said. "London crowds insist on having their money's worth, which means one is never certain what time the curtain may be brought down!"

Eva shuddered, a look of intense pleasure on her face. "He's such a strange gnome, and his performance puts me in mind of the most horrid Gothic novels!"

Holton and Vanora exchanged amused looks.

"That's as accurate a portrayal of Kean's acting style as I've heard," Holton said to Eva, unwilling to look away from Vanora.

Warmed by their shared recognition of Eva's youthful pleasure at being horrified, Holton leaned closer to Vanora. "Does Kean's performance please you as well?" he asked.

Vanora felt Holton's warm breath tickle her ear, sending undulations shivering down arm and back. She couldn't recall his question. "Quite!" she said desperately, hoping the general observation answered well enough.

Vanora couldn't say that she took in much of the remainder of the act, but her agitation's focus had shifted from the past to the present. At the interval, she sat staring at the empty stage, bemused, until the door to their box opened. Turning, Holton removed his arm from the back of her chair, and Vanora was set free, as from an enchantment.

Lord Holland escorted his lady into their box, and Holton hurried to place chairs for them. Lord Holland desired that Lady Fenmore give her husband a message. This errand out of the way, conversation descended to *on-dits,* as it normally did among members of the *ton,* Vanora had noticed.

Holton had brought the sisters to the visitors' attention when they first entered, which Vanora expected from a man of such exquisite manners. However, he seemed to make a point of bringing her into the conversation beyond that.

Vanora found herself more at ease in exalted company than she had felt previously, with Holton's support. She began to enjoy Lady Holland's outspoken tongue as characters were sliced up like apples, more out of wit than malice.

"Byron was lost to the ladies for naught," observed Lady Holland acidly. "Marriage has neither settled him nor rescued him from debt!"

"Salvation is a poor task for matrimony!" Vanora observed to appreciative laughter. "Byron might better live in his abbey than sell it. Surely the rent of his mansion in Piccadilly would set a few rooms right!"

Nodding agreement, Lady Holland allowed that keeping to his country estate might keep Byron out of more than debt. Talk turned to political topics, especially Napoleon's recent escape from Elbe, and Vanora found her interest increased. This was the part of a London season she found gratifying, though Eva must be sadly bored.

As if Holton caught her thoughts, he murmured to Sir Edward, who invited Eva to stroll in the corridor for the remainder of the interval. Holton was considerate of every member of the company's comfort, Vanora mused. He had encouraged her to join the conversation, knowing the pleasure it gave her. Mindful of Eva's different tastes, he had arranged for her entertainment as well.

Vanora was pleased Holton stayed to talk politics beside her, instead of escorting Eva through the throngs crowding the corridors. Despite his denial, she had known all along that Holton hid a genuine interest in affairs of state.

13

Knee to knee with Holton in the carriage two days later, Vanora wondered at how little space even luxurious coaches allowed. Holton had offered to escort Lady Fenmore and her charges to a Saturday breakfast at Chiswick House, claiming they were less select under the auspices of The Bachelor Duke than in his mama's day.

As the Fenmore's coach-and-four turned between columns topped with facing lions, Holton directed their attention to the vast courtyard garden, then to the house as the carriage crawled toward it in a long line of vehicles.

"A stream winds round the house," Holton said, leaning forward to engage Vanora's attention, "and one forgets London's smoke amongst trees and flower gardens."

Vanora forgot to breathe as Holton's knee brushed hers.

Eva bounced once upon the well-sprung seat beside him, for she had insisted on sitting with her back to the horses so Vanora and Lady Fenmore could ride more comfortably. Vanora hadn't properly appreciated Eva's consideration, between concern over Holton's shoulder making contact with Eva's and a concerted effort to draw in her own knees.

They were set down shortly before four o'clock between matched pairs of steps on either side of the raised portico entrance at first-floor level. Standing beside Holton as his mama and Vanora were handed out of the carriage, Eva asked, looking up in awe, "Does one man live here quite alone?"

"William actually resides at Devonshire house when he's in town," Holton replied. "He uses the villa mainly for ruralizing and entertaining."

Vanora turned with her sister to look up toward the main entrance. There, earlier arrivals bent forward over the railing, gazing out upon the front garden. One particular face blazoned itself upon Vanora's attention.

Charles!

He leaned back again without looking directly down, but Vanora needed no second sight to know that her past had caught up to her. The man who had stolen her heart eight years ago was present, here, today.

Sunlight that had seemed no more than pleasant the instant before now glanced off the mellow, golden surface of the structure to dazzle Vanora's eyes, so that they took in no further impression. Sounds of carriages and conversations melded into a mad cacophony of senselessness. Feeling deafened and blinded by too much noise and light, Vanora was buffeted by a windstorm of emotions that allowed no time to sort them out. Remaining erect was effort enough.

Her next sensible impression was of a strong hand under her elbow and Holton's voice speaking near her ear.

"Vanora!" he said, as though he had repeated her name several times. "Do you feel quite the thing? Take my arm, and I'll have you comfortably inside in a trice!"

Vanora leaned into his hand for an instant, wishing to throw herself into the protection of both his arms. Then she straightened, looking about in sudden recollection of where she was. She must offer no display for prying eyes.

"Thank you, I'm quite recovered now," Vanora assured Holton, stepping away from his supportive hand. "I merely felt the effect of standing too quickly after a prolonged spell of sitting in the carriage. That and the glare of sunlight quite overwhelmed me for a moment!"

Holton took in her white visage and could easily believe she felt faint. "Take my arm up these steps," he directed. "Miss Eva will see Mama safely inside."

Eva agreed readily, looking on in anxiety.

"The sun is quite strong, indeed!" said Lady Fenmore. "Let's make our way indoors as quickly as may be."

To go forward was to meet Charles, somewhere in front of them, Vanora thought wildly. She didn't know how to face him again. Vanora felt a seesaw of longing and dread at the thought of meeting Charles. She couldn't bear to speak with him for the first time in eight years before this assembly, but neither could she make explanations to Holton and Lady Fenmore that would permit departure immediately upon arrival.

Vanora allowed Holton to take her arm and guide her progress, feeling like an aged crone mounting the steps. Vision and hearing had returned to the point that she took in events around her, but none of it appeared any more real than a dream's unfolding. She felt removed, as though she observed and listened from another room.

Mercifully numbed, Vanora found herself inside, where she greeted her host in some fashion and was seated at one of three long tables in an elegant chamber. Sir Edward attached himself diffidently to their party, sitting by Vanora.

Lady Fenmore covered Vanora's lack of conversation

as breakfast was served in a long procession of dishes. Lamb, veal, hams, chickens, prawns, pines, strawberries, and cherries were passed, and Vanora ate without taste.

From another room, chamber music wafted like memories from a former time, faint and sharply sweet. Vanora didn't raise her eyes for fear of meeting Charles's gaze. The nape of her neck prickled with certainty that he was in this room, that he had no doubt found her out already.

Finally, the interminable meal concluded.

"Shall we stroll into the gardens?" Holton asked Vanora. "I dare say we shall find a shady seat under the pines, perhaps by the stream, where you may be quiet."

Vanora managed a smile and nod. At last she was settled on a bench outside with the pungent scent of pine trees acting as vinaigrette. She recovered herself enough to say to her party, "Don't hover like so many hens with one chick! Go off and enjoy the gardens, please!"

Sir Edward offered, "I should be honored to keep you company, Miss Chalmers, if you will permit it." He moved to the bench beside her, awaiting permission.

Patting the cushioned seat at her side, Vanora said with relief, "Yes, do. We shall have a comfortable coze, and the others will know they've left me in good company." Knowing Sir Edward could ramble aloud through his thoughts with very little encouragement, Vanora waved Holton, Eva, and Lady Fenmore away with as much show of ease as she could muster.

Vanora needed time to think, to adapt herself to facing the reality of Charles instead of the elaborate mental screen she had constructed between them during the past eight years. Sir Edward's gentle prosing required only an amiable expression to keep it wafting past her ears.

"Have you attended routs at Chiswick House before?" she asked, to set Sir Edward off.

As his droning voice flowed round her like a stream

round a stone, Vanora retreated mentally to springtime eight years previous, to her first season. To her first love. This time, she must try for clarity of recall.

Charles had taken her eye at once, with his fair good looks, easy manners, and well-dressed form. At first he had shared his attentions equally between the cousins, but Margaret had paid little mind to anyone once George had taken her hand to lead her out in a first dance.

Then Charles's attentions were wholly Vanora's. Bouquets arrived each morning, with scraps of poetry tucked into the wrappings. Somehow, he learned Aunt Lauder's invitations, and he met them at every rout.

Vanora never attended a ball without Charles signing her card for a dance and begging for another. She never sat down at a musicale without his holding her chair and claiming one beside her. And though Vanora was flattered by the attentions of other gentlemen, she was as singlehearted as her cousin Margaret, for never did she think seriously of another but Charles.

Charles was an older man, all of thirty to her eighteen years, with an easy command of the ways of the *ton*. He was known for flawless attire and sought out to settle questions of taste. His eyes were more alive than any she had known, and they spoke to her.

Many ladies fluttered fans and eyelashes at Charles. Vanora was flattered beyond expression that Charles singled her out to receive his attentions, and she paid no mind to Aunt Lauder's gentle warnings that gentlemen's flirtations weren't always to be taken seriously.

When Charles urged her down the Druid's Walk at Vauxhall as they strolled about in a large party, she went as trustingly as she would have followed him to the ends of the earth. When he led her into a dark, leafy alcove and took her into his arms, she went there without question as well.

His arms folded her against him, his kisses claimed her for his own. She knew the trembling excitement that Margaret had described in rosy confession of George's stolen embraces.

That Charles would speak for her, she never doubted. He had kissed her; he would marry her. Vanora expected that he had written to Papa and awaited only a reply before making her an offer in form. Charles's attentions grew ever more assiduous as spring progressed, and he found privacy at most events to press his devotion upon her willing lips. How difficult it grew, to hold rising responses in check as he pressed her to further demonstrations of their mutual regard.

Aunt Lauder spoke with satisfaction of how fortunate Margaret was, to be settled in her first year out, and Vanora secretly hugged the same sentiment to herself. Papa wouldn't be put to the expense of a second season for her; Charles had awakened her sentiments and claimed her for his own.

That private satisfaction swelled when Charles whispered that his mama would arrive in London soon, and he wished them to meet at the earliest opportunity. A week later, Charles wheedled her into the garden at a ball, where he revealed that he would bring his mama to the Theater Royal two days hence. His hands caressing her back hotly through a thin sarcenet gown, he murmured into her hair that he could hardly wait to display his bride to his mama.

Vanora must arrange to attend the performance as well, Charles instructed. He would come for her at the first interval and bring her to his box to make her known to her new mama. The Dowager Lady Marchand would love her, without doubt. Vanora melted into transports that hardly contained his straying hands in time to keep her bodice up. She hardly knew how she resisted his importuning that night.

Two nights later, she entered the Drury Lane Theater in a tremble, begging Margaret and Aunt Lauder to assess her appearance every few moments. Only Margaret suspected why the question plucked so insistently at Vanora's nerves.

Because of the press of carriages crawling to the Brydges Street entrance, the Lauders arrived well past six o'clock. The first act had commenced when they entered their box. Vanora sank down on a chair at the front railing beside Margaret and George, shaking with anticipation of the meeting to come. The scene was little more than a kaleidoscope pattern to Vanora's feverish gaze in the dim candlelight.

Vanora looked expectantly across the horseshoe-shaped area, wondering which box held her future. Even when she heard Margaret's indrawn breath, Vanora suspected nothing.

After searching the boxes opposite eagerly, Vanora glanced past Margaret to the boxes toward the stage. She wondered why her cousin sat rigidly, staring straight ahead. Vanora looked the other direction.

Charles! He sat in the next box, his back to her for the moment as he leaned forward to address his guests. The lady with grey curls and tired eyes must be his mama, for the shape of her nose repeated his. And the young lady must be a sister, though Vanora didn't recall Charles speaking of one.

Vanora fended off pity for the girl, whose round face inclined to spots, for an unprepossessing appearance wouldn't keep her from loving a new sister. Then Charles lifted the girl's pudgy hand to his lips. Vanora's mind groped for a comfortable explanation, the first step in self-protection.

Aunt Lauder spoke softly to her husband in the shadows behind Vanora. "Isn't that the wealthy Miss Hatcher with Sir Charles Marchand and his mama tonight?"

"Indeed," answered Lord Lauder. "And from the smiles Sir Charles and his mama bestow on the little cit, you may assume he has engaged himself to a fortune at last!"

The words penetrated Vanora's awareness but made no impact on sensibilities gone numb. She still stared with the same eager smile when Charles turned for a moment toward the stage and caught her eye. If she had doubted her uncle's words, the dull color rising over Charles's shirt points as he bowed to her distantly told all that she didn't want to know.

Vanora never stopped smiling, publicly, for the rest of that horrid season. Retreating inside herself like an injured creature into a cave, she shrugged off Margaret's private sympathy with assurances that Charles had been no more than a pleasant flirt. She heard talk that Sir Charles would have languished in Fleet Street but for his hasty marriage, with no sign of personal interest, let alone agony.

But no other man made an impression on Vanora's shocked, grieved sensibilities, for none was allowed near during the remainder of the season. Whom could one trust, including oneself, to know the genuine from the counterfeit in loving?

Little by little, her battered spirits wove a supportive explanation of events that put a lid on anger and permitted Vanora to look upon herself in the glass again. She had loved Charles and he had loved her. He couldn't have kissed or touched her in the way he had, unless he meant to give her the protection of his name. Family duty required that he pledge himself to the heiress; he had no other choice.

Fate might rend them apart, but her heart was his for eternity, as his must be hers. Platonic love was the only form left to them, so she must cherish and honor it always.

Pervasive as the scent of pines, a question crept through a crack in Vanora's protective shield. *If she loved Charles, why dread meeting him once more?*

Her mind shying like a horse refusing a fence, Vanora escaped to the present. She became aware that Sir Edward sat at ease beside her, his voice still humming on the scented garden air like a bee that couldn't let itself alight.

Finding a tear on the end of her lashes, Vanora turned from Sir Edward to finger it away. Almost immediately, she found Holton and Eva beside her. Bending, he murmured, "Shall I call for the carriage?"

"No, indeed!" Vanora said bracingly, putting on a face to match the tone. "I should be most unhappy to interrupt the afternoon's pleasures for the rest of you. Perhaps the sun on the water is too bright, for I seem to have a hint of the headache from squinting. I believe I'll step inside the villa to look over its furnishings for a while."

"We shall come with you," Holton said at once.

"When Eva has been saying this age how she misses the open air at home?" Vanora said brightly. "I think not! I shall just step directly across to that entrance by myself; you may keep me in view if you fear for my safety."

"Mama entered that door not two minutes since; promise me that you'll find her at once," Holton begged.

Seeing the entreaty in his eyes, Vanora agreed and rose, thanking Sir Edward for his company. Promising Holton and Eva to stroll or sit quietly inside, she walked off quickly.

While Eva asked Sir Edward if he knew the grounds, Holton watched Vanora's progress along a path between cultivated flower beds. The vandyked flounce of primrose skirts rippled behind her as she moved, the salmon bodice like a flame topping a wax taper. He saw her enter Chiswick House, concerned for the pallor she had worn since arrival.

Hard on Vanora's heels, a gentleman approached the villa. He turned quickly to glance behind him, then slipped inside furtively. Holton recognized Sir Charles Marchand.

Holton searched his mind for an earlier glimpse of the same face. Of course! Sir Charles had leaned out from the balustrade above them, just before Vanora came over faint. Holton's lips twisted as he wondered what the man was to Vanora, that she would be undone on sight of him.

Sir Charles was undoubtedly the dandy who had given Vanora a distorted view of the type. Holton discovered he didn't care to be bracketed with this bounder by Vanora.

He turned to Sir Edward. "Miss Eva hasn't had the pleasure of being rowed upon the serpentine lake as yet, old man. Take her along and see that she enjoys herself."

Without waiting to see if the proposal suited either party, Holton plunged along the path after Vanora and Sir Charles. No doubt she was safely ensconced beside Mama, but it didn't hurt to assure himself that all was well with her. Protecting Mama's charges against well-known libertines like Sir Charles was more his business than Mama's.

Inside, Holton waited an instant for his eyes to adjust to the dim room. Groups sat about at tables playing whist or on sofas matching wits. Vanora wasn't here, though Mama stood in conversation across the room.

Catching her eye, he raised his brows in a silent question. She inclined her head toward a door to the left. Holton stepped quickly in that direction, smiling grimly at acquaintances in his way.

Holton reviewed the layout of the house in his mind as he crossed another room, recalling nooks to which he had escorted ladies in days past. Taking to the passage, he followed its dim length until he heard a low murmur nearby.

Turning into an anteroom near the end of the passage, Holton quietly approached a reception room beyond. A familiar voice assured him that Vanora occupied the inner room, so he kept out of view of the door.

A man spoke suggestively. "And you are still Miss Chalmers. Have you remained heart-whole such a time?"

The man's insinuating voice gave Holton an urge to storm the room, plucking Vanora out like an apple off a tree. He couldn't interfere before he knew if she would welcome it.

Vanora's voice came, recognizable, but not the tone Holton knew from her. "You were used to call me 'Guinevere.'"

"And are you still my Guinevere?" Holton heard footsteps among the silken words, as though Sir Charles approached Vanora, and his hands clenched into fists.

"You must not ask that, Charles; your wife—"

"My wife, sweet Guinevere, is far away, on my estate, and we are here. May I not be allowed a moment to think only of you in eight long years?" Sir Charles spoke persuasively.

"You haven't forgotten me either?" Vanora sounded bemused, as though she spoke in a dream, Holton thought grimly. His ribs ached with tension and self-restraint. Much as he abhorred interference in others' concerns and his own, he began to doubt that he could allow Vanora to make a cake of herself for a second time over this aging profligate.

"You fill my thoughts every moment of every day of my worthless existence," Sir Charles answered smoothly.

"I knew how it was," Vanora said in a rush of faltering words. "I knew that duty must have forced you to wed where greater fortune lay than mine. I've prayed that you could learn to be content with your lot, as I've endeavored to be with my life."

She was begging the rake's case for him! Holton stared at a spindle-legged desk, feeling that he must break it, or Sir Charles, apart. If she insisted on excusing the cad's outrageous treatment of her youthful self, she might just as well fling herself onto the couch Holton knew was part of the inner room's furnishings. That image nearly took him inside.

"To think that you remained faithful to a dream that couldn't be," Sir Charles intoned. "Eight long years, and I find you more lovely than before, a Scotch rose just coming into full blossom." Silence riveted Holton's attention.

"Please, darling, let me but hold your hand," Sir Charles murmured persuasively after a shuffle of feet.

Holton felt every muscle in his body bunch. He wanted to storm the inner room, smashing his fist into the rake's oily mouth and carrying Vanora off for a good scolding. Her intelligence should put her above being taken in by this smooth-tongued seducer a second time, if not the first!

From inside the room, Holton heard the slight whisper of slippers, followed by heavier steps.

"You mustn't!" Vanora said breathlessly. "All that remains to us is the purity of a platonic love, and we must never despoil it with an unworthy act!"

Holton almost snorted aloud. Vanora must read more Minerva Press pap than any Bath Miss to harbor such notions. How could she speak such drivel to this dandy when she heaped abuse on him? Holton's pride and an unnamed area hurt.

"Don't refuse an opportunity to recover all that the years have denied us," Sir Charles pled. "If you but knew the sacrifice of finer feelings to my estate's needs which I endure! Nothing remained to me, not even Mama's portion, or I couldn't have given up our hopes!" The man's voice sank to tragedy. "And having renounced your love, to find that the torment of that betrayal could never cease! My darling, you can't imagine how I've suffered."

Holton heard heavier steps once more and clenched his teeth as well as his fists. Vanora had the right to choose her own actions, he reminded himself. He wasn't her father, to instruct her on how to go about her life.

Sir Charles spoke again. "Nothing is left to us now but to make all that we may of snatched time together. Let me feel your heart beat against mine once more!"

Muted sounds from the inner room, a gasp and scrape, suggested displaced furniture. Holton envisioned the couch.

Vanora's rights be damned, Holton decided, as he pictured Marchand's practiced hands pawing at a salmon-colored bodice. Holton stormed the inner room.

The scene that met his eyes was so far at odds with the dialogue he had overheard as to provide amusement to one inclined to see humor. Sir Charles held Vanora by the wrists in an effort to pull her to him, but she had flung herself back, looking like a shirt hung to dry by the sleeves, billowing in a high wind. Vanora's expression, far from passion, revealed the liveliest dread. Holton wasn't amused.

Reaching the struggling pair, Holton seized Vanora's arm above Sir Charles' hand. He locked gazes with the startled baronet, hoping the man would defy him.

"How kind of you to look after Miss Chalmers for a moment," Holton said in a voice that conveyed an entirely different message. "However, that privilege is mine, and you'll recognize that it's one I don't surrender lightly!"

Holton stabbed Marchand with hot eyes. The threat Holton invested into his tone removed Sir Charles's clasp from Vanora's wrists as though they scorched him.

Taking Vanora's hands into his protection, Holton demanded, as he examined her pale face, "You're unharmed?"

"Quite!" she replied, clinging to him as she had when one of his greys nosed her off balance in Cavendish Square.

Holton yearned to cradle Vanora safely against his chest, but before a man who had just endeavored to embrace her, he couldn't. Holton tucked Vanora behind himself, standing squarely between her and the baronet. Never had he wanted with such bloodthirst to call out a man.

Sir Charles extended a hand toward Vanora, beseeching, "My dear, we must talk over this coil! May I call on you?"

Holton didn't wait on her answer. "Miss Chalmers's time both now and in future is entirely taken up," he said frigidly. "No doubt you'll find your presence required on your estate immediately."

Sir Charles bowed to Vanora and said languidly, "Perhaps not so precipitously as that." He quitted the room.

Holton heard a small sigh behind him and wondered with a spurt of anger if Vanora would have preferred that he leave.

Rage crested in Holton's chest like a ship tossed in a storm. He wheeled on Vanora, clasping her wrists in a grip like manacles. "You secluded yourself with the greatest rakehell of the past twenty years! Have you no care for your reputation, or the reflection you cast upon your sister and my mother by your totty-headed behavior?" Relief at having her safe made him scold like a nanny who had just snatched a heedless child from a coach's path.

"You dare judge my behavior or Charles's when your own friends decry your libertarian propensities to your face?" Vanora gasped, struggling to free her wrists for the second time in three minutes. Being caught in a compromising situation with a married man, by Holton of all people, left Vanora feeling dirty and defensive.

Vanora felt unprepared to cross verbal swords with Holton at present, shocked as she was by a new view of the dandy she had idealized for eight years. Forced to face what her youthful self hadn't consciously admitted, that Charles was no gentleman, Vanora's fire of self-assurance burned low.

"My behavior isn't in question, for I'm not a lady with a reputation to ruin!" Holton raged from unaccustomed fear for a lady. "How could you sully yourself with a known seducer, either eight years ago or today?" Hurting in a way he hadn't experienced, Holton cast away Vanora's wrists as though he held something distasteful. He wanted to pull her into his arms in spite of his charges, but he wouldn't behave like the cad who had just quitted the room.

Stumbling backward, Vanora retreated behind a chair, out of countenance and confused. Charles had just demonstrated how mistakenly she had viewed the first dandy she loved. When Holton entered the room, she had felt the relief of a child waking from a nightmare to his nanny's soothing hands.

Now Holton's scold was a plunge into worse torment. He appeared to think so poorly of her as to imply she had allowed herself to be seduced. She would neither address nor forgive unspeakable insult. "How could you imply to Sir Charles that you have any right to protect me?" she said hotly. "You aren't my brother as yet!"

Holton felt the leash on his self-control snap as Vanora's color and chin rose. "By Gad, I'll teach you better care for your honor when I am! To hear you posturing about platonic love in that sick-making way! Haven't you sense enough to know that a man doesn't follow a female into a secluded room alone to mew about platonic sentiments?"

Defiantly, she said, "And how shall you teach me,

sir—by example? Were I to follow your lead, I'd be off to the country in a trice with Sir Charles, where you're known to cavort with females during the hunting season! Little you know about platonic love, or of any sort except the profane!"

Anger being safer than emotions he hadn't sorted out as yet, Holton's temper flared like a smithy's fire under the bellows. "You waste your energies charging me with normal male pastimes, just as you've wasted eight years on self-pity, wearing the willow for a fellow not worth a fig!"

"Charles isn't a whit worse than you!" Vanora leaned over the chair to aim the accusation, stung by a dart too near bull's-eye. "At least he married before his thirty-fifth year, even if not the lady he loved!"

Perceiving a hit himself, Holton sneered. "Love! How easily you toss off the term! You aren't in love, spiritual or otherwise, with the debaucher who just left us. More like, you simply can't bear to be wrong. You'll waste your life in a silly drama of devotion to a cad rather than admit your calf-love was nothing more than girlish self-delusion!"

Befraddled, Vanora pounded the chair's back with both fists. "Self-delusion! Calf-love! You make light of the tragedy in another's life because your affections are frittered away in meaningless flirtations! You offer pieces of your heart to every chit you dance with in order to avoid keeping it whole for one!"

Vanora shot from behind the chair to shake a trembling fist in Holton's face. "And the real tragedy is that you're so self-satisfied, you think you have only to offer the pitiful remnant of your regard to snare an innocent! That innocent won't be my sister, sir! I'd rather give her into a crofter's keeping; at least his heart would be hers alone!"

Vanora stumbled out of the room sightlessly, bumping

a table in passing to send a porcelain piece crashing to the floor. Overwhelmed with anger and loss heaped upon loss, she hardly registered the mishap.

No wonder facing Charles had inspired fear, Vanora thought as she hurried away from Holton. Now she must face the truth of what she had been to Charles. And truth forced her to give up the precious illusion of loving him and being loved by him. Racked with anger like hot chills, Vanora began to recognize how little of it Holton had inspired.

Behind her, Holton stood staring at the shattered object long after she had departed, wondering if his fury fed on fear that Marchand had indeed ruined Vanora before jilting her eight years back. Myriad fragments littered the floor, giving no clue to what had been broken. Some unknown part of himself felt in much the same state.

14

Head down as she fumbled for a handkerchief in her indispensable, Vanora fled across the anteroom and into the passage, swerving to avoid two approaching figures.

"Vanora! What's amiss? Where do you go in such a rush?" asked Eva, extending her hands.

Vanora evaded her sister's touch, turning away down the passage. "This pestilent head—forgive me, I must be alone to recover myself!"

Eva turned quickly to Sir Edward. "Thank you for accompanying me, but now that I've discovered Vanora, I perceive I may look after her best on my own. Won't you find Lady Fenmore and tell her that Vanora and I are together, looking about the villa? I wouldn't have her worry unduly."

Eva followed Vanora swiftly down the passage, entering a door through which primrose skirts had just whisked. Pots of flowers brightened the cozy sitting room as they did the rest of the villa, indoors and out. Finding Vanora plucking leaves off a scarlet geranium near the window on the opposite side of the room, Eva closed the door behind herself.

Quietly, Eva observed, "I've never known a headache to give you such high color. Does your obvious agitation have aught to do with the gentleman who followed you inside?"

Without turning, Vanora said repressively, "I haven't the slightest notion to whom you refer!"

Eva moved toward her sister. "Naturally, I noticed that Holton didn't care for the dandy who entered on your heels. Sir Edward recognized him as Sir Charles Marchand, a rake who frightened Sir Edward's wife during the season in which they met. He said you were in London then, as well. Were you escaping unwelcome attentions just now?"

Vanora laughed without feeling humor. "You might say as much, though my judgment was under attack, rather than my virtue, when you saw me quit those rooms so precipitously."

Vanora bit off the tirade spewing up from her anger. She must call her wretched temper to heel like an unruly hunting hound, for it was unfair to prejudice Eva against the man she appeared to favor most.

Vanora passed a hand over her eyes as though to clear inner vision. What a confusion of feelings clamored for attention this afternoon, one crowding upon the other before she could sort them out. Vanora realized that she had never viewed Charles clearly before today. Learning how little he respected his wedding vows had convinced her of his unworthiness at last.

Holton, too, had changed character before her very eyes. Vanora had thought him a trifling dandy, but he had come to her aid like a protective friend. Next thing she knew, he was an angry accuser, upbraiding her at a time she wanted comforting. An image of herself in Holton's arms appeared unbidden, and Vanora stifled it at once.

Eva touched Vanora's sleeve. "I've closed the door so we won't be interrupted, for you seem unlike your usual calm self. Perhaps if we talk quietly for a time, you'll feel more the thing?" Eva gestured to a small sofa near a tiled fireplace where a fire was laid but not lit.

Vanora allowed herself to be persuaded to the sofa.

Eva watched Vanora intently. "In every *snarle* of my life, large or small, you've heard my misery. Can you not allow me to lend my ears, even if you believe me too young to offer advice? I can care, even if I can't set things right."

Vanora turned away from the concern in Eva's face. "I shouldn't speak of such experiences to you, for I've just learned how unfit a guide I am for a young girl."

"Don't be a ninnyhammer, Vanora," Eva answered. "Do you think by wrapping me in cotton wool you keep me from harm?" Eva forced Vanora to look at her. "I shan't blacken my hands just by looking upon coal! Tell me what transpired at once, for you needn't bear burdens alone, now that I'm grown up."

Vanora yielded to Eva's unexpected good sense and her own need to talk out thoughts snarled in her head like yarn tangled by a cat's paws. Bowing her head, Vanora began, "When I was just your age, I fancied myself in love."

Eva nodded once, looking wise. "Sir Charles?"

"Just so," Vanora confessed in embarrassment. "He was as great a dandy then as Holton is now, though a dandy was called a 'beau' in my come-out. Charles was wickedly charming, the most elegant dancer of my season, both alarming and attractive to us young ladies. I was exceedingly flattered to be marked out for his attentions."

"Then you could hardly avert a tumble into love," Eva defended. "Don't blame yourself so sorely."

Vanora shook her head, tracing the design of the

printed chintz covering the sofa with one finger. "I've avoided blaming myself too long, Eveleit, for it was easier to invent banbury tales than to admit that I had been taken in."

"But you never talked about your come-out at all!" protested Eva, laying a hand over Vanora's.

"My tales were told to myself," Vanora admitted sadly. "Instead of being angry with Charles for misleading me, or with myself for being foolishly blind about him, I convinced myself that I had suffered the loss of an unmatched love."

"Surely that harmed only yourself," Eva objected.

"I wish that were true," said Vanora, feeling heat rise in her cheeks. "But some part of my mind knew my pose for the pretense it was. When we met Holton, I saw him as a deceiving dandy such as Charles, and poured the pent-up anger of eight years upon him! That was most unfair."

"You berate yourself too far," Eva commiserated. "You must simply put the whole unfortunate period out of mind!"

"I'm afraid Holton's good opinion is lost forever," Vanora said. "I haven't told you all." The next admission was more difficult, so she rushed the words. "I permitted liberties that convinced me Charles meant us to marry; I'm so ashamed!" Vanora's throat hurt from holding back tears.

Eva placed an arm about Vanora's slumped shoulders. "What sort of liberties do you mean?" Eva asked urgently. "Did he merely kiss you, or was there more?"

Vanora stiffened and her inclination to tears dried at once. "What do you know of more, let alone kissing?"

"I was first kissed when I was fourteen, you wet goose," said Eva impatiently, "by Jamie MacElvain during a children's ball. Were you not so pokered up, you'd know that a kiss isn't a declaration, let alone the end of the world!"

"Mama and our governesses said it was," Vanora objected, looking at her brazen sister in horror.

"You were ever the goody Miss Prim, preaching proper conduct," Eva observed. "No wonder you believed every lecture read us. I didn't listen to the half of them, and I dare swear I've had more pleasure of life than you! Tell me the straight of it: *Should* Sir Charles have offered for you?"

Looking at Eva doubtfully, Vanora said. "Certainly he led me on to believe that he intended to do so, but though he pressed me to more, there were just kisses and—and warm embraces between us."

"Men's hands stray more readily than do sheep," Eva observed impatiently. "That doesn't make you a doxy!"

Relieved to have early indiscretions received as less shocking than she had thought, at the same time Vanora was chagrined. Attentions she had hugged to herself all these years as unique were more commonplace, less out of the ordinary, than she had liked to believe.

Worse than commonplace, Charles's attentions might be thought common, Vanora realized. She leaped from the sofa and went to stand by the window, wishing to escape the heavy mantle of shame settling over her. While she had no idea how long Holton had listened outside that room, he had overheard enough to convince him that she was wanton. No wonder he put the worst construction on her past relations with Charles!

"When did Sir Charles jilt you?" Eva interrupted thoughts that Vanora set aside for later self-torment.

Haltingly, Vanora described the devastation of learning without warning that Charles would wed another. "I convinced myself that he was forced to marry an heiress against inclination," Vanora said. "I've harbored an image all these years of him living bravely with a woman he couldn't love in order to keep up his estate and provide for his mama."

"While underneath, your anger grew like mushrooms in dank cellar frames." Eva nodded wisely. "A pity you can't poison Sir Charles with a dish of them stewed just for him! I think you much abused myself, first by a man who used you ill, and then by Aunt Lauder, for not guarding you better!"

Fingers worrying the geranium again, Vanora urged herself to honesty. "I was silly, not abused or neglected. I doubt Charles would have taken you in for a moment, for you knew Holton's worth from the start. Then to take myself in for another eight years! My pretense simply allowed me a comfortable, exalted picture of myself, you must allow!"

"You're in a self-castigating frame of mind!" Eva said, coming to tuck up a fair tendril ruffled from the wing dipping onto Vanora's forehead. "Naturally one would wish to put a good face on such a lowering occurrence! Don't we all see our own views of circumstances?"

"Speaking of lowering considerations," Vanora said, "now I must enter into a carriage with Holton and ride four long miles to London with a man who not only has learned the horrid circumstances I've just revealed to you, but also has rung the most humiliating peal over my head on the subject!"

Eva looked thoughtful. "So he concerns himself for your welfare! Never you mind, for I shall keep dear Holton fully engaged in conversation every turn of the wheel, so he can't spare a glance in your direction. You may be comfortable chatting with his mama."

Vanora pressed her sister's hands. "What a comfort you are, Eva. Now I can credit that you've grown up. But how lowering to think I came south to play gooseberry for you, and I've acted the veriest goose instead!"

"Looking out for you is most diverting," Eva said, setting her sister's appearance to rights, like a child's. "Now we had best hide ourselves in another room until time to depart, for you've stripped that poor geranium to its stems while we've talked, and I don't care to be caught with the evidence of a murder!"

"Perhaps my fingers acted their impulse toward vile dandies," Vanora jested feebly. Though she was ready to admit that Holton was a totally different sort of dandy from Charles, she still smarted from his tongue-lashing.

Vanora inclined her sunflower head to a Turk who ogled her unabashedly. No doubt she took the eye, in a costume afire with gold spangles worked over India muslin. An orange silk half-mask and braids wired into petals behind her head added to the illusion of a sunflower masquerade dress.

Lady Fenmore had suggested that Vanora attend the Mildmay masquerade as Clytie, who loved Apollo and was turned into a sunflower by the gods. Not caring overmuch what dress she wore, Vanora had readily agreed.

Eva had added her persuasion, saying that with Vanora in gold and herself in silver, they would outshine every lady in attendance. Since both were besieged for dances as each set formed, Vanora had to accept Eva's assessment. No dance cards were provided, as Lady Mildmay informed them that, with guests incognito, no names might be written beside the dances.

Vanora had dithered over the propriety of exposing Eva to the excesses of such an entertainment, and Lady Fenmore had shared her concern. Eva, never having attended a fancy dress ball, begged so prettily to attend that Holton added his entreaties to win his mama's reluctant approval.

Seeing the frown on Vanora's countenance during that discussion, Holton had said, "Mildmay's pretty wife hostesses this event, so one mustn't fear a rackety affair like his Dandy Balls at the Argyle Rooms. I'm certain Vanora would never wish to see Eva exposed to Mildmay's set."

Sir Charles was a part of that set eight years earlier, Vanora was well aware. She and Holton had circled one another warily since The Bachelor Duke's breakfast, exchanging only the most civil conversation, underlaid with insinuations such as this barbed thrust.

A sylvan bower beckoned Lady Mildmay's guests for this evening, as the ballroom resembled a forest glade. Fir trees in tubs surrounded and centered the dancing floor, festooned with ivy tendrils and banked by flowers in pots. While the effect was charming, the arrangement screened chaperones' watchful eyes from their charges half the time and couples appeared to make use of sheltering firs in shadowy corners.

Vanora found it difficult to keep Eva in sight every minute. As she had feared, the Mildmay ball was less circumspect than most routs they attended.

An hour after arrival, Vanora seethed as Eva turned under Holton's arm in a second dance. Not even half way through the evening, Holton made Eva conspicuous by standing up with her a second time. She must remind Eva not to put herself beyond the pale by taking the floor with the same gentleman a significant third time, without a declaration.

Sir Edward spoke to gain her attention, holding a cup of orgeat away from his toga. "Thought I'd never find you again," he complained, "for 'crush' doesn't begin to describe this mob. Can't believe I allowed Holton to persuade me to attend, for normally I don't go in for this sort of thing!"

Taking the cup and sipping gratefully, Vanora teased, "More accurately, he half-persuaded you!"

Sir Edward chuckled, extending shirt-sleeved and pantaloon-clad limbs. "Be grateful I insisted on dressing decently beneath my toga, for clad only in Roman costume, I embarrassed myself and should have contracted a chill!"

Vanora reflected that she would have enjoyed Holton's comments when he stopped by his friend's lodgings to bring him to the ball. Obviously, Holton had no influence on what Sir Edward wore tonight, unlike Eva.

"Miss Eva appears most charming, though I haven't a notion what her costume represents," Sir Edward said, as though he'd heard her thoughts.

Vanora's ire rose as she agreed that Eva's costume suited admirably. Garbed in silver gilt-worked draperies and ribbons that reflected colors from Holton's brilliant costume as they danced, Eva flashed under massed candles in the chandeliers like light off a sheet of water.

Naturally, Holton had suggested that Eva dress as Echo, constrained to reflect Narcissus's love, Vanora mused. The dratted man meant to remind them of his first meeting with the Scotch sisters, though Vanora had hardly forgotten how unflattering the event had been to herself. Perhaps she should have attended the masquerade dressed as a governess, Vanora seethed to herself. Doubtless, that guise would suit his notions of propriety for her behavior!

The music scraping to an end, Holton escorted Eva toward Vanora. He moved lithely in a loose tunic over full trousers, and fluid folds of silk revealed the contours of long limbs as sensuously as the knit pantaloons Holton often wore. A colorful turban and jewels suggested a character from Byron's *Corsair*. Vanora imagined Holton on an Arabian steed, snatching a golden maiden onto the saddle before him, then galloping into the night.

Appalled at such foolishness, Vanora reined in her imagination as the laughing couple approached. The revelation of Charles's true character should have cured her of romantic notions for all time. Obviously, fancy dress balls inspired fanciful thoughts and were best avoided.

"Have you spoken to Miss Chalmers?" Holton inquired of Sir Edward as Eva reached for Vanora's orgeat.

"Hadn't found the courage as yet," Sir Edward admitted.

"Noble Roman, speak! Don't let those paltry pantaloons mask your courage, whatever else they hide!" Holton intoned with a wicked glint of blue-grey eyes through a jeweled mask.

Laughing reluctantly, Sir Edward turned to Vanora, adjusted woolen folds over one shirt-sleeved arm, and begged, "Will you do me the honor of stepping the supper dance with me, then going down to supper afterward?"

"Please say you will, Vanora," Eva pleaded, "for Holton has solicited me already, and we may form a small table. How merry we shall be!"

Provoked by Holton's presumption, Vanora spoke sharply. "You mustn't dance another set with Holton, Eva; to stand up three times together looks entirely too particular!"

Holton's eyes glittered a challenge to Vanora through the slits in his silk mask, but his tone sounded almost civil. "Undoubtedly it could, were my intentions only to disport myself with a lady. However, you must acquit me of raising expectations I don't intend to fulfill."

Vanora noted his faint emphasis on personal pronouns and felt her face heat as though she stood in the sun behind a window's glass. How dare the dandy make public reference to her unfortunate experience with Charles! Then she felt cold to her toes, as she realized the other implication, that Holton was ready to declare himself to Eva.

By then Vanora had stood mumchance too long to deny Eva the proposed dance absolutely, for Eva had already turned away to take the floor with a masked youth whose voice marked him as Fothcringay. Vanora continued silent as Sir Edward engaged Holton in conversation, too mazed in a mire of discontent to find words to fling at Holton.

Vanora felt hot resolve mold in her mind without being certain of the form her objection took. Even if she must threaten Holton with the jeweled dagger he wore at his waist, she was determined the dandy wouldn't claim Eva!

A hand touched her elbow, and Vanora turned to a Tudor-clad gentleman observing her closely through a black velvet mask. Making her a leg with consummate grace, he begged, "Won't you do me the honor of joining the set forming now?"

Vanora caught her breath as she realized that the low tones, velvet as his mask, identified Charles. Eyes flying toward Holton, Vanora realized that he, too, had recognized the invitation's issuer, if taut, lips were any indication.

Giving a hand to Charles instantly, Vanora flashed her sunniest smile. "I should be vastly entertained, sir," she said warmly. Vanora walked onto the floor without looking at Holton again, but she clearly heard the oath he loosed.

Charles led her into the set Eva had joined, and Vanora met Eva's curious eyes. How would she explain this dance to Eva, when she couldn't justify it to herself?

Vanora noted the significant pressure on her hand before Charles left her in line with the ladies to stand opposite for the country dance. When he turned toward Vanora in a movement as graceful as a dance step, Sir Charles's smile was a caress and his eyes stroked her face and form.

Vanora stiffened, recalling the days when such dalliance had turned her knees to water and her blood to wine. Now Charles was just another partner, more proficient than most, but sending no electrifying tingles down her arm as they took hands to turn half around.

The most satisfying part of dancing with Charles was knowing that she annoyed Holton, Vanora admitted to herself, looking for him out of the corners of her eyes each time the movements of the dance changed her position. She smiled brilliantly upon Charles as they met to cast off.

By the end of the dance, Vanora was dissatisfied with retaliation, for Holton had disappeared round the floor's glade before she had flirted through the second figure. Thanking Charles civilly for the dance as he led her off the floor, Vanora wondered how she was to be rid of him.

Pretending not to know him, she said, "If you'll excuse me now, sir, I must seek my party."

Leaning to breathe the words against her ear with suggestive warmth, Sir Charles said, "You surely recall how easily we avoided doing just that in days gone by."

"Those days are just that, sir, in the past," Vanora said in considerable embarrassment. She now regretted encouraging the man to false notions by dancing with him, let alone flirting. Masquerades clearly inspired madness.

Speaking urgently, Sir Charles said, "I wasn't permitted to take proper leave of you at Chiswick House, my love. As much as we were to one another, may I not hope for a kinder parting between us? I owe you what explanation I may offer."

Culpability twined with embarrassment within Vanora. One could hardly cut a man dead after flirting with him through a country dance. She didn't fear Charles, whatever Holton had implied of his reputation. No doubt Vanora could manage the man more easily now than as a chit of eighteen.

"Let's seek out a sofa," she said reluctantly. "Half an hour's dancing makes a rest for conversation quite welcome."

Charles led her through the crowd, and before she realized it was there, deftly propelled her into a curtained alcove behind the ubiquitous potted firs.

Looking about in near darkness, Vanora doubted that either rest or conversation was the purpose of this space.

Urging her gently toward a couch against one wall, Sir Charles smiled down upon her with the tilt of full lips that had mesmerized Vanora in her come-out.

"As I suggested a sofa, I prefer to stand," Vanora said firmly. "What little remains between us doesn't require a couch for expression." A green girl might not recognize the difference between furniture for sitting and that for reclining, but Vanora was no longer a green girl.

Sir Charles held up both hands to demonstrate lack of constraint. "I wouldn't impose myself upon you for the world! My only desire is to assure myself of your good opinion once more."

"To what purpose?" Vanora inquired. "Surely married ladies fill your requirements for female company in town more nearly than a spinster like myself."

"Never name yourself by such a term," Charles said fervently, seizing her hand, uncovering the pulse between glove and transparent sleeve to press his lips to it.

Curious, Vanora allowed the intimacy. She remembered Holton saluting Eva's wrist in this way at first sight of her, so perhaps it was a standard move in a dandy's repertoire. Charles's lips were quite as warm as she recalled them, but her present lack of response must disappoint. She felt nothing beyond impatience and reclaimed her hand.

So swiftly that she hadn't time to fend him off, Charles swept an arm about Vanora, crushing the ribbons trimming her bodice against his chest. Even in the twilight of the alcove, she saw his eyes warm to his purpose and his lips part in approach to take hers. Vanora found Charles *ugsome*. She was diverted to think that one's perceptions of a man could change so far, for eight years ago, she had never wished that she carried a weapon more weighty than a fan.

Without conscious decision, Vanora grasped her folded fan, suspended from one wrist by its gold ribbon, and poked Sir Charles squarely in the eye with its ivory sticks.

Muttering an oath, he released Vanora and leaped back, cupping the offended orb with one hand. "Is this the way you answer lovers' attentions now?" demanded Sir Charles.

"You flatter yourself too far," Vanora said, backing toward the curtain. "You're no more than a reminder of girlhood folly. Had you wished to cry friends, I might have listened with some complacency, but you know only one way of approaching females! I recommend you stay closer to your wife, that being the case."

"My wife never inspired the ardor that one glance at you arouses," Sir Charles intoned, looking out of one eye.

Vanora thought unexpectedly how Holton would laugh with her at a dandy who flirted like an automaton, after such a rebuff. She schooled herself to severity. "Perhaps if you put a fraction of the effort into inspiring passion in your wife that you devote to your flirts, you'd be amazed at the warmth to be found in your own house!"

Feeling for the curtain's parting, Vanora added, "If I encouraged you to believe that I haven't outgrown my calf-love, forgive me, as I forgive your odious behavior to me eight years ago. However, you might as well not ask me to dance in future, for I shall certainly decline."

Stepping through the curtain quickly, Vanora let it fall behind her, both on Sir Charles and the girlish folly he represented. She evaded the potted firs to regain the ballroom. Not two paces away, Holton stood staring, his classical lips firmed like marble under the half-mask.

Heart slipping to her sandals, Vanora froze and flamed in an agony of chagrin. Defensive, she challenged Holton. "Do you follow me about for a reason?" At her back, she heard the curtains whisper, and Holton's face, despite its mask, told her that Charles had stepped out from the alcove.

"For no good reason, I see," Holton said through shut teeth. He wanted to shake Vanora until her braids fell down, while he dragged her into the alcove himself. "No doubt you've shared a laugh at my previous, misguided rush to your rescue!" Eyes and posture bespoke opinions a gentleman would never voice to a lady, before he walked on, making a conspicuous arc to avoid Vanora.

Sir Charles stepped to Vanora's side, murmuring regretfully against her ear, "You waste yourself, my dear, for he's but another such as I!" Bowing in an exaggerated fashion, Charles also took himself off.

Vanora stood staring at the dancers blindly. If Holton had wondered if she were wanton before, he had no doubts now.

Later that night, each suffering from perceived betrayal, Vanora and Holton cast aspersions across the supper table like snowballs.

Aggrieved at Vanora's rejection of his protection, Holton asked Vanora sweetly, "Will you have a slice of *goose,* or have you made a surfeit of that dish tonight?"

"Thank you, but it doesn't tempt," Vanora returned dulcetly. Smarting from Holton's barbs at herself while he lavished attentions upon Eva, she determined to get her own back in this duel of tongues. "Did the buffet offer no wilder game to suit your own sophisticated tastes?"

"Take more of these sweets," Holton offered, handing a plate of comfits toward her across Eva, "unless over-indulgence has already palled this night!"

"You must instruct me on the subject of indulgence," Vanora replied in honeyed tones, "for you've mastered it to an extent I could never hope to attain."

Looking bewildered at the cross-currents between two of the foursome, Sir Edward said jovially, "You must forgive me if I don't follow your banter. Holton keeps me out until dawn to the point that my understanding gives way at midnight these days, and here it is nearly two of the clock! Where were we at this hour last night, Holton, Drury Lane's Green Room?"

Holton frowned at his friend. "We hadn't left Watier's, if you must rehash events of no interest to present company. Switch to lemonade, if you mean to talk before ladies!"

Sir Edward objected, "I an't in my cups; I recall well the little filly whose sash you used as reins last night!"

"Ha!" said Vanora in a tone of satisfaction, though hints of Holton gambling and wenching the previous night inspired feelings far from that.

Eva listened, roundeyed, spoon suspended above an ice.

Realizing how improper it was to encourage this conversation before her sister, Vanora turned on Holton. "Please don't let us delay you, if you're expected in more dashing quarters," she said with heavy sarcasm.

"At times it's difficult to see a difference in one place and the other," Holton said deliberately, leaning back in the gilded chair as he fingered the stem of his glass.

Vanora felt her color rise at the remark, much as she hated to show Holton she cared for his opinion of her visit to the alcove with Charles. "Since you confess to confusion, perhaps I may offer instruction on what to avoid, if you mean to pursue inclinations toward decent company," Vanora answered, flicking her glance to Eva meaningfully.

In spite of the turban, which could have rendered the salute ridiculous in a man of less elegance, Holton inclined his head. "Don't flatter yourself that men may be led by sashes, Miss Chalmers. Most have an aversion to instructions from lovely lips that sound like orders."

From a distance, the sound of the orchestra striking up provided contrast to the discord twanging between Holton and Vanora. He lifted his head as though called by the sound.

Extending a hand to Eva, Holton stood. "Shall we

return to the ballroom?" he asked with a defiant glare at Vanora.

Vanora took Eva's arm. "Stay, Eva," she commanded. To Holton she said, "Three dances in one evening are more than sufficient. I shall call for the carriage and take Eva home if you try to lead her out again this night. As usual, your behavior is excessive, sir."

Eva blinked between the two of them, wearing an expression of fascination, without uttering a word.

Holton slammed his fist on the table so hard the plates jumped, along with nearby guests. Heads turned and voices trailed into silence, but Holton, the master of social niceties, failed to notice.

Hearing only the throb of hot blood in his head, Holton said with none of his usual restraint, "Don't believe you control my behavior, Vanora. I won't be bound by bonnet strings!" He bent across the table, leaning on both fists. "As for excess, you don't half conceive the scope of the term. You will oblige me by not using the word in my hearing again, whatever tales appeal next to your selective hearing!"

Turning abruptly, Holton strode from the supper room, scattering guests before him like a flock of hens.

Gripping Sir Edward's shirt-sleeved arm, Vanora begged, "Please go after him, to keep him safe! No telling what folly Holton may commit in this uncertain mood, and the streets are too dangerous of late for one alone at night!"

In a quake of fear for Holton's welfare, Vanora realized that her feelings for Holton were hardly those of a sister-to-be. Vanora could no longer deceive herself: Imprudently, she loved a dandy once more.

Why can't I love where love's returned? she thought in despair. *For doubtless this night's doings have set his mind even more firmly on Eva.*

·15·

Resolutely, *Vanora rapped* upon Eva's chamber door. She couldn't go to bed with this question pounding in her head like a woodpecker. Late as it was after the masquerade, she must learn the extent of Eva's attachment to Holton, in view of the discovery of her own feelings for him.

Entering without waiting for an invitation, Vanora found Eva standing beside her posted bed, tying the strings of a fetching night cap jauntily under one ear. "Whom do you mean to entrance with that fetching bow?" she asked jestingly.

Eva shook her head. "One must begin as she means to go on, so I'm practicing appealing attire for the night."

How easily the subject arises, though Vanora. "And have you a particular bridegroom in mind to bedazzle?" she asked, crossing to the dressing table as though checking her braid, but watching her sister closely in the glass above it.

Eva flung her arms wide and fell backward onto the bed. "One always has gentlemen in mind, Vanora! Whether anything will come of it is the stuff of dreams!"

Approaching the bed to keep Eva's face in view, Vanora asked playfully through her dread, "Gentlemen in the plural? Have you not centered your thoughts on one gentleman as yet?"

Eva sat up, hugging herself so that the ruffle at the neck of her nightdress kissed her chin. "Why limit myself to one gentleman in imagination! Have you settled on the one man you hope to rivet me to?"

"Much good it does me, I've come to think!" Vanora said, plumping onto the bed beside Eva as she hadn't permitted herself to do since she was thirteen. Facing one's true feelings must free one in various ways, she thought, and prepared herself to confront Eva's sentiments.

Vanora fished, "After standing up three times with the man tonight, you must have warm sentiments toward Holton, at the very least!"

Eva sighed gustily, moving her arms in the feather quilt as though she were making snow angels. "Didn't he look the most dangerous sort of dream in turban and tunic? How could I refuse to stand up with the gentleman who took every lady's eye, no matter how many times he asked me?"

Vanora felt a draft that had nothing to do with the predawn chill of the room. "You wouldn't accept a gentleman's suit simply because other ladies sigh over him, surely, Eva? That's hardly the best measure for a husband, love."

Eva bounced up on the feather comforter, tucking tiny feet underneath her gown. "Then how would you suggest I go about selecting a husband, Vanora?"

"With your head as much as your heart, I should hope," said Vanora, Holton's image filling both parts of herself. "Choose a trustworthy man whose honor you can never doubt, as well as a thoughtful gentleman who may enter into your sentiments," Vanora said carefully, wishing she had never undertaken to guide Eva's choice. If only conscience allowed her to guide Eva away from Holton!

"How prosey that sounds!" Eva laughed, leaning forward to tweak Vanora's long braid. "Don't you wish for a husband who curls your toes when he kisses you?"

Vanora's heart performed peculiarly, like a newly landed fish. How many times had Holton kissed Eva? "I fear that choosing a husband by kisses alone leads one sadly astray. Gentlemen with the most practice at kissing are perhaps the least likely to remain contentedly at home, don't you agree?"

Eva said roguishly, "That depends on how one returns his kisses, I should hope! Even though we're sisters, we may not share the same views on every subject, Vanora."

"We may always speak our different views openly to one another, however," Vanora said. "Do I appear to expect you to think just as I do?"

"Perhaps more than you know," Eva said seriously. "It's as if you sit down to take my likeness and look in a glass, instead of at me, as you sketch. I'm not you, Vanora, and I doubt that the man I mean to wed will suit you in the least."

In view of tensions obvious between Vanora and Holton from the Christmas house party through supper tonight, Eva could only mean that her interest was fixed on Holton. Eva assumed Vanora still held him in dislike. If only she did!

Yet since Eva loved Holton, how could Vanora even consider intruding between them? Loving him herself, Vanora admitted sadly, she knew how bleakly life loomed without him. Eight years of mourning Charles were less than one moment's tortured consideration of life without Holton.

She couldn't attempt to attract Holton, for she might lose a dear sister in that way. Vanora knew with certainty that she would allow no one to keep her from Holton, were she in Eva's enviable position of having won his regard.

Vanora forced herself to speak generously. "What I think of the man who merits your regard doesn't signify. Endeavor to consider life's realities in relation to a husband, though, and not just the pleasure of kisses."

One fleeting touch of the lips under the kissing ball was all she would know of that pleasure, Vanora thought mournfully. In a feeble effort to dissuade Eva, Vanora said, "You must realize that Holton, for example, entrancing as he may be on the dance floor, might make a shockingly bad husband on other occasions. He's sadly in the habit of flirting with ladies."

Eva went off into fits of giggles, patting Vanora's cheek as though she were the younger. "I should think Holton entirely diverting, on any floor! Can't you imagine him striding about a bed chamber, delivering himself of an ultimatum upon one's behavior as he did tonight, wearing a simple nightshirt instead of tunic and trousers?" Eva fell back onto the featherbed once more, convulsed with mirth.

Vanora sat quivering at the conjured image, not amused at all. So Eva had undressed Holton to his nightshirt in her thoughts. If Eva confessed to so much, no doubt she had harbored wifely visions long enough to be comfortable with expressing them aloud.

Eva must be determined to accept Holton. Certainly he had all but declared himself tonight with three dances, so that settled the matter. Vanora mustn't allow herself to think of Holton again, except as a brother-in-law.

Hopelessness fastened about Vanora's throat like a neck iron. Nothing was left but to live out dreary days with her brother at Keathley, learning to subdue an over-weening urge to order others' lives. That fault had brought about all that had befallen her.

Bravely, Vanora kissed her sister goodnight, saying, almost as though it were true, "I'm happy you've determined to form so eligible a connection, love."

Before retiring, Vanora retrieved from its hiding place the handkerchief Holton had lent her on Christmas Eve at Keathley. As she fell asleep at last, its faint citrus scent both tormented and comforted her.

Lord Fenmore leaned idly toward his carriage window as his coach drew into Cavendish Square. He had sat until the early hours of the morning with Liverpool and Robinson over the Corn Bill, but the closest they had come to a solution was the brandy they imbibed as they deliberated.

Feeling the carriage slow, Lord Fenmore peered though misty darkness. A curricle and pair trundled under a garden lamp glowing faintly from its iron-caged globe, and he would swear he knew the groom up on the seat.

While he waited for the vehicles to draw even, Lord Fenmore watched the groom walking the pair. The man had his cap low over his eyes, and he hunched his face into his collar, but Lord Fenmore had known Jem man and boy, and he'd not be fooled by shadows. The spirit of the greys held in by the groom confirmed Lord Fenmore's first impression. Holton visited in the square.

Bending to the other side to peer ahead to his own house, Lord Fenmore found it dark. Looking across to the Plewes house, he saw similar darkness there. Puzzled, he tapped the toe of his pump absently with a clouded cane. He signalled his coachman to stop in the cobbled street.

When Jem pulled slowly along side, Lord Fenmore had let down the glass, ready to hail him. "Where's

Holton?" he called softly through the damp predawn air.

The groom spoke respectfully toward the dark carriage. "In the garden, your lordship."

"Went over the fence, did he?" Lord Fenmore observed with satisfaction. "I'm of a mind for a stroll myself, so take Holton's pair round to the stables with mine. He'll send for you when we're through."

Jem fingered his cap and drove off to turn into the mews. Lord Fenmore slid open the panel into the box, addressing his coachman. "Get me the key to the garden's entrance, then deliver me there," he instructed. The carriage dipped as a footman stepped down.

Within minutes, Lord Fenmore was inside the garden with the gate secured behind him, listening for his son's movements in near darkness. Away from the path circling the garden, where lamps in iron standards dotted its perimeter with gently lapping pools of yellow light, one could easily stumble into a tree. Lord Fenmore wondered if Holton had come here in a state to stumble already. He looked back to the house where Vanora no doubt slept by now. No sense in leaving the boy out in the damp, were he in his cups.

Lord Fenmore spoke in normal tones, knowing how sound carried at night. "Holton! I'm near the gate. Make your way to me here, if you please."

He waited without doubt that Holton would come, listening to covert sounds that bespoke insects and vermin before hearing the firm step that brought his son to him. Holton advanced steadily, a dark patch taking form as sounds of approach preceded him from the center of the garden. The boy walked soberly enough.

"You must have the eyes as well as the habits of a tomcat, to make your way through the garden's center in darkness," Lord Fenmore observed neutrally.

"You're slinking about late yourself, Pater," Holton returned. "Or one could say early, depending on which day is under consideration. What brings you to seek me out at this hour of the morning, in so unexpected a place as this?"

"I won't ask what you do here," Lord Fenmore evaded, taking in the tunic and full trousers his son wore and refusing to remark on them. "Jem has stabled your curricle, for I wish a word with you, if you'll spare me the time."

Lord Fenmore spoke courteously, without the sarcastic bite to his voice that Holton expected to hear. "As many words as you like," Holton said quietly, falling into step beside his father.

The older man took to the path with a gait that belied the hour and his age. Night's relative silence magnified the soft shift of sand and gravel beneath their feet. Darkness added an intimacy that their confrontations generally lacked, Holton thought whimsically, noting that his own hands were folded behind his back in the same manner as his father's.

"We need a few more votes our way on a matter of some consequence," Lord Fenmore said in a tired voice.

Holton looked at him curiously as they neared a lamp. His father had never mentioned the business of the Lords to him except to complain that his son would never be suited to it, Holton thought. He waited.

"Permit me to mention names to you, and be so good as to tell what you may of *on-dits* that might reflect each man's present mood," Lord Fenmore requested in statement form.

Holton discovered that he liked having his cooperation assumed by his father on this subject. "Say on," he responded quietly.

For the next fifteen minutes, Lord Fenmore named both Whigs and Tories sitting in the Lords, and Holton gave brief resumes of debts or lack of them, wives behaving decorously or not, daughters about to receive declarations or languishing without hope of an offer, sons racketing about town in the normal style or nearly done up. He used these factors as concise indicators of members most likely to be open to a reasoned approach, and those too distracted by family affairs to concentrate on those of the country.

When no further names came out of the darkness beside him, Holton was content to walk the length of three shifting pools of light from the garden's lamps in comfortable silence. He felt closer to his father than ever before.

"Have I told you how I came to marry your mother?" asked Lord Fenmore musingly from near darkness.

"Not that I recall," Holton said, caught off balance.

A quiet laugh answered him. "You'd recall, if I'd shared the tale. I couldn't decide, most of our early years, whether to choke her or kiss her, you know."

Holton wheeled toward Lord Fenmore in amazement, but his father walked on placidly, his face in the light of the next lamp fixed on the past.

"Your mother was as headstrong as a donkey, and as a girl, she hadn't learned to hide it. Thought she knew just what I should do, and set her mind to seeing that I did it."

Holton stiffened, seeing direction to this reminiscence and disliking it.

"Don't get on your high ropes; I've learned better than to endeavor to instruct your thinking," Lord Fenmore said in amusement. "Just as you told me what you know of society as it might affect my business, I should like you to know certain experiences of mine." Lord Fenmore looked toward the center of the park, where the statue of the Duke of Cumberland stood in darkness.

"I've finally been brought to realize that interference is anathema to you," Lord Fenmore continued. "Perhaps if I speak of myself instead of you, I will seem less intru-

sive. You may glean what you want from my tale, politely leaving the chaff to blow away with the next breeze."

Lord Fenmore eased his top hat back on his head, and
Holton felt the lack of his turban for the first time in the
damp air. He realized that, in this minimal light, his
father's silver hair probably resembled his own fair head,
increasing a new sense of kinship.

"Your mama is a managing woman, always has been,"
observed Lord Fenmore. "Probably interferes with your
life as much as mine, although she's learned to go about it
with more subtlety over the years.

"We grew up on adjoining estates, and though I was
the elder, she directed our path when we rode out together
as children and informed me whom I would stand up with
at local assemblies later. I was set to propose marriage to
her cousin, when your mother convinced me that a silly
young wife would bore me into the arms of a mistress
inside of a month. I don't doubt she decided to marry me
and permitted me to discover that I wished to wed her."

Holton laughed softly in the darkness. He'd felt Mama's
teasing prods enough to know what his father meant.

"The point is that she was quite right that we should
suit, for a strong man indeed needs a strong lady beside
him," Lord Fenmore said.

"Or standing out against him on occasion?" Holton
inquired with a laugh, recalling the smiling statue that Lady
Fenmore could enact when she had formed a firm opinion.

"Exactly," agreed Lord Fenmore with a snort. "Life
might be simpler without tollgates, but one pays a price
to travel better roads, in order to improve the journey.
Were Hester less strong minded, I should have only one
head with which to think, one view from which to observe.
She saves me from the complacency of believing myself
always right and keeps me from the despair of thinking
myself the most stupid man in existence on occasion."

Holton found a face before his mind's eye, that of a lady who never hesitated to fault him, but one who had eased his view of himself as well, on occasion.

Their steps on fine gravel were the main sounds against the night's quiet chorus for a few moments. "A strong wife suits me," Lord Fenmore said almost as though speaking to himself. "Hester can occupy her own mind and time with interests and accomplishments so I may pursue my goals without constant need to oversee her well-being like a child's. She expands my life by living her own, instead of just mine. She increases my interest in her by finding her own concerns, rather than making mine her sole focus."

Lord Fenmore laughed softly. "What joins us together is being content to share the journey, not a need to occupy the same saddle. Neither of us holds the other's reins, for each of us trusts the other to ride toward the same destination."

Holton waited for his father to speak again, then asked apologetically, "Does Mama never seize your reins, or gallop off in the wrong direction entirely?"

Lord Fenmore groaned piteously. "You must know that she does! We've aired our differences loudly enough over the years. Hester's human, as am I, and patience doesn't come naturally to such creatures. But as a man of strength I can choose not to be led when it isn't right for me."

"Sounds uncomfortable, when constrained to journey with a person, to find yourself interpreting the milestones differently," Holton observed. He had never realized that Pater could talk easily in this way, without ripping up at him or setting him straight with every breath.

"Strength married to strength requires a stronger bonding to keep together, I dare say," Lord Fenmore allowed. "Perhaps it's my place in the House of Lords that leads me to the notion, but I believe that bond to be persuasion. I don't command the members of the Lords to my way of thinking; I must convince them to cooperate.

"And sometimes, when no view prevails, we must argue our way to a compromise. But whether persuasion or compromise brings us to a common road, people must communicate to travel forward together."

It was Holton's turn to groan. "Some confounded women are so set on their own paths one can't sway them, Pater!"

Lord Fenmore smiled not just at the words, but because, for the first time, Holton had used the Latin title without it sounding like a cold stone tablet.

"I confess to riding you hard on the subject of marriage," he said to Holton sincerely, "and that's at an end. What I wish for you, son, is not just a wife, nor yet a conformable, biddable mate. Seek out a lady with the strength of mind to demand your best self of you, one who requires you to think and to convince her of the rightness of your thinking. And until you believe you've found her, don't let your mama push you into just any pretty chit's arms!"

Holton burst into laughter with the unexpectedness of that statement and this meeting of minds. He felt as though he dreamed the entire encounter, as though he must awaken with his valet pulling back the curtains whilst he nosed his pillows for a few more minutes of this close comfort.

He listened to his father join his laughter and thought how little he had laughed in concert with this man. They must laugh together more often, while time allowed.

Recalling conversations with Vanora, parts of them as comfortable as this strolling talk in the darkness, Holton asked, "Can you say what makes you friends with Mama?"

Lord Fenmore turned toward him briefly. "A most perceptive question; I have great hopes of you!" He walked on, wrapped in thought, but not apart from

Holton. "I believe Hester and I are friends because we can talk, really talk, not just converse in word games that placate or thwart real understanding. I had to learn to listen, you know, to hear truly what Hester felt beyond the words, when I was impatient at the concentration it required. Listening is a knack women seem to acquire easier than do we men.

"Another cornerstone of any fast friendship is politeness," Lord Fenmore said. "Hester and I expect the courtesy from the other that we receive from any friend. Good manners are a matter of consideration, not affectations. It sounds overly simple, does it not?"

As they rounded the curve at the north end of the garden, Holton looked toward the Plewes's house. Vanora lay behind one of the dark windows, no doubt ordering her dreams to her own satisfaction. Mama could never have been as stubborn a donkey as Miss Vanora Chalmers. Friendship, let alone warmer sentiments, must surely be impossible with a despot, he thought.

"Did Mama lead you to believe my opinions useful?" Holton queried, harking back to the start of this unexpected meeting of the minds with his father.

"Not at all," Lord Fenmore answered. "I was abducted at a ball one evening by an excessively strong-headed young lady. She wouldn't let me go until she had explained exactly how a man who had learned to lead the *ton* should manage the Lords easily enough when his turn came to do so."

After a moment's stunned silence, Holton found himself laughing once more, his heart suddenly lighter than a balloon in ascension. This talk with Pater started some hares of thought. Mayhap the heat of dealings with Vanora indicated a different kind of fire had ignited.

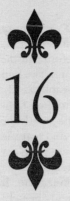

16

Vanora watched from her bed as the door closed behind her sister. She had begun to think Eva might never finish her chocolate and take herself off to dress for the day.

Maintaining even a semblance of normalcy before Eva was a drudgery of the spirits this morning. Last night's masquerade ball had proved Holton's scorn for herself and his intentions toward her fortunate sister, even as it revealed her hopeless attachment to a more worthy dandy.

Setting aside the tray with its chocolate pot and cups, Vanora swung her feet to the floor. Lying abed feeling *doonset* didn't send misery to the rightabout.

For a few minutes, Vanora busied herself with undoing and brushing out her braid. She might decide what gown to wear this morning and lay it out, except that she didn't care. The abigail she shared with Eva would be in presently to help her dress, and Mysie could choose a gown.

Pulling the brush in distraction through thick hair, Vanora paced the room. She was restless, unsettled, aimless.

As a loving sister, she should be in alt for Eva, Vanora scolded herself. Finding Eva a *tonish* husband had been the goal Vanora set for this visit to London, and before half the spring flowers pushed their heads above ground, she had accomplished just that. Holton was a most desirable *parti*.

The match did honor to Eva and must add to their family's credit as well; no doubt Mama and Papa would be pleased. Holton's breeding, manners, person, and fortune were of the first consequence. His parents were pleasant and more than ready to welcome their son's bride.

Eva could hardly form a more eligible connection. If only Vanora didn't long to connect with the dandy herself!

Setting her teeth together, Vanora flung the hairbrush across the room. It flew straight at a window, struck the drapery in a muffled whack and fell to the floor.

Feeling guilty at still another ungoverned fit of temper, Vanora hoped that the window hadn't cracked. As she hurried across polished boards and rugs to inspect for damage, Vanora reflected that her emotions had slipped from control more often in the short weeks since Christmas than in the eight long years previous to the holidays.

"And I must credit myself for that!" Vanora assured herself, kicking the brush against the wall on reaching it.

Picking up the abused brush, Vanora pulled aside the drape. Fortunately, the glass was intact, unlike her heart.

Cool air hung at the window like glass curtains, and Vanora leaned her heated forehead against a pane as the drape dropped behind her. She looked out toward Cavendish Square's garden with unfocused eyes. Spring made the area blush a pale green, with leaves half furled against the gaunt, grey bones of trees and shrubbery.

Eva was still but a green girl; could she truly know her heart enough to be trusted to make the best choice of mate? At eighteen, Vanora had believed herself ready to make that commitment, and Charles was the man she had chosen to trust with her future. Surely this proved how little faith one should put in a young girl's inclinations.

Perhaps Vanora could insist that Holton not speak before June, giving Eva more time to unfurl, if not bloom. Another gentleman might recommend himself to Eva, were she allowed the remainder of the season to form further impressions.

Hardly any flowers nodded to spring in the garden as yet; why push Eva to early blossoming? Vanora placed a palm against the chill glass and thought morbidly that her present position symbolized the rest of her life. She must remain an onlooker, observing life at second hand from behind a glass, if Eva indeed were to wed Holton.

Tears welled in Vanora's eyes, and the green and grey of the garden ran together in her view like a watercolor left out in a rain shower, except for the scarlet patch on the edge of her blurred vision. A scarlet patch?

The bright red blob distracted Vanora from further indulgence in self-pity, and she stretched to see the source of the hue. She blinked away tears for a clearer view. Flowers of such brilliant color would hardly bloom among treetops, and she realized that the colorful spot seemed suspended in midair. What centered the garden?

Even as her mind asked the question, it answered it. A statue centered Cavendish Square's garden. A statue she had called an insult to Scots the day she walked with Holton there, for it honored the Duke of Cumberland, that hated Butcher of Culloden!

Hands gripping the window sill, eyes staring, and face pressed against the glass, Vanora identified the colorful headdress the horrid statue sported. The turban Holton had worn at the masquerade last night screamed mockery at her from the center of the square this morning!

No other reasonable explanation than insult presented itself for Holton to climb the base of the statue in darkness, mount the horse the duke rode in effigy, and exert himself so outrageously as to place his turban on the statue's head. Obviously, the odious Mr. Holton, recalling her stricture against the statue, and being far gone in his cups last night, had chosen this course to express his disdain for her and her opinions on excess!

The door to her room flung open, and Vanora turned from the window to find that Eva and Mysie had tumbled through together. "Vanora! What hubble-bubble erupted in here?" Eva cried in consternation. "Did you spy a mouse?"

Vanora discovered that her throat rasped raw with strain. Only then did she realize that she must have uttered the battle cry of clan Cameron.

An hour later, Vanora paced the morning room, making no pretense of reading the papers she had hurled across the room shortly after they were brought in. The house was quiet, for Squire Plewes had accompanied his lady to her accoucheur, not caring for her to be out without him in a delicate condition.

Vanora composed scathing denouncements to Holton in her head, but none of them had taken adequately vitriolic form to be committed to paper as yet.

Perhaps it would be more dignified to ignore the insult offered, pretend she hadn't even noticed the schoolboy jape. A note was hardly expressive of the havoc she wished she could wreck upon the wastrel. For a man of Holton's superior abilities and intelligence to squander himself in childish taunts was the outside of enough.

His parting words last night had been that she had no notion of excess. Only an excess of drink could lead him to believe that stupid larks with a statue demonstrated his freedom. Perhaps she could wound most by ignoring his display entirely.

To a faint knock on the door, she called, "Come!"

Entering apologetically, a footman bearing a mixed bouquet of spring flowers extended a folded, sealed sheet to her on a tray. Dismissing him, Vanora broke the seal and flattened the heavy, cream-colored paper as she read.

Uttering an unladylike oath as she reached the spiked *H* ending the brief scrawl, Vanora called sharply to the footman scurrying out of the room. "Wait! Whose are those flowers?"

"They was left for Miss Eva, with that message addressed to you," the tall footman said diffidently.

The man grew visibly nervous as Vanora stared, and she realized that she scowled horribly at him. Forcing her expression to civility, Vanora extended a hand. "Leave them here, and send me a running footman in five minutes' time."

The footman opened his mouth, then seemed to think better of speaking. He handed over the bouquet meekly and hurried from the room.

Vanora stood considering the lovely flowers, a faint, fresh scent rising to tease her nose from white anemones, purple irises and pink clemantis, stems enfolded in silver paper. Holton should have them back, with a piece of her mind on the subject of men who were unworthy to offer posies, let alone themselves, to an innocent like Eva! She wouldn't need to mention the insult of Holton's turban after all.

When Eva poked her bonnet round the door minutes later, Vanora had written her missive and was just sanding it, thinking that even a bucket of sand wouldn't smother the fire in this message. She slipped Holton's note under the blotter to prevent Eva's seeing it.

"Lovely!" Eva said, tripping across the room to lift the bouquet lying across the writing desk beside Vanora. "Who sent you flowers so early in the day? One of your dancing partners from the masquerade last night?"

Guilt assaulted Vanora at her peremptory handling of this matter, but she wrestled it into submission. Flinging back her head, she looked Eva squarely in the eye and said, "Yes, indeed! But they come from one whose attentions I don't mean to encourage, so I'm having them returned straight away."

"Sir Charles, I apprehend," Eva said with a nod. "You act entirely for the best. I'm on my way to Hatchard's. Do you wish to come along and see what new Gothics may be in?"

"You'll find something horrid enough to scare us both into nightmares, no doubt," Vanora said. "Take a maid or footman along, Eveleit."

Pulling a pouting face, Eva said, "I know I must do so; Mysie comes with me."

When Eva had departed, Vanora sat glowering at the flowers and her note to Holton. Then she retrieved the stiff sheet from under the blotter on which Holton had scribbled the briefest of messages:

> *I beg leave to inform you that my petition on the subject of matrimony has been addressed to your father, as is proper. I shall do myself the honor of calling later this morning.*

Vanora crushed the sheet in her hand and flung it toward the grate. His words were as arrogant as his nature. Eva would be grateful one day that she had been saved from a man who scorned the Scots and indulged in despicable excesses.

Lifting the posey to tuck her scorching note among its sweet blossoms, Vanora wished she could observe Holton's reaction to her message. She had informed him that she was writing her father post-haste to reveal why Holton's request to address Eva was an insult to the entire family.

*   *   *

Fifteen minutes later, Vanora pretended to pursue Shelley's *Queen Mab* in her room. A thundering knock upon the front door caused her to put down the slim volume in satisfaction. Running to the window, she peered down into the square, where Holton's greys were just moving away from the front of the house. Smiling grimly, she tiptoed to her open door, leaning into the passage to listen expectantly.

Holton's angry tones reverberated up the stairs. "Inform Miss Eva Chalmers that I wish to see her at once!"

He must have been told that Eva had gone out, Vanora surmised smugly during an unintelligible reply.

"Then see that these flowers are taken directly to her room and left there!" Holton ordered at the top of his lungs.

Vanora whisked out into the passage. When the footman arrived on the first floor and checked at sight of her standing ready, arms crossed, she hissed, "Return that bouquet to the gentleman at once with a curt refusal of it!"

After one agonized look, the man retreated down the passage and slowly descended the stairs again. Vanora heard first his low murmur, then Holton's explosive oaths.

"Inform Miss Chalmers that I require her presence at once in the drawing room!" Holton ordered, words resounding like a series of blasts during a group bird shoot.

He wasn't so jug bitten this morning that he couldn't deduce that she was at home, Vanora thought. Hearing Holton in a rage was doing wonders for her own disposition. Vanora returned to her room to await the footman in comfort.

When he appeared in the doorway to her chamber, Vanora said from her chair, "I heard, as must the entire household. You may inform Mr. Holton that I'm not at home!"

The footman's face was a study in indecision. Staring at him implacably, Vanora had the satisfaction of seeing his shoulders slump as he turned to take her message belowstairs.

Listening avidly, Vanora heard the low murmur of the footman's voice again and a renewal of oaths. Then her pulse beat a devil's tattoo at the sound of clattering footsteps, as though booted feet took the stairs two at a time.

The footman's helpful cry was almost drowned out: "Last door on the right, sir!"

Vanora leaped from her chair, heart lurching with each step pounding down the passage. She put a hand to her throat, then snatched it away. She refused to appear as frightened as she felt of a sudden. It never occurred to her that Holton would so far forget himself as to intrude into a lady's bedchamber!

Holton slammed the door wide against the wall as he strode in upon her, and he was reminded of the morning Vanora had slammed a door into his shoulder. The memory fueled the fury that blazed within him at her wrongheadedness.

He thrust the bouquet forward as he advanced on Vanora, shaking it under her nose as he spoke. "These flowers are not yours to dispose. They were sent for Miss Eva, and your sister shall have them. Show me her room so I may leave them there or, by Gad, I'll plant myself on you until she returns to receive them directly from my hands!"

Vanora was quivering from rage, she assured herself. She wasn't the least afraid of this bully who invaded her virgin room. Hoping her voice held steady, she said, "You go beyond the line, sir! You can't be aware where you trespass! This is a lady's chamber, and you have no place in it!"

"Don't flatter yourself that I want a place in it!" Holton snorted, determined that Vanora shouldn't best him in this encounter. "I wonder that you dare refer to yourself as a lady. After going off with Sir Charles last evening, you'll find me hard to convince of your finer feelings!" Holton cursed himself. He had no intention of dragging out that subject. His fists clenched as he growled in self-anger.

Thinking herself under increased threat, Vanora shrieked and darted round Holton and out into the passage. Retreat was an honorable battle strategy, she decided, for Holton's wrathful expression convinced her that a bedchamber was hardly the best ground on which to continue this conversation. The dandy was clearly demented!

Fleeing down the stairs, Vanora ran toward the porter's room across the entry hall, then changed direction. Holton might expect her to take refuge behind the first door across from the stairs. She scurried for the morning room at the back of the house instead, flinging round to close its door quietly and reach for the key.

No key waited in the lock. She threw herself against the closed door and listened as for her life. Perhaps Holton would put down the flowers abovestairs and leave quietly now that he had routed her.

Over the pounding in her chest, Vanora heard steps descend the stairs in a purposeful march. "In the morning room, sir," she heard the footman say in an ingratiating voice. No doubt he was pointing the way! She would see the gabble grinder lost his position before the day was out, if she survived this encounter.

Increasing pressure against the door from outside told Vanora that Holton had found the morning room. She threw all her weight into holding the door closed, only to feel her slippers skating over the polished floor as he exerted greater pressure from his side. Slowly, she slid in a quarter arc with the door as it opened into the room.

When Holton stepped inside, letting go of the door, she

very nearly fell on her nose, and the door slammed shut upon them. Vanora was trapped in the morning room with a madman.

Holton advanced upon her, jaw jutting dangerously.

Vanora ran for the sofa, choosing the largest piece of furniture in the room to place between them. Holton came on, never stopping for a moment, until she did.

Facing her across the chintz sofa back, which he noted that her fingers marked deeply, Holton said, "You won't escape the consequences of your meddling so easily on this occasion, Vanora! You will hear every word I say to you, and this time, the Snapdragon will be scorched!

"Item one: You will not dictate to me! If I wish to present flowers to a lady, or to a hundred ladies, I don't require your permission to do so! Do you understand me?"

Feeling braver now that she was in more seemly surroundings, Vanora leaned across the sofa back to snatch the bouquet from Holton's hands. "Very well!" she said in starched tones. "If your favors to females must include flowers to my sister as well as romps with opera dancers, I shall see that she gets these!"

Holton yanked the flowers back, shaking a few blossoms loose. "Opera dancers aren't at issue here, and they're no concern of yours at any rate!" he bellowed.

Vanora whisked the bouquet out of Holton's hands again, or at least a sizeable handful of it. "Opera dancers are precisely the issue, for you're no fit companion for my sister, due to your excesses with demireps!"

In exasperation, Holton threw his remaining flowers onto the sofa between them. "A lady wouldn't know the term "demirep," let alone mention it to a gentleman! Is this what you learned through your association with Sir Charles?"

Infuriated at Holton for daring to refer to her youthful mistake, Vanora flung a handful of the flowers she held full in his face. "A gentleman wouldn't use a lady's unfortunate experiences of the heart to humiliate her beyond endurance!"

Determined that Vanora wouldn't heap guilt upon him this time, Holton grabbed a fistful of the flowers he had dropped on the sofa and hurled them at her stubborn head. "No lady would choose a rakehell like Sir Charles to waste affections on! You dare set yourself up to judge other people's excesses, when no female could put herself in the way of receiving his attentions without losing her reputation!"

Vanora gasped at the effrontery of the repeated charge. Holton's previous hints at misconduct on her part had been painful in the extreme. But this man above all others couldn't truly believe that she had gone beyond the line!

Vanora threw the flowers she held straight at Holton's head, stooping over the sofa back to scoop up fallen flowers to cast at him again. "How dare you speak such charges! As if I'd so far forget myself as to allow more than a kiss!"

Holton was ashamed of his words' implications, but he was convinced that if he backed down now, he would never hold his own with this termagant. Plucking a pink clemantis from the strewn flowers on the sofa, he leaned over to caress Vanora's quivering lips with it. "Do you expect me to believe that so great a libertine as Marchand had you in his arms, and you allowed him no more than a few paltry kisses?" he asked provocatively.

Snatching the flower away, Vanora crushed it in her fist before plastering it against Holton's cruel lips. "What you choose to believe is of no interest to me whatsoever! A lady doesn't respond to kisses as wantonly as your opera dancers, I assure you, sir!"

Seeing Holton's jaw jut again as he spit away bits of clemantis and leaf, his eyes like steel, Vanora knew that she stood in greater danger than she had in her bedchamber. Before she could act on that realization, Holton had her wrist in a grip that nearly brought tears to her eyes. His voice slashed past her ears like a sword's whisper when he finally spoke.

"Do you truly believe that, you little innocent? Do you doubt that you can perform the same sweet dance as your sisters of the stage, indeed? Perhaps Sir Charles wasn't the man to teach you the steps!"

Holton was certain that he had lost his mind, but this baggage had maddened him to the point that he no longer cared. One knee sinking onto the sofa, Holton got both arms about Vanora and halflifted, halfdragged her willy-nilly across its back and onto her knees upon the sofa. In spite of Vanora's struggles, Holton settled her firmly against his chest, enjoying the way her eyes widened as she realized his ungentlemanly intentions.

Ignoring slaps and shrieks, Holton captured the golden loops of braids to still Vanora's head. He put his lips firmly to hers, determined to persuade a response from this lady. As he set about it, he realized this pursuit had been in the back of his mind since that chance kiss under the mistletoe.

Holton soon discovered that an effort to inspire passion was a certain way to increase it for oneself. He forgot that he was showing Vanora he wasn't a man to be trifled with.

Vanora had been shocked to find herself hoisted in the air like a sack of grain and hauled unceremoniously over the sofa back. She would have fought the dandy more strenuously, but it was essential to keep one's skirts decently down while sailing over the furniture!

Then she was kneeling off balance on the sofa's seat, and Holton was pressing unwelcome attentions on her, trying to prove that she was no better than a bit of muslin from the stage. Let him but try! He could maul her about all he liked, but he would learn that she was a lady, indeed!

Vanora squeezed both eyes and lips shut to avoid sight and taste of the debaucher taking liberties with her person. Unfortunately, she could still smell his sharp citric scent, and it made her feel quite dizzy.

Vanora gripped Holton's shoulders, simply to steady herself on the uneven mound of the sofa seat, then found herself slipping both arms about him as a sensation of falling down a bottomless well followed on the insistent pressures of his warm attack. It would hardly do to allow herself to fall at this wicked man's feet.

A strange lassitude weakened Vanora's resolve. She couldn't permit Holton the satisfaction of a response to his demanding lips, and now his tongue and teeth were teasing her unmercifully as well. Feeling her treacherous lips succumb to his insistence, Vanora knew that this was a battle she couldn't win by fighting Holton.

One surely must be as honorable in defeat as in victory, Vanora thought wildly. She pressed herself bravely against Holton's chest, took his head between her two hands, and gave her entire being into the surrender.

Holton felt the moment when Vanora's rigid resistance melted and was moved to greater efforts. When her sweet mouth opened to him, he could have claimed the victory, if a renewed attack hadn't seemed a better notion. When he felt Vanora press her warm length against him and begin to match his ardor, he found himself too caught up by her response to declare himself the victor.

It was far too late to discuss who was a lady or gentleman, for they were fully occupied with the discoveries of a well-matched man and woman. Holton turned Vanora under him tenderly, lowering her onto the sofa among the flowers without letting her free of his lips' demands.

Holton was thinking in a dazed frenzy that he must

never let Vanora out of his arms again, when the only event that could have separated them occurred.

The door opened.

Eva danced into the room and stopped dead. Dropping the books in her arms onto the floor, she clasped both hands to a gaping mouth and emitted one tiny sound, much like a mouse's squeak. Then she dashed from the room.

By then, Holton had forced himself to release Vanora. She lay dazed on the sofa, hair and dress in disarray, lips swollen with his kisses, staring after her younger sister from among crushed flowers as though trying to bring to mind the identity of the intruder.

Holton helped Vanora to sit up, removing from the sofa with the greatest reluctance he had ever felt in leaving a woman's arms. He was both grateful and desolate that Eva had interrupted them.

Vanora swept a fallen wing of hair out of her eyes, breathing as though she had run a footrace. She looked about in distraction, then gazed at Holton in horror.

"Look what we've done to Eva's flowers!" Vanora wailed.

17

"*How could I?*" *Vanora* whispered, scrambling off the sofa in horror at being found horizontal, in Holton's arms, by the sister whose beau he had been from the beginning. "I must go to Eva at once!" Embarrassed and confused by her passionate response to Holton, who had undoubtedly proved he could make her react as he wished, Vanora was appalled.

"I'll wait for you here," Holton said, reaching for Vanora's hand to offer reassurance. He, after playing at love as a social game for years, was shaken to find the lady he wished to cherish and brangle with for a lifetime cowering away from him.

Had he forced no more than a physical response from an unwilling lady? He knew how much more than that he wanted from Vanora. The fear of having failed was a humbling experience and a deucedly unpleasant one.

Vanora avoided Holton's hand and eyes. "No! You had best go," she said hurriedly. "I must face Eva as best I may, and I can't imagine that she will care to see you soon."

"But I shall care to see you as soon as may be," Holton said with certainty. He couldn't consider leaving in such doubt, before he had put his chances to the touch. As a dandy, Holton had practiced flirting as an art form. He found nothing artistic in the anguish that threatened his happiness were Vanora to refuse his addresses.

"I don't know—I can't stay!" Vanora cried, torn between rushing abovestairs to repair what she could of relations with her sister and casting herself into the delicious debauchery of Holton's arms again.

Holton spoke to reassure Vanora. "Your sister is doubtless far less overset by what she observed than you believe."

Would that it were so! Vanora thought, rushing out of the room and down the passage. Her slippers scurried up the stairs, but her conscience malingered under its load of guilt and embarrassment.

My own sister's beau! Vanora castigated herself. To be found in a wanton position with any gentleman was shaming enough; but to be discovered in the arms of one for whom Eva had just last night revealed her partiality was beyond begging or receiving forgiveness.

As Vanora walked the corridor toward Eva's door, her steps faltered. She excused her reluctance on the grounds that repairs to hair and costume would permit her to present herself, if not her actions, in more seemly fashion.

Outside Eva's door Vanora paused, hand on the brass knob, without courage to turn it. Vanora's thoughts spun without slinging out anything useful. What could one say to a sister who had just discovered the man she loved in abandonment with one's self?

But Vanora could hardly seize happiness at the expense of a beloved sister.

Vanora bowed her head against the door's panel. Not one of the three of them could hope to be comfortable again, for she had made a fine mull of their lives by her interference. Vanora had urged Eva, who had never formed a desire of her own to come to London, to a *tonish* marriage. She had goaded Holton into standing up with Eva three times, tantamount to a declaration in form, by delivering ultimatums to him. Worst of all, she had failed to recognize in time that the strong sentiments she experienced toward Holton indicated a growing attachment for a far more worthy dandy than the first one she had known.

Vanora's wrong-headed tendency to drive all before her without reference to their inclinations had brought the three of them to this impasse. She couldn't mend matters, but she could own to her faults, and Eva need never know how deeply Vanora's heart was engaged.

It wasn't as though Holton loved her. He was simply proving a point, and she had allowed herself to be carried away. Were Holton truly attached to her, matters would be still worse, for Vanora doubted she was strong enough to renounce the man she longed to link her life with.

But he had written their father and sent Eva flowers, with only a note to Vanora to warn of his intentions. Holton preferred Eva. Vanora felt fiercely glad to have had a few moments on a sofa, memories that were hers to keep.

Setting her mind to soothe Eva into forgiving Holton's meaningless lapse, Vanora opened the door.

Eva lay across her bed in a flurry of white flounces, shoulders heaving, one small fist beating the coverlet feebly. Choked sounds emanated from the sprawled heap she formed, like a load of laundry dropped by a careless maid. Vanora's heart twisted painfully with remorse. Sight of her sister's grief was even more affecting than Vanora had thought it would be, but no more than she deserved.

Selfishly, she had considered only her own anguish and culpability, while Eva lay in the throes of the deepest humiliation and distress a female could endure. Minded of her own heartbreak at eighteen, Vanora knew that even Eva's sunny disposition couldn't recover itself easily. Eva had discovered Holton in scandalous embrace with her own sister! This was infinitely worse betrayal than Vanora had known.

Stumbling toward the bed with her eyes brimming, Vanora stretched herself beside Eva. Laying an arm about Eva's shoulders, she murmured, "I shan't ask for forgiveness, for I know I don't deserve that. Just please, don't cast me off entirely. I'll do whatever you wish, leave for Scotland today, if it will ease your hurt!"

Eva's slim form went rigid under her hands. Vanora prepared herself to face the worst acrimony and revulsion possible between sisters. Eva made an odd gulping noise and turned a scarlet face toward Vanora.

She was laughing.

"As long as you don't intend to carry on in that fashion without wedding Holton, I haven't the least objection to your excesses!" Eva said, choking off in another gale of laughter.

Vanora lay propped on an elbow, bereft of speech or rational thought. "I beg your pardon?" she asked stupidly.

"Yes, I gather that's what you're doing, though why you think there's the least need in the world is beyond my poor powers of comprehension!" Eva replied, eyes twinkling.

"Did you not see me—Holton!" Vanora said feebly.

"It hardly seemed polite to stand and stare," Eva said roguishly, "but I flatter myself that my powers of observation aren't lacking! You, Holton, indeed!"

Eva collapsed onto the bed in laughter once more. "The preachy, proper Miss Chalmers actually disporting herself upon the sofa like a milkmaid in a hayloft! I never knew you had it in you, Vanora!"

Flushing, Vanora pushed herself erect on the bed with a sense that the world had gone mad. No one acted sensibly, let alone normally, today, including herself. "Aren't you overset at finding me in close embrace with Holton?" she asked, bewildered.

"Why should I object when you let your hair down with a most unexceptionable beau?" Eva sat up again to tuck up Vanora's tumbled hair as she spoke.

"But don't you love Holton yourself?" Vanora asked bravely, thinking that Eva sacrificed her own interests.

"Of course I love him, you great ninny," Eva declared affectionately. "As a brother, that is. You're quite welcome to him as husband, for he's entirely too old and sophisticated to be amused by me, except as a little sister!"

Vanora swept off the bed in a surge of chagrin. "You pesky brat! Then how could you pretend to me that you meant to accept the man, in this very room, just last night?"

"Did you assume so?" Eva giggled and sprang up to catch Vanora's hands in a chassé about the room. "I thought you jumped to that conclusion at the time and found it vastly diverting! That's when I was certain beyond doubt that you loved him, you know."

Vanora felt the room spin for more reason than Eva's romping. Hope was too painful to encourage lightly. She grasped Eva's arms, forcing her to stand still. "Do you put on a brave front, sacrificing your own happiness to me? I won't have it, my dear!"

"Never!" Eva insisted. "Only you would be so crack-brained as to languish silently for years over a star-crossed love. Were my heart set on a man, I'd take him by the ears and refuse to let go until he promised me my heart's desire!"

"But I had formed the intention to look after Mama and Papa in their last years! I couldn't possibly leave them to age alone," Vanora protested, off balance from the speed with which recent events had transpired.

Eva made a face at Vanora. "You truly consider yourself indispensable, the only one to assume responsibility for all your acquaintances! Our oldest brother and I can see to our parents, and you may tend to your own knitting for a change!"

Vanora collapsed on the bed again. "Think how this must look to the *ton*, though! Holton all but declared himself at the masquerade, by standing up with you three times. Even were I so selfish as to endeavor to attach your beau, you must become the subject of excessively painful gossip, Eveleit. I can't expose you to odious conjecture, for I know too well how lowering an experience that is to endure!"

"Much I care for wagging tongues," Eva declared stoutly. "And Holton was only my flirt, never my beau. I assure you that I'm quite experienced enough to feel the difference, even if you aren't capable of observing it."

"I doubt I'm the only person to observe the particularity of Holton's attentions to you since we've been in town, however," Vanora argued.

Eva walked to a tallboy and rummaged in its cabinet, producing a ribbon-tied parcel of letters from under a stack of bonnets. Flourishing the packet at Vanora, she said, "Unexceptionable as I find him, not even for Holton will I act the part of a jilt!"

"Whatever do you mean?" asked Vanora in disbelief.

"I mean to wed Jamie MacElvain, as soon as ever I return home," Eva said smugly. "Papa said I might, if I were of the same mind after a season in London."

"You haven't been corresponding with Jamie the entire time we've been in England!" Vanora wailed. "How improper! Mama will be excessively vexed."

"You have more culpable matters to consider than a few harmless letters," Eva said piously. "If you're going to kiss Holton with such abandon, you might just as well march belowstairs and propose marriage to him as well."

Vanora felt her color rise as her heart plummeted. What must poor Holton be thinking, waiting below to make the best of a bad situation. Her horrid temper had provoked him to act in an ungentlemanly fashion. Once he discovered Eva pledged to her Jamie, no doubt he would insist on doing the proper thing by herself, since they had been discovered in highly compromising behavior.

The blame was entirely hers; she couldn't allow him to sacrifice his own best interests to her wanton loss of control. Eva could be persuaded never to reveal what she had observed; matters could still be put right for Holton.

"You must never mention what you saw in the morning room, Eva," Vanora begged as a first step to protecting the dandy from her excesses. "It was entirely my own foolishness that brought about the scene."

Eva seemed inclined to go off into spasms of laughter.

"I provoked Holton past endurance and we argued," Vanora explained, ignoring Eva's levity. "He was simply overcome by the fervor of our argument and forgot himself for a moment." She stood, resolute, straightening her skirts for departure. "I must go down immediately and assure Holton that it meant less than nothing to either of us."

"As Mama has often warned you," Eva said, "if you persist in putting words in others' mouths, you'll surely choke on them!"

As much as Vanora had dreaded walking up the stairs to face her sister, she felt no more inclined to step down them again to confront Holton. Besides the memory of her shameless behavior of a short time past, she couldn't bear to hear Holton offer for her hand solely to save her reputation. She loved him too much to live with him in an arrangement required only to satisfy honor, and she knew very well that Holton considered his honor of the first consequence.

At the bottom of the stairs, Vanora found a footman facing her across the long entry hall, the one she had earlier determined to see turned off without a character. Here was another victim of failure to govern her emotions. By her excesses, Vanora had embarrassed a servant unable to protect himself against her unreasonable demands.

Stepping across the tiled floor toward him, she said, "My orders this morning were most unreasonable. I regret that I forced you to bear the consequences of my own ill humors."

The footman inclined his head correctly. As she turned away, he said, "May I wish you happy, Miss. He's just the right gentleman for you, if I may say so."

Feeling the burden of the footman's forgiveness, Vanora crept down the passage. Indeed, Holton was the very gentleman to make her toes curl and her heart open wide. But it was hardly fair to entrap any man into unwilling matrimony, which appeared the outcome of her hoydenish behavior this day.

Vanora paused outside the morning room door, found her handkerchief in one sleeve, and applied it quickly to nose and eyes. Assuming a bright expression, she opened the door and swept into the room.

"So you still are here, Holton! Quite unnecessary, I assure you," she said in her old managing manner. "Eva is fully recovered, and so am I, so you may be on your way without another thought to the morning's nonsense."

Vanora didn't quite meet Holton's gaze after one quick look into his frowning face. She folded her hands at her waist primly and looked past his right ear, where a tolerable representation of one of the lakes hung. Perhaps a holiday to the Lake District would provide a suitable setting to drown oneself.

Vanora's words nearly stopped Holton's heart. She couldn't sound so unconcerned, as though she had never lain in his arms, if she cared a farthing for him. Where were his practiced phrases of lovemaking when he needed them? His mind was as empty as his life stretched without her.

Holton advanced until they were nearly touching toes and took her chin in his hand so that she was forced to meet his eyes again, if only briefly. "Still trying to fiddle my ribbons, little despot?" he drawled, cursing himself for offering a challenge instead of his heart.

Vanora wished to melt and soak into the carpet, as she easily might under his touch, to escape from Holton's teasing voice and eyes. Holton was a consummate dandy. He meant to pretend an attachment to ease her embarrassment over acting so a gentleman must offer for her. His generosity of spirit and sense of honor increased her determination not to allow him to sacrifice himself.

"Please!" said Vanora. "You mustn't feel constrained to take any notice of the mare's nest I provoked you into this morning. I brought the entire circumstance about by meddling where I had no right to do so, and you were justified in any retaliation that occurred to you."

After a considering look, Holton walked away, and Vanora was bereft. Seeing him turn his back marooned her in a sea of woe. Holton stood at the window, lighted as though upon a stage in a shaft of sunlight. Curves of fair hair caught the sun like threads of spun gold, entangling Vanora's heart. She put her whole mind into memorizing every line of the man as he stood negligently, tantalizingly, about to walk out of her life forever.

"Do you mean to throw me over so easily?" he asked without turning round. "How do you recommend I proceed now, beg Miss Eva's pardon for making love to her sister, and see if she'll have me instead?"

His doleful suggestion brought worse pain than Vanora felt on her own behalf. Holton loved Eva, whatever her sister might think, and now he must be disappointed in his attachment. Vanora had ruined his life.

Holton turned quickly, staring directly at her with a reproachful expression, and Vanora reached for her handkerchief. The poor man! He didn't yet know that Eva's heart was bespoken.

Speaking to her hands to avoid seeing the agony she dealt him, Vanora said, "That won't be possible, I'm afraid, for you see, Eva had formed an attachment even before I persuaded her to come to London for a season."

Holton moved toward her again, laughing in a way that brought her eyes to his face once more. "How like you, to drag your sister south to find a husband she didn't want! My dear, managing despot! Don't you feel honor bound to manage something on my behalf now?"

"But it's madness to think we could live together in any approximation of harmony!" Vanora protested, wishing she dared manage for Holton what she most desired for herself.

At least she hadn't rejected him out of hand, Holton thought. He stopped by the sofa, strewn with spring blossoms, and looked at it significantly before speaking. "Equally mad to think either of us should be left loose on the world without the other, I should think. I don't doubt we'll pitch flaming rows instead of flowers at intervals, but I believe we must pitch in together for all that."

He couldn't woo his prickly love with pretty words. "I require a lady to hound me toward responsible pursuits. And you require a safe target for your tendency to ride roughshod over others, a man who's strong enough to stand out against you."

Not caring to have her faults flung in her face so directly, Vanora let her eyes stray to the sofa as significantly as had he. Looking back to him with a lift of her chin, she said, "As you stood out against me this morning? Don't deceive yourself that I should tolerate your opera dancers!"

Holton laughed, his eyes glinting dangerously as he came forward again. Vanora retreated behind a handy chair.

"I have no intention to require opera dancers," Holton said languidly, "but don't deceive yourself that I shall renounce them from fear of your hot head."

"I shouldn't think you would care to yoke yourself to a lady who had so little care for her reputation as to encourage Charles Marchand!" Vanora taunted, ready to deal with Holton's earlier insulting insinuations, since he seemed inclined to pick up hammer and tongs again.

"My dearest love, that wasn't handsomely done of me," Holton confessed, stopping his advance toward her chair. "Only an innocent could have cloistered herself for eight years over the man. And even if I weren't fully convinced of your maiden state, I should love you anyway."

Drunk instantly on the sweet wine of Holton's endearment, Vanora trailed her fingers across the chair's back. "Do you think I should disappoint your friend, Sir Edward, when you've led him to believe me the perfect mate for a widower?"

"Hang Sir Edward!" Holton said, staring at her mouth. "Wed anyone but me, and I'll be forced to make you a widow."

"But you have no regard for my heritage!" Vanora protested, pouting at Holton in a way that brought a groan from his throat. "I know very well who placed that turban on the Butcher's statue in the square garden, where I couldn't help but see it first thing this morning."

Holton cursed softly but advanced another step on Vanora's chair. "The tiresome thing slipped my mind entirely! I confess to placing it there in a temper, thinking to provoke you. Then more interesting thoughts about you distracted me to such an extent that I was too bemused to retrieve it."

"This is just so much clever banter," Vanora said in a rush, afraid Holton would drag her from behind the chair's protection at any moment. "The truth is that you need another sort of mate than I could act, for as a future member of the House of Lords, your wife must be a political asset. My regrettable failure to control my emotions makes me most ineligible for the position."

"Composure is most difficult to keep with those we care for deeply; and overcontrol of emotion might choke off healthy exchanges entirely! Besides, at present I've no seat in the Lords," Holton said quite reasonably, arriving before the chair she used as barricade. "I'm just a dandy and, as you have persisted to name me, a rake. And you're eminently suited for a rake's wife."

Holton leaned forward, hands on the chair's back on either side of Vanora's. "You're intelligent enough not to be taken in by nonsense, principled enough to demand my best self, vulnerable enough to inspire my protection, and," his voice resonant with intimation, "most certainly provocative enough to exhaust sensual energies at home. A few of those qualities wouldn't come amiss for a member's wife, as well."

Toward the end of his list, Vanora had abandoned the chair for the far side of the room, sheltering behind the sofa once more. Holton stalked her at leisure. •

"Nothing gives a man a greater disgust than a managing female, however," Vanora said from her vantage point. "And you can hardly deny that my propensities in that direction go beyond what is pleasing."

Holton was silhouetted against sunlight for a moment as he passed the window. "Perhaps all of us are subject to meddling in the lives of those we love, for I couldn't stay out of the room when I feared you might make the wrong choice with Sir Charles. We'll have to remind each other when concern strikes more as interference."

Nearing the sofa, Holton said, "I have it on the best authority, from my esteemed father, that managing ladies can learn to channel interfering ways into worthwhile endeavors."

"Indeed?" said Vanora in satisfaction, diverted by his revelation from Holton's approach. "Then I expect that you've spoken more comfortably with your father of late, for that's hardly a discussion you would have entered upon earlier." Vanora started round the sofa, away from Holton.

"You see what a settling effect you've had upon my character already," Holton cajoled, moving across the front of the sofa to intercept her. "Surely you don't begin a task, only to abandon it before it's well underway."

"You needn't pretend to make love to me, truly," Vanora assured Holton as they met at the end of the sofa. "Last night you stood up with my sister three times and would have danced a fourth set, had I not put my foot down. Who will credit that your sentiments could veer round like a windmill from one day to the next!"

Holton picked up an anemone from the sofa and trailed its white petal down Vanora's cheek, "I'm no longer looking at a reflection in a glass, my dear. I've seen the real, incorrigible, adorable you for some time now. My sentiments are no illusion of my mind or yours."

"But how does one know when to believe a dandy?" Vanora cried, seizing the flower impatiently. "You've made a study of saying and doing the most devastatingly agreeable things, so how does one know when to trust them?"

"Do you recall the note you received from me earlier this morning?" Holton inquired, picking up a pink clematis for an assault on her nose and strong jaw.

"Yes, indeed!" Vanora retorted. "And how do you propose to explain to my father that you now wish to wed me, when you just wrote him, seeking permission to speak to Eva?"

"You must learn to read correspondence more precisely if you're to help me with government papers," Holton warned. "I didn't mention Eva in my message to you, and certainly not in that to your father."

Holton observed with delight that Vanora's complexion shaded gradually to match the pink blossom with which he stroked her cheek, as the import of his words became clear.

"You wretch!" she cried out at him. "You've given me no indication that you held me in other than the greatest aversion of late!"

Tucking the flower behind her ear, Holton said affectionately, "You must never believe that you know what's in my mind better than I do myself, love. Allow me an opportunity to tell you. Even if I must live on a battle field, I'll not fly a flag of surrender on this point!"

Having learned earlier in the day how pleasant surrender could be, Vanora determined to share the lesson with Holton. Placing her hands on his broad chest, she looked up adoringly, then, as she felt him relax toward her, pushed him backward onto the sofa. Before Holton could speak the objection registering on his dear face, she joined him there.

After an indecent interval, Vanora demanded, "Tell me what more an opera dancer can do for you than that, sir!" Holton raised languid lids to reply, speaking carefully so as not to disturb her determined kisses to his cleft chin.

"Give me but time enough to secure a special license, and I'll show you, love!"

Desert Song by Constance O'Banyon

The enthralling conclusion of the passionate DeWinter legacy. As Lady Mallory Stanhope set sail for Egypt she was drawn to the strikingly handsome Lord Michael DeWinter, who was on a dangerous mission. From fashionable London to the mysterious streets of Cairo, together they risked everything to rescue his father, the Duke of Ravenworth, from treacherous captors.

A Child's Promise by Deborah Bedford

The story of a love that transcends broken dreams. When Johnny asks Lisa to marry him she knows it's the only way to make a new life for herself and her daughter. But what will happen when Johnny finds out she's lied to him? "A tender, uplifting story of family and love...You won't want to miss this one."—Debbie Macomber, bestselling author of *Morning Comes Softly*.

Desert Dreams by Deborah Cox

Alone and destitute after the death of her gambling father, Anne Cameron set out on a quest for buried treasure and met up with handsome and mysterious Rafe Montalvo, an embittered gunfighter. They needed each other in order to make their journey, but could newfound passion triumph over their pasts?

One Bright Morning by Alice Duncan

Young widow Maggie Bright had her hands full raising a baby and running a farm on her own. The last thing she needed was a half-dead stranger riding into her front yard and into her life. As she nursed him back to health, she found herself doing the impossible—falling in love with the magnetic but difficult Jubal Green.

Meadowlark by Carol Lampman

Garrick "Swede" Swensen rescued a beautiful young woman from drowning only to find her alone, penniless, and pregnant. He offered Becky his name with no strings attached, but neither of them dreamed that their marriage of convenience would ever develop into something far more. When Swede's mysterious past caught up with him, he was forced to make the decision of a lifetime.

Oh, Susannah by Leigh Riker

Socialite Susannah Whittaker is devastated by the death of her best friend, Clary, the sister of country music sensation Jeb Stuart Cody. An unlikely pair, Jeb and Susannah grow closer as they work together to unveil the truth behind Clary's untimely death, along the way discovering a passion neither knew could exist.